The Fall of America

Book 3 — Enemy Within

WR Benton

LOOSE CANNON ENTERPRISES
Paradise, CA

Ingram Edition
ISBN 978-1-944476-57-1

Edited by:
Daniel Williams, Bobbie La Cour and Juanita Druyea

Author photos, © 2012 Melanie C. Benton
Cover design and layout © 2014 by DancingFoxPublishing.com
all rights reserved.
Cover Photo: Shutterstock.com used with permission
Logo fonts [*Shortcut, Dirty Ego*] by Eduardo Recife, misprintedtype.com

www.loose-cannon.com

Books by W.R. Benton

War Paint

Fur Seekers (Co-authored with Grady Clark)

Red Runs the Plain

Blood Mountain

The Fall of America, Book 1, Premonition of Death

The Fall of America, Book 2, Fatal Encounters

Jake Masters, Bounty Hunter

Jake Masters, Bounty Hunter 2: The General's Wife

Nate Grisham, Black Mountain Man (Co-authored with Grady Clark)

Nate Grisham, Renegade Trapper (Co-authored with Grady Clark)

Nate Grisham, Revenge (Co-authored with Grady Clark)

The Youngest Mountain Man

Missouri in Flames

War Paint

James McKay, U. S. Army Scout

Hired Gun

Blood Money

Hell Comes To Dixie

Alive and Alone (Young Adult)

Simple Survival, a Family Outdoors Guide (Non-Fiction)

Impending Disasters (Non-Fiction)

Bubba's Dawg Might be a Redneck (Southern Humor)

Adrift

W.R. Benton
The Best in Post-Apocalyptic

Dedication

To Judy Maben, Billie Trout Patterson, Kimberly Kucera Luke, Firecracker LM, Stacie Burns, Linda Vee Sado, Lila Sue Riley, Kristie Tucker West, and Marilyn Lenaham-Fischer, all special friends on Facebook and good people.

A special dedication to Wendy Hartman, Wendy Gay, and Lynn Marie Gilleran Eisen, three caring women who are always there when I need someone to listen or to keep my spirits up.

A Note from the Author

Many folks who read *"Fall of America: Premonition of Death"* asked why I had shotguns as the primary weapons used by the main characters. There are a number of reasons, but the principal one is the cost of assault rifles versus shoguns. Additionally, the most commonly found long gun in American homes today is a shotgun. Shotgun empties can easily be reloaded quickly and at a much cheaper cost and ease than rifle shells. The shotgun has choke and every single time you pull the trigger, you create a cone of fire filled with lead, with different types of chokes controlling your spread. Anyone hit within the pattern of fire will feel the shot, although it may not kill your adversary, depending on shot placement and distance, along with other factors. Shotguns can also fire lead slugs, which many folks have used historically to hunt deer. Slugs have fair accuracy, but nothing like a rifle. Additionally, since I prep for survival, it just makes good horse sense to me to stick to the more commonly found weapons, because if push comes to shove, the most common ammo found following a collapse will be for these weapons. Also, a shotgun can be sawed off, which is hard to beat in clearing rooms or in close contact with an enemy.

If a fall or collapse does happen in the future, most of us will be stuck with what we have on hand, so we'll either die or survive with what we own, can steal, or take from the dead hands of our enemies. I suspect military weapons will quickly make an appearance, but only after folks have gathered together and organized to fight for freedom. I suspect, little by little, weapons will change as they're taken along with ammunition, following raids, killings, and hijacked truck convoys.

There were also some doubts a man would cry over the death of his dog and then viciously maim a man for life during an interrogation. I happen to be a man that loves my dogs dearly, which I cannot say about many people I've met. I strongly suspect, when the end comes, folks will love their pets even more than now, because animals give us unconditional love and ask nothing in return and love will be hard to find. Actually, simple kindness will disappear. Interrogations will be crude and bloody affairs and don't think they won't be. When lives may depend on information gathered, and quickly, the means will justify the end. Human life will be of little value, but knowledge of what a potential enemy may have planned will be great wealth. I, for one, will do what it takes to get information needed to protect myself and family.

WR Benton
Jackson, Mississippi

"We can't all be Washingtons, but we can all be patriots."
—**Charles F. Browne**

"My God! How little do my countrymen know what precious blessings they are in possession of, and which no other people on earth enjoy!"
—**Thomas Jefferson**

"The government is merely a servant—merely a temporary servant; it cannot be its prerogative to determine what is right and what is wrong, and decide who is a patriot and who isn't. Its function is to obey orders, not originate them."
—**Mark Twain**

Table of Contents

BOOK 3

ENEMY WITHIN

CHAPTER 1

Colonel Sokol stood in ankle deep mud on the edge of a swamp, as his radio operator stood beside him, and yelled into a handset, "Look for the Americans, you damned fool! Of course they'll not be easy to find, but intelligence said there is an old mansion deep in the swamp, so find it and do the damned job quickly. Out." He stepped over the body of a dead American and never noticed the man's unseeing eyes or the puddle of blood under his ripped apart torso. The man had died from multiple gunshots to his chest and stomach.

Sokol was a short man with a bald head and bad teeth. He was a heavy vodka drinker and his once brilliant mind was only a shell of his previous intelligence, due to alcohol abuse. He was fat, and only five feet three inches tall, and two-hundred and fifty pounds, so he was a big man. His troops often laughed and called him 'Barn Door,' because he looked wider than he was tall. While he saw himself as a genius, in reality, he barely functioned. His assignment to Edwards, Mississippi, as the Russian anti-partisan commander, came with a warning; wipe out all resistance in the state within one year or be removed from command.

He tossed the handset to his radio man and thought, *Damned fools. All Moscow sends me are drunks and fools.*

"Colonel, we caught this man on one of the swamp trails." Major Falin, his executive officer said as he neared with a partisan.

The partisan had his head lowered and his hands were secured behind his back.

"You mean to tell me after four hours all we have to show for our searching is one man?"

"So far, but we know there are many more at the mansion."

A bright flash filled the sky and when Sokol looked up, a sharp crack of thunder was heard. *Damn it, now it will rain and make it even harder to locate the partisans. But, maybe this man can lead us to the mansion.*

"Uh, you speak English, don't you, Major Falin?"

"Yes, sir, I was college educated in the United States and had four years of English lessons while here. My excellent command of the English language is the main reason I was assigned to intelligence, sir." Falin was the propaganda officer and as such, he was a good writer, and understood the psychology of Americans better than anyone else in the command. His suggestions on how to handle Americans, however, were often ignored as being too soft or lacking in sound military reasoning. He was a tall and thin man, with his brown hair worn in a crew-cut for ease of cleaning.

"Tell this bastard to take me to the mansion or he'll be tortured to death. It's important that he understands I will do exactly what I say to him if he refuses."

"Sir, I don't think —"

"Major, you work for me, and I'm not interested in what you think. If I need your opinion, I will ask for it. Get his name and then ask him the question about the mansion."

The Major spoke for a moment and then said, "His name is James and claims he has no last name. He also demands to be treated according to the Geneva Convention as a prisoner of war."

"Tell him to lead us to the mansion or the torture will start in a few minutes."

The American and Russian spoke and then Falin said, "Uh, he said go to hell and you can kiss his red, white, and blue, ass."

Sokol slapped the prisoner hard enough he fell to the mud.

"Did you tell this Yankee bastard about the torture?"

"Yes, sir. He knows."

"Master Sergeant Rusak, have two men tie this man to a tree and do it now."

"Yes, sir. Corporal Babin and Junior Sergeant Shubin, secure this man to the big tree on the left." Rusak ordered and then thought, *We are doing this all wrong. Hell, it is more than likely this man has no idea where the swamp mansion is; I have heard the whole swamp is a maze of trails. A man cannot tell what he does not know. This death will just add more fuel to the flames of anger the Americans already have for us.*

Once James was secured to the tree, Sokol moved to the man and pulled his bayonet. He gave an evil grin and then with a quick slash of his knife, an ear fell to the mud.

James screamed and jerked at his bonds, but he would go no place and his thrashing around splattered blood on the Colonel, Major, and Master Sergeant.

"Shubin, you and Babin, hold his legs open. I will remove his penis next."

The two soldiers looked at Master Sergeant Rusak, who nodded.

Once his legs were pulled apart, Sokol said, "Tell this damned fool of an American, I am going to remove his penis and balls next, if he does not talk."

James yelled, "Tell yer Russian Commander to untie me and I'll kick his ass! He's a damned coward!"

"James, you must take him to the mansion in the swamp or he will make you less of a man. He is not making an idle threat. He is most serious."

Knowing he was a dead man, no matter what he did, James closed his eyes, raised his head and prayed, "Lord, I'll be seein' you in a short spell. I've always lived as good a life as I can. I —"

"What is he doing? Is he telling you how to get to the mansion?"

"He is praying."

"Praying? Is he asking God to spare his life?"

"No, actually, he is letting God know he will soon be there. He knows we will kill him no matter what he does."

The knife in the Colonel's hand flashed in the dim light and the long blade entered under James's rib cage at an upward angle, so it went in deep. A horrendous scream was heard from the captive and then Sokol jerked the knife from side to side. The scream grew louder as his whole body shuddered violently. Suddenly the scream died, a loud sigh came from James, and as his bowels emptied, he quivered, and then died. His upper body was leaning away from the tree, with blood pooling at his feet.

"These sonsofbitches never talk!" Sokol said in anger. He wiped his knife blade clean on the grasses and then ordered, "Get the men moving into the swamp and do it now!"

Corporal Babin looked at the dead American and thought, *Why are we here? I see nothing here that I need or want. This war is confusing to me, but I must follow orders. I am only a Corporal and not paid for my thinking. He died bravely, but praying to God did him no good at all. There must be something about this country I do not understand. These people, these Americans, they are determined, only why?*

"Vodka, you are our point man." Master Sergeant Rusak said to Private Alvang, who detested the strong tasting alcohol, thus his nick name. "Keep your head out of your ass and you will survive the day; daydream and we will send you home in a box."

As the men started moving, Rusak called out again, "Dvorkin, you are my drag man. Let us move, and keep your eyes and ears open. Make a mistake today and some of us will die."

The point man was understandably nervous and after a few minutes, Lieutenant Markov said, "Alvang, increase your speed. Hell, it will take us all day to cover two kilometers as slow as you're walking."

That is easy for him to say, because it is my ass that will get blown up or shot if I overlook something. I am expendable to these bastards, the Private thought as he scanned the trail and increased his speed.

The morning passed uneventfully and it was at their noon meal when Private Konfer had to pee; he'd taken two steps from camp when his world exploded into flame and smoke. The men scattered, which resulted in another explosion, followed by a loud scream. Konfer had not made a sound since the first detonation. Then a second scream was heard and Rusak yelled, "No one move! Konfer set off a mine. Medic, check out the three men, but look for trip wires or bumps in the soil as you move."

A thin man, actually little more than a boy, eighteen year old Private Elout moved slowly forward, scanning the ground around him. He moved to Konfer, rolled the injured man on his back and felt for a pulse on the bloody neck, "Konfer is dead. I will now check the other two men."

When he neared the victim of the second mine, he could see the man's right leg was gone from the knee down and his right arm was mangled badly. He examined him and called out, "We need a helicopter for this man, he has suffered the loss of a leg and arm. I see some smaller injuries, but none look to be life-threatening." He applied tourniquets and bandages to the injured man, a Private named Flits. He then shot him full of morphine and his screaming soon stopped.

"Medic! Private Gise has stepped in a stake trap and has a sharp stake through his left foot and another in the calf of his leg." Corporal Babin said from beside the injured man.

"I'm coming, but don't move the man until I get some morphine in him. His pain is severe and it will become worse as we remove him from the pit." Private Elout said as he gathered his medical bag and started moving.

As the medic moved, he could hear the Master Sergeant on the radio and finally the man said, "The helicopter will be here in about ten minutes. In the mean time, all of you check yourselves and each other for injuries. In this swamp, infection will come quickly and to even the smallest wound."

Private Elout squatted beside Gise and pulled a syringe with morphine. He injected the powerful painkiller and then pulled a tag out and began filling it out with a pen. The tag identified the medic, date, time, known injuries, and what drugs were given to the wounded man in the field. He then attached the tag to Gise's shirt pocket.

Once the tag was complete, Gise was feeling no pain, so Elout said, "We have to jerk his leg from the pit. It will cause extensive tissue damage, but there is no other way to get him free of the stakes. I need two strong men to pull him from the stakes, using his shoulders."

The Master Sergeant ordered two of the biggest men to help removed Gise. They both moved forward cautiously, suspecting other traps, but discovered nothing. Once in place, they grabbed the injured man under his shoulders and pulled him from the pit.

Thanks to the powerful analgesic, only a few grunts were heard from Gise.

"Damn, he is in for a long hospital stay." the medic said to no one in particular.

"These stakes are smeared with shit?" Master Sergeant Rusak asked.

"Yes, so he is infected. At the hospital, they will run an IV with antibiotics into him for a few days and see if it clears up. I'm treating him with penicillin right now, too."

"Will he live?" Corporal Babin asked.

Looking up from his medical bag, where he was looking for his antibiotics, Elout replied, "I think he has a better than average chance, once I get some penicillin in him, but it will still be a difficult injury to treat." He pulled out a syringe and raised it, pushing the plunger just enough to release any trapped air, and then gave the injection into the injured man's good leg.

"I see the helicopter approaching from the west." Junior Sergeant Shubin said as he pointed at the aircraft.

The radio operator said, "He is unable to land, of course, so he will hover next to this trail. He wants the dead and wounded loaded quickly. He will return to base once loaded, refuel, and then come back out."

Glancing at Lieutenant Markov, Master Sergeant Rusak said, "Sir, he must suspect we will have more trouble or he would not have said what he did." Then glancing around, Rusak said, "Get the dead and wounded ready to travel and do it now."

Soon the *whop-whop* sound of an approaching helicopter sounded and the men made ready to lift their loads.

When the chopper neared, Rusak saw Warrant Officer Paley was the pilot, so he waved, and then spotting for the bird, he lowered it by hand signal, until about a foot above the water. The dead and wounded were quickly loaded and the aircraft lifted almost straight up, then the nose lowered, and away the chopper flew.

Paley was known to Rusak as a trader, thief, and man that all units needed and most had on hand. He'd take things they didn't need and trade with another unit for something they did need. All organizations did it and in many ways it made life easier for the soldiers, because it provided things the normal supply system couldn't or wouldn't. It was faster, too. Paley drank and smoked too much, and played a lot of cards, but he was also a brave man. When combined, these traits made him the ideal man to trade things and often his trading was desperately needed.

"Move them down the trail and now, Master Sergeant." Markov said.

The rest of the day was uneventful, but with a lot of stress. Twice, booby-traps were marked on the trail and the men stepped over them and continued on, their senses on guard for danger. It was an hour before dark when the Lieutenant had them move off the trail a little and make camp for the night.

Sergeant Bluska, the line NCO, said, "If you want to eat, do the job now. Before dark all fires will be extinguished and covered with mud."

Rusak didn't like being in the platoon leading the invasion into the swamp. He knew they'd start having more and more problems the deeper they went. The American traitor didn't know the location of the ancient mansion, but had revealed the number of men, their arms, and also the names of some of the leaders. As far as the Master Sergeant was concerned, he didn't want to tackle any group led by the prior Green Beret, Willy. He'd heard them compared to Spetsnaz, and they were some coldblooded men in his mind. He suspected they'd not do much except move around in the swamp and get the hell shot out of them, or be blown up by mines.

He'd just placed his canteen cup on the flames to boil water, when a man to his left gave a short scream and fell to the mud jerking with half his head gone. Then everyone heard the shot.

Going to ground and crawling behind a log, he thought, *since it took some time to hear the shot after our man was hit, the sniper must be at a great distance.*

Another man fell, with a long finger of blood shooting from his back, and then the shot was heard. Unlike the first man, this one continued to scream as his fingers dug into the mud and his legs kicked in all directions. Private Elout moved to the injured man and, as he was dragging him to safety, a bullet burned his ribs. The minor injury just made him move faster.

"Does anyone know where the sniper is?" Lieutenant Markov asked.

"I would estimate a thousand yards or more, to the north of us, sir." Rusak replied.

"Sir, we need another helicopter, if we can get one." the medic said.

"Give me a minute." Markov replied.

He took the handset from his radio man, stood and spoke. A few minutes later, he said, "Rain due to hit at any time, huge front with high winds, so the helicopter commander and operations officer declined our request. Can you keep Private Gavlik alive?"

"He is lung shot and I can keep him alive, only I am not sure for how long."

It was growing darker now and Rusak knew the sniper was long gone or he would have killed the Lieutenant when he stood to make the call for help. "Two of you men get a shelter over our injured man and medic. Then, each of you buddy up and construct shelters of your own. Sergeant Bluska, see that this is done properly."

"I'll see to it, Master Sergeant."

A bright flash of lightning filled the sky and a dull *boom* was heard a second later. Rusak felt a gentle breeze and then rain began to fall. He glanced at the western horizon and saw a long finger of light and as he watched, it exploded into many smaller fingers, and an earsplitting crack was heard.

This will be a rough storm from what I see, he thought as he pulled his poncho from his gear and put it on. He watched as shelters were completed and men crawled under scant protection offered from the storm.

He moved into his shelter and seconds later hailstones began to fall. They were small at first, about the size of the tip of his little finger, but soon grew larger. Before long, the hailstones were huge, near baseball size and men began to scream as their poorly made shelters fell apart. Most moved into shelters of their friends, while a couple stood under trees. Rusak had never seen stones of ice so large, and he knew the American weather was dangerous too. As a professional soldier, where the Master Sergeant was assigned mattered little to him. He'd do his thirty years and retire to a small village or farm. He started his career unmarried, not wanting a wife to worry about while serving, but enjoyed the company of women, so he married Esfir. *I need a drink of vodka,* he thought as he pulled a metal flask from his coat pocket. Taking a healthy gulp, he then pulled out a ration and began to eat his supper.

Once the hail stopped, Senior Sergeant Shubin was up and moving in the rain, telling his troops to fix their battered shelters because heavy winds and rains were due to hit again and any minute. Men scurried in all directions to prepare, but Rusak knew some of the men would sleep poorly this night.

Morning came with a veil of white mist covering the swamp. While the rains had stopped, dark gray clouds were hanging low overhead, and all knew they'd be wet again before this day was done.

Lieutenant Markov walked to Rusak and said, "A helicopter overhead last evening, just before the rain, discovered the partisans have broken into small groups and are moving quickly in all directions. Our infrared gear picked up their body heat, only the storm hit before we could attack. I have a map here with marked locations of trails they were on and the one we are on now had about fifty partisans on it yesterday."

Glancing at the map, the Master Sergeant said, "Sir, there are countless trails connecting to this one, so it is hard to say if they are still on this trail or not. I will alert our point man, but there is little we can do."

"I realize that, Sergeant, but during the night some big guns were brought forward in the event we run into more than we can handle."

"What kind of guns, sir?"

"I was told by Colonel Sokol that a dozen T-90 tanks are available if we have the need for cannons."

"I suspect they are on the edge of the swamp, so let us pray if we run into any large groups of Americans, we are within range of the tanks. I don't know their range, but I think it would be smart not to depend on them for help. I learned years ago, in battle, the only man I can fully trust is myself."

"Get the men moving and let us get this over with, but warn our point man."

"Sergeant Bluska, get the men moving. Intelligence reports large groups of partisans may be on this trail, so have the point man use caution. Also, slip another man between us and the point man as well."

An hour later as they moved over the trail, one of the new men said, "Look at the size of that snake."

"Which one?" an unknown voice asked.

"On the right, about thirty meters."

"Stop the small talk. Save this shit for later once in camp." Junior Sergeant Shubin said and then thought, *Damn, that thing must be over two meters long, and fat too. I do not like spiders or snakes.*

Suddenly the point man stopped, as well as the middle man, and both had their hands in the air, indicating trouble. The main group came to a stop and heads turned, scanning the swamp. Shubin noticed a half-dozen gators and three snakes, but nothing human moving.

The second man moved toward the main group and when at Lieutenant Markov, he whispered, "Large group spotted moving toward us. I would estimate contact with their point man in five minutes or less."

CHAPTER 2

Bright search lights flashed as they circled the gulag in Edwards, Mississippi, but nothing was spotted moving. Men with huge dogs, walked in the middle of two fences, and both barbed barriers were charged with high electrical current. Razor wire lined the top of both fences, all the way around the camp perimeter, and so far, no one had escaped. The gulag now had ten unheated barracks for the prisoners, and they needed more. At last count over three thousand prisoners were held captive, with most having committed no crime other than being rounded up as hostages for retaliation of partisan actions. Some were used for executions, while others were used in experiments at the base hospital, but most were simply starving to death. It was an hour before daylight.

Mark, like everyone at the gulag, was thin, had bleeding gums from scurvy, and his eyesight was poor as well, all the results of malnutrition. There were three others with him and they were sitting beside a small fire outside the barracks. The barracks were so overfilled that a good thousand slept on the ground, unable to squeeze into the crude structures, and being exposed to the elements led to many early deaths.

The other three were Lewis, who was tall and had once been a police officer, George, a retired Air Force Lieutenant Colonel, and May, who'd been captured as she carried messages for the partisans, but she'd managed to eat them before being seized. She'd played dumb and after being raped numerous times by the troops who'd caught her, was locked up with the rest.

"The Colonel says we're to go out tomorrow night."

"I'm ready." Lewis said and then grinned.

May said, "Me too, but I worry about finding partisans."

George grinned and said, "We'll find them, and then come back and kick some Russian ass. These sons-of-bitches owe me. I live for revenge."

Adding another twig to the ever hungry flames, Mark said, "Revenge is fine, as long as you control it."

"What's that suppose to mean?" May asked.

"It means it has it's place in life, unless you become preoccupied with revenge, because then it becomes dangerous. It can make a man take dangerous risks or do things that otherwise he'd never do, and all in the name of avenging a wrong. I live for life, I want revenge and every chance I get, I'll kill Russians. Nonetheless, I'll not place myself or others at risk to exact my revenge, understand?"

People began to assemble for the morning meal, which consisted of water-downed cabbage soup with some kind of meat and rice in it. As near as Mark could figure they were slowly dying, being starved to death on a diet of less than 900 calories a day. However, the four of them were eating better than the average prisoner and it was because of the mission they were selected for. Prisoners who did all the manual work in the kitchen of the camp, most were prior chefs or professional cooks, stole as much food as they could safely take out. This food was brought into the concentration camp and fed to the four of them. Even with this food, they were getting little, when compared to times before capture.

The four stood and moved through the serving line, each eating everything in the cup, even gristle, fat, and even hairy skin at times. They had to eat in order to be strong enough to escape and leave they would, just as soon as the tunnel was complete. According to the Colonel they were to be within a few inches of the surface tonight. If so, then tomorrow night, a little after midnight, they'd make a break.

It took little time to eat the contents of the cup and once done, the four sat by the fire. Mark looked around quickly and then said, "We need to reach help or many of these people will be dead within a month. One cup of slop the Russians call soup twice a day will not keep them alive. At least when they were feeding them three cups a day a person had a chance, but it was a slim one."

"According to the Colonel, the rations were cut because the partisans were attacking truck convoys running between Edwards and Jackson." May said.

"Bullshit. Most of the food comes up the Mississip' by barge, not into Jackson by air."

"How do you know this?" George asked as he turned to face the man.

"Simple, I used to attack the convoys. I was once part of the resistance. I was picked up in my brother's home, gave a fake name and here I am."

"What happened to your brother?" May asked.

"He'd been hanged early on and I was there providing for his family."

"Was his wife still alive?" Lewis asked with a grin that suggested much more.

Mark grew angry and said, "It was nothing like that, not at all, so wipe that smile off your face. I stole some vegetables and bought some meat for them is all. I had no one except his family and I don't know what happened to them after I was arrested."

The Colonel walked from around one of the corners of a barracks and made his way to the small group. Once there, he squatted by the fire and held his palms out to warm. Looking around he said, "There's been a change in the mission. You'll go out tonight. Apparently the Russians have some sophisticated electronics that may have picked up the sounds of our digging. They've been out all day probing, so we've moved the schedule up. It's imperative that at least one of you gets to the resistance and informs them of our situation here. Understood? All else is the same, except you leave this evening."

All four nodded, the Colonel stood, and then he walked away.

"I'd suggest we all try to sleep for a few hours. God only knows what we'll run into tonight." Mark said, and then curled up in the dirt beside the fire to sleep.

The night was dark and the spotlights were once more stabbing into the darkness, looking for movement or something out of place. The escapees were late and it was almost an hour before sunrise. None of the four saw the lights; they were underneath the earth crawling through a tunnel toward an opened hole just outside the wire. A shortness of air and dust being kicked into the air caused an occasional cough. Finally, Mark smelled fresh air and the tunnel curved toward the surface. Looking straight up, he could see stars.

He crouched beneath the opening and slowly stood up. When his head cleared, he watched the lights hoping to spot a pattern and, after a couple of minutes, he noticed the guard always moved the beam left first and then right. He moved the light slowly with many long minutes before he'd return to the same spot.

"When we go, we all go at the same time. Rush out as quickly as you can." he whispered, knowing one or two would not make it out before the light was near the tunnel again.

"Okay." May whispered and she was right behind him.

He waited until the light moved over the hole and then moved up. In less than a minute he was up and out of the hole running hard for the woods. Once in the trees, he stopped to see what would happen to the others. He saw May up and out, then Lewis, and they were both moving for the trees.

George was half out of the hole when a machine-gun in a tower opened up just as a bright beam of light struck him. Dirt was knocked high into the air and the man's body danced insanely as bullets passed through him. A loud scream filled the night air. His left arm flew from his body and when each bullet struck, a long finger of blood followed as it exited his back. He fell back into the hole, dead, with the one remaining arm sticking up and his hand balled into a fist. One finger slowly moved to open and it quivered a few seconds before stopping. The hand cast an eerie shadow on the grasses.

"Move! Move and do it now!" Mark said and started running north through the woods.

"Follow me," May said, "I was raised in Edwards, remember?"

"Sonofabitch, did you see what that big gun did to George? It tore his ass to pieces!"

"Lewis," Mark said, "shut the hell up and keep it shut. Right now we need some distance between us and this gulag."

At that point, dogs were heard barking and a siren went off.

"May, lead the way; let's go."

Once deep in the woods, it became harder and harder to see, so Mark said, "Do you know a quick way out of here?"

"Sure, off our left, oh, maybe five hundred feet, is the town."

"Move there, now. We can't see well enough to walk in this shit. And, move faster."

The leaves made noises as they moved and Mark was terrified at the thought of being caught. *The Russians will torture us to death in a minute, just to get the names of everyone involved.*

Soon they were beside the macadam road leading into Edwards from the main highway. A new day was being born, with the sun just starting to rise. No traffic was seen, but the dog barking was getting louder, and Mark was growing desperate. When they were in the woods both men had picked up pieces of wood to use as clubs, which was better than nothing, but just barely. They sent May around the corner of a building and instantly heard a voice in Russian.

May heard the Russian but ignored him and kept walking. Finally, the man walked to her and grabbed her by the shoulder. All May carried as a weapon was a rock in her hand and when he pulled her around, she swung her arm with full force, seeing the rock strike him in the forehead. The soldier fell to the concrete where he lay twitching as May called out to Mark and Lewis.

Mark neared the guard, pulled the man's bayonet and stabbed him up and under his ribs, hearing him grunt. Three more times he stabbed and the Russian finally gave a loud sigh and voided in his trousers. He then stripped the man of anything of use and felt much better with the Bison sub-machine gun in his hands. The pistol he gave to Lewis and he handed May two grenades.

At that point two guards with a German Shepherd rounded the corner and were as surprised as the Americans. Mark fired first, dropping both men, and then the dog made a mad run for the small group. Lewis fired twice with his pistol and the big beast dropped to the ground about two feet from May, who was petrified with fear. The animal attempted to raise his head, but was unable to move, and in a few seconds was dead.

"Get their weapons and gear. Get it all and quickly!" Mark said.

"Packs too?" Lewis asked.

"All the gear. There might be some food in the packs. Hurry, we need to get out of here and now!"

They quickly stripped the dead men of all useful gear and took off at a trot, south. They'd gone but a half of a block when Lewis said, "Motorcycle with a sidecar off our left. We can all three ride, but once out of town a few miles we need to separate as instructed."

They ran to the motorcycle, where May climbed in the sidecar, Mark would drive, and Lewis would be the passenger. The key was not in the ignition, but Mark had been a cop before the fall and could hot wire any vehicle. Less than two minutes later, they were moving down the road toward the main highway.

"Stay off the main roads, if possible!" Lewis yelled to be heard.

"We'll use the overpass, go about five more miles, and then find a dirt road if we can."

"Sounds like a good plan."

May found dog hair in the sidecar, a pistol, canteen, and a bag. When she opened the burlap bag, she found huge dog biscuits. *This stuff must have belonged to the dog handlers we just killed,* she thought, as she pulled out a biscuit and took a bite. She then handed one to each of the men, who accepted the snack with big smiles on their faces. *A person has to be pretty damned hungry to eat dog food,* she thought and then smiled, but it's not bad at all.

They crossed the overpass and looking in the mirror, Mark spotted a staff car behind them, and wondered why they were after him, or where they. He kept his distance and at the next side road, braked hard and turned right, giving the motorcycle more gas as soon as the turn was made. Hitting 100 KPM, or roughly 60 MPH, he began to scare his passengers. He glanced in his mirror and discovered the car was gone. He slowed down to about 10 miles an hour and yelled, "There was a staff car on our ass."

May looked behind them and yelled, "There still is a car on our asses!"

The car was moving so fast that it almost ran into the rear of the bike. A soldier leaned from the passenger window and was attempting to get a clear shot at the three on the motorcycle.

May opened up with her pistol and sent bullets flying into the windshield. She saw blood splatter on the glass and the car suddenly went out of control and crashed into the tree on the right side of the road. The passenger went airborne and his body landed in a field near the car.

Mark, didn't hesitate, goosed the motorcycle, and soon they were moving at 100 KPH. After about twenty minutes, he slowed down and asked, "May, any idea where in the hell we're at?"

"Yep, coming up you'll see a dirt road on the left; take it and continue down about three miles. Once there, you'll see a four way intersection, take a right. After that, the road will end completely in about four miles."

"You'd better slow this sonofabitch down on a dirt road, or let my ass off now." Lewis said.

Mark laughed and replied, "Sure, and I've been thinking, it might be smarter if we remained together."

Mark turned onto the dirt road and Lewis said, "We've got weapons, but no food and only a little water."

"We have canteens and we have no idea what's in the packs we took. Only, I think staying together is a better idea." May said.

Mark said, "We'll talk about it once at the end of this road coming up." He turned right and after about three miles, it turned into a mess and looked more like a logging road than a county road.

May, reading his mind said, "My dad used to log back in this country. He died during the fall, when he couldn't get his prescription medications."

No one spoke until the road ended and then Mark asked, "So, we stay together?"

"I think it's smarter now that we have some guns." May replied.

"I agree." Lewis said, and then added, "I think our survival chances are better in numbers."

"Okay, the Colonel stated the last know position of the resistance was about ten miles due south of Edwards, right?" Mark asked.

"Yep, but I don't have idea where the hell we are."

May grinned and said, "I do. We're close to ten miles south, but more east than where we need to be. I think we should cover some ground today and then travel at night. By morning we'll be close to where we can start looking."

"Well," Mark said, "make sure we have some distance between us as we move. We'll take turns moving in the front position, because it's the most dangerous. I'd say step in the persons footprints in front of you as we move. We have no idea who has been in this area, if there are any mines, or even if there are Russian or resistance members on the prowl. We'll treat everyone as an enemy until we know better."

"How do we know which way is west?" Lewis asked.

"Keep the rising sun on your back and start walking. The sun comes up in the east and sinks in the west, or didn't you learn that in school?" May asked and then giggled.

"No, I must have slept through that part."

"Keep the noise down and no more talking unless it's important. Keep a good twenty feet or more from the person in front of you. Let's move, and we need to cover some miles."

Meanwhile, back at the gulag, the Colonel was being interrogated by the vice camp commander, Lieutenant Colonel Alvang, who was selected for his position because he spoke passable English. The American Colonel and two other prisoners were shackled to metal chairs and were unable to move their arms or legs. The two men, Bill and Joe, secured with him were his friends, but they had no knowledge of the escape. They were selected because they were speaking to him when the Russians came searching.

"Tell me about the escape and tell me now." Alvang said, his tone an angry one.

"What escape? I know nothing of an escape." the Colonel lied, knowing he'd be dead if he told or not. *I have to hold out for as long as I can, so maybe Mark and the others can reach safety,* he thought.

Another Russian, Private Budian, stood in the room holding an iron bar in his hand. Alvang met his eyes and nodded. Budian moved forward and swung the bar hard, striking the Colonel's left leg between his knee and ankle. The Private was huge, closer to seven feet than six and well over two hundred and fifty pounds, most of it muscle. His intelligence was limited and was what psychologists would call borderline functional. His mind was simple and he was an uncomplicated man, except cruel and nasty, which was the reason he was the muscle behind the interrogations.

A loud warbling scream filled the small room as Alvang moved to a desk and removed a pack of cigarettes. Removing a cigarette, he ignored the painful cries of the Colonel and waited. A minute or two later, he pulled a lighter from his pocket, lit his smoke, and then inhaled deeply. He exhaled and then looked his three captives over closely.

The other two captives were horrified and filled with fear. Alvang moved to Joe, the thinner of the three and asked, "What do you know of the escape?"

"N . . . nothing and I swear!" Joe's eyes were huge in fear.

Looking into Joe's eyes, Alvang believed the man, but he had to scare the Colonel enough to speak. He pulled his pistol and asked, "What do you know of the escape? If you do not answer me truthfully, you are a dead man."

"Nothing! I had nothing to do with it, but the Colonel did, or so I heard. Don't kill me, please."

Walking to Joe, Alvang placed the barrel of his gun near the side of the man's head and said, "I want answers and I want them now."

"I know noth—"

The shot was loud in the small structure and a long thin finger of blood blasted from Joe's head, splattering the wall beside him, as pieces of brain, bone and gore flew through the air. The man's body quivered a few times, as his central nervous system shut down, and then he slumped forward—dead.

Lieutenant Colonel Alvang moved to Bill, took a drag of his cigarette, and then asked, "And what do you know, my friend?"

"I heard rumor that the Colonel had selected four people, three men and one woman, to escape and try to link up with the resistance. Their names are Mark, Lewis, May, and George. One was killed by the guards. I don't know which died, but the Colonel was the brains behind it all."

"Tell me more!" Alvang demanded. "Where is this resistance group at right now? Who is their leader? How many men do they have? I want to know everything you know."

"I d . . . don't know more! I've told you all I know! Don't kill me, please!" Bill said and Alvang could see the man pleading for his life with his eyes, as well as his trembling voice.

"Private, this man is yours to play with, but make his death slow and meaningful. I want to see him suffer and hear him speak the truth. This sonofabitch knows more than he is telling us."

Budian swung the bar and came down on the Bill's left arm, breaking it just shy of his wrist. A scream sounded and the big Russian smiled, showing brown broken teeth. The guard was happy, because inflecting pain on others stimulated him sexually, and he could feel it starting to affect him. He would help kill these three Americans and then find a whore for the night.

The Colonel was no longer screaming, but whimpering like an injured animal. He knew as long as they were playing with Bill, he was buying time for his people. He was no hero, not in his eyes, simply a man determined to remove the Russians from America, regardless of the cost.

Budian swung the pipe once more and struck Bill's left leg. As Bill started to scream, the guard raised the bar again and brought it down on the prisoner's right leg, which brought a loud scream of anguish. The bone on the right leg was clearly seen sticking through the flesh. Dropping the bar, Budian grabbed Bill's severely injured leg and twisted. The prisoner's screams immediately stopped and his head dropped to his chest; he was unconscious.

Handing his knife to Budian, Alvang said, "Cut his throat and be done with it."

The guard grasped Bill's filthy hair, raised his head, and then cut his throat. A fountain of hot crimson shot from the injury and the man's body jerked violently, followed by choking as blood flooded his lungs. Two minutes later Bill was dead, and the growing puddle on the floor under him was rufescent. A strong smell of copper, from the blood, filled the room.

Alvang enjoyed toying with his captives and all were to die anyway. He moved to his desk once more where he rubbed his cigarette out in an ashtray. Opening the top drawer, he removed a pint of vodka, took a long drink and, still holding the bottle in his hand, said, "Tell me about this Mark, May, George, and Lewis, Colonel, or your death will not be a pleasant one." He took another sip of the strong drink and then tossed the bottle to Budian.

The big guard guzzled about a pint and threw the empty bottle into a trashcan beside the desk.

Gritting his teeth against his pain, the Colonel replied, "Kiss my Yankee ass."

"Private Budian, pick up the Colonel's chair and bring him outside, away from the building. I have a special death planned for him." Alvang said and left the building.

The big Russian moved to the back of the chair and grasping the back, he tilted the chair and dragged the Colonel from the room and out the door. Once outside, he pulled the chair to the middle of two buildings, well over fifty feet between them.

Seeing movement, he spotted the Lieutenant Colonel returning with a gas can in his hands.

"Now, Colonel," Alvang said once beside the chair, "I want to know everyone who knows about your organization in the gulag and I mean everyone, or I'll burn you to death."

"Go to hell!" the Colonel yelled.

The Colonel said, "Pour the petrol on him and make sure you cover him well."

Budian took the can, but before he could move, the Colonel said, "Wait!"

CHAPTER 3

Willy looked at Esom and said, "Instruct the partisans to break into small groups and try to break free of the Russians. It's not likely they have every single trail marked, but expect a fight. We'll lose some people, but I think most will survive."

"I still can't believe we have a traitor within our group." Esom said.

"Well, by God, we do, but who? I have no idea." Willy replied.

"Me either."

"It has to be someone who knew we were moving to the mansion." John said, as he stroked Dolly's back slowly. The dog had her head resting on his thigh.

"Hell, John," Willy said as he turned to look at his friend sitting on the floor, "that is a good two dozen men and women."

"We'll weed 'em out, but it'll take time. Now, we'll all split in a minute and we'll go out by teams. We'll regroup near Edwards, due south about ten miles, at an old sawmill." Willy rolled up his maps and yelled, "Let's move, people! The more time we sit on our asses, the more time the Russians have to surround us."

As Willy left the room, Sandra looked at John and then asked, "Are you fit to move?"

"I'm okay, but regardless, we need to be moving. If we can't break out of the Russian ring, we'll play hell surviving."

"Esom, when we leave, I want you on point. Margie, you'll be my drag; let's move and do it now. Dolly, come with me." The big German Shepherd moved toward him.

They no sooner cleared the old house, moving down a trail, when an explosion was heard. Looking over his shoulder, John knew the Russians had just taken out the mansion. He watched the ball of flame roll into itself and hoped the remaining people he'd seen had gotten out in time. *Well,* he thought, *that's a safe house that's no longer safe. I grow so tired of this shit and would love for Sandra and I to have a quiet evening together, like in the old days.*

Esom raised a balled fist and squatted on the trail.

"Let me see what he's got." John whispered and slowly moved forward.

Once beside the black man, he whispered, "What?"

"Russians, maybe a hundred meters from us and moving this way. I spotted them moving through the cypress trees on the left."

"Plant two mines here. One where it's easily seen and the next about a foot behind it."

"Will do, but move back to the last intersection and wait for me."

John returned, moved the group to the next intersection and waited. Ten minutes later he saw movement on the trail, flipped his safety off, and smiled when Esom appeared.

"It looks like a big ass bunch of Russians, a company or more would be my guess."

Suddenly a loud explosion was heard and a minute later a second sounded.

"Damn, how'd that happen?" Margie asked.

"Not sure," Esom said, "because the first mine should have been easy to see."

"I think they were using a cherry for their point man."

Seeing confusion in the eyes of the others, except Esom, he said, "New guys in combat are called a cherry, because it's their first time. Now, let's haul ass down this other trail."

"This trail will take us out, too." Mollie said.

"Tom, you pull drag and try to cover as much of our passing as you can." John said.

"I'll lay some surprises, too."

"Good, now let's move. I want no talking, and all of us need to keep our heads out of our asses as we travel."

The first half mile was uneventful and just as they started to turn north, the whop-whop sounds of a helicopter were heard.

"Chopper." Mollie said and moved to the trunk of a huge cypress tree. The others scattered in all directions as well.

A chopper flew over them a few minutes later, then banked sharply to come back and take another look.

"Don't move, they're returning." John said.

The chopper flew over once more and then they continued on another course.

"Damn me," said Margie, "I almost filled my pants on that second pass."

"Let's move, folks." John ordered, then adjusted his backpack, and started walking.

They'd moved about a hundred feet when off in the distance they heard three gunshots and Tom approached from the rear. The big dog, Dolly, growled and looked at their back trail.

"The Russians just found the shotgun shells I had resting on nails, so someone is short a good set of balls or leg right now."

"Those toe-poppers are good. Had they turned onto this trail?"

"No, they continued toward the mansion."

"I planted the poppers down the other trail a ways and then planted others on this trail. I don't think we'll ever be in this swamp again. But, if so, we damned sure want to avoid this trail."

"I'll mark my map. Let's increase our speed. I'll move forward and tell Esom."

"I think we need to move a hell of a lot faster, because I've never seen so damned many Russians in my life."

John didn't reply but trotted to his point man, who he saw stopped near a big stump.

"Damned gators." Sandra said as she pointed to a huge one swimming near the bank.

"Don't bother 'em and he won't bother us none." Mollie said, and then grinned. She was comfortable in the swamps and knew most of the others weren't. She'd discovered the biggest fear in the wetlands, was fear of the unknown or ignorance of the place.

Most of the gators, snakes and other animals would leave a human alone, except for mosquitoes and they'd attack anything with blood.

Soon they were moving quickly down the trail and it was soon mid-afternoon. Since the earlier explosions, they'd heard nothing, except the sounds of the swamp, and not even the sounds of aircraft searching were heard.

Suddenly, Esom froze.

Everyone stopped and after a few minutes John moved forward.

"What's the matter? Why'd you stop?"

"I . . . I think I'm standing on a mine. I heard a noise when I put my foot down and if so, it'll not blow unless I take my weight off."

"Shit! Which foot? And, your ass is lucky it's not a contact mine, or you'd be hurtin' right now."

"My right one."

"Okay, the key is to replace the weight of your body on the depressed part of the mine. If it snaps back again, it'll blow."

"H . . . how can we do this?"

"How much do you weigh?"

"Hell, I don't know, maybe 150 pounds."

John motioned Tom forward and said, "He's standing on a mine. I'm thinking of placing weight on his boot and then having him remove his foot. The boot will have to stay behind."

"Esom, unlace your boot and pull the laces out, so they hang loosely." Tom said.

"I'll look for some large rocks or logs."

"W . . . what if this doesn't work?" Esom asked.

"Uh, we'll be shy a sniper, but I'm sure you'll be fine." Tom said and then added, "Relax, I've seen this done before."

"Did it work then?"

"In one case yes, but not in the others."

"H . . . how many others?"

"Two. In both cases the victim moved before the weight was lowered."

"Shit."

"I've a huge rock here, but need some help moving it." John said. Dolly stood behind him and moved when he did.

Esom unlaced his boot and sweat was starting to form on his face. He'd never been so frightened in his whole life. *Damn me*, he thought, *I've been through a lifetime of pure hell since the fall and now this shit. Lord, I ain't much of a man and I ain't going to promise you a bunch of things I don't intend to do, but save me right now and I'll try to be a better man.*

It took three of them to move the rock to the mine and once there, John said, "Do not remove your foot until I tell you. If you move before then, you'll end up killing all of us. Do you understand me?"

"I . . . I hear you loud and clear." Esom said, his voice trembling with fear.

"I think, but I'm not sure, these mines require only 30 pounds of force to keep the plunger down." Tom said and then added, "So just the tip of this rock will do the job, I hope."

"You hope? Hell, what about me?" Esom asked, his eyes huge.

"We're at risk here too, buddy, so remember that."

"I know y'all are and I appreciate you helping me, too. I'd rather be in a firefight any day than step on a damn mine."

John grinned and replied, "We're all in this together. I know beyond any doubt, we'd all try to help each other if need be.

Now, close your mouth and keep it closed, until I get this rock on the boot, and you're free." Tom said.

Tom lifted the front of the rock and said, "Y'all help me drag it to the boot. Once in place, I want all of you to move to safety."

Three minutes later, John said, "I'm moving away from you now, Esom. When you remove your foot, do not let the rock fall or shift weight. Try to come up and out. Dolly, come."

"I'll t . . . try."

Once John was at a safe distance Esom tried to remove his foot, but it refused to move at all. Looking over his shoulder, he said, "My foot is stuck and won't move."

"Damn." Tom said.

Standing, John said, "I'll go cut his boot off. I don't see any other way."

"It's your funeral, but I think you already know." Margie said.

"Margie, what in the hell do you expect me to do, let him blow up? Damn, you're a pain in the ass at times." John said as the stood and moved forward.

"Be careful." Sandra said.

Once at Esom's side, John explained his plan.

He kneeled beside the boot and pulling a skinning knife, started cutting the leather. Ten minutes later, Esom's boot was removed, with just the leather of the toe caught under the rock.

"Try to pull your foot out now."

"You move first." Esom said.

"No, I may have to tilt the rock to free your toes."

"Okay, here goes."

John watched as the foot backed out of the toe and actually quivered when he realized Esom was safe. Esom's ebony face was covered with sweat and it ran down his cheeks like tears.

"Now, let's get back to everyone else and let you rest a minute. In the mean time, we'll try to make a shoe of some sort to allow you to move."

"I can fix him up a crude shoe from some of the canvas I have in my pack. He'll still feel every pebble and stick, but not as much. At least he'll be able to walk."

"I'll get some new boots from the next Russians we kill." Esom said without a trace of a smile.

Ten minutes later, Tom returned from watching their back trail and said, "No Russians heading this way yet, but I don't like being here this long. We need to be moving and now."

John nodded and said, "Saddle up, and let's move. Tom, you take point and Mollie, I want you on drag. Keep the pace fast."

Near dusk, just as they were about to walk from the swamp, a bright light flashed in front of them and a sharp crack followed. Rain was coming. Tom raised his right hand and the group stopped. John moved forward, Dolly at his side, and asked, "See anything?"

"No, but we need to check it out before all of us walk from this swamp. This clearing would make a perfect ambush site."

Taking Dolly with him, John moved forward, knowing the big dog would alert him to any dangers. After circling the area slowly, he returned and said, "It's clear."

It was then they heard the sound of a helicopter flying near. Each went to ground and Dolly was now conditioned to remain unmoving. The chopper moved over them fast, banked hard and then returned—hovering to the left of them.

Esom, pissed at the Russians in general because of the mine, raised his sniper rifle, looked through the scope and sighted in the pilot. He took a deep breath, held it and as he slowly released it, he began squeezing the trigger. The door gunner must have seen movement or suspected something, because the barrel of his machine-gun came up as the sound of Esom's shot echoed in the swamp.

Esom was watching his target in his scope when the aircraft commander's head exploded, so he moved his sights slightly to the left and lined up a shot at the co-pilot.

The door-gunner opened fire, but he had no idea where the threat lay, so his firing wasn't anywhere close to the group.

Just as the chopper started to raise, Esom squeezed the trigger and the co-pilot slumped forward. The chopper, now out of control, nosed down, due to the dead co-pilot's body on the control stick and crashed into the swamp. As it fell, John saw a body fall from the door, but knowing the danger of an explosion, he buried his head in his hands. A huge fireball developed and the heat was intense for the small group, but they stayed in position as the flames rolled. A Russian ran from the flames, looking more like a miniature ball of fire, than a human. One shot from Tom dropped the man.

"Let's move, people, and at a trot." John ordered, and they began to move away from the swamp. As they ran, all could hear the munitions going off and then a loud explosion as something explosive went off from the heat.

After moving for over a mile, John said, "Okay, Esom, take point and I'll take drag; we need some distance between us and the crash site, so keep the pace fast. Avoid all trails and move overland. Let's move, people."

It was near daylight but a couple of hours of darkness remained, when John said, "Four hours of rest, then we'll move again until dark. Keep the noise down and no talking. I want three claymore mines put out and that should be enough. We're off the beaten trail and I think we're as safe as it gets here."

Moving to some large oaks, the members of the small group began looking for food in their backpacks and hoped to eat before falling asleep. John sat under a huge oak and opened a Russian ration. He pulled out crackers, beef stew and a can of meat spread. He opened the cans and fed the meat spread to Dolly, dipping crackers in the meat. She wasn't crazy about it, but ate anyway. She was as tired as he was and sleep weighed heavy on her mind. John ate the beef stew without much thought and was eating to live, not for enjoyment.

"Tom," John said as he gathered his emptied meal and placed it in his backpack, "You guard an hour, then me, Esom, and last Margie. At the next break, I'll rotate so Sandra and Mollie will start first."

Not a word was spoken as folks stretched out in the grasses and fell asleep. Less than an hour later, the mosquitoes were so bad that John awoke cursing under this breath. Finally, pulling a rag from his backpack, he opened it and then placed it over his face. A few minutes later he was back asleep. The shift John pulled was rough, not because of a light rain that fell, but because he was still tired. He remembered the days before the fall, how he'd sleep in late on Saturdays, and now there was no rest, unless a person was seriously injured. His mind jumped from thought to thought and he spent a lot of time thinking of foolishness. He passed his shift and then woke Esom.

He had no idea how long he'd been asleep when Esom touched his ankle and whispered, "Movement."

John sat up and listened, knowing his mind was still heavily drugged by sleep. He heard metal striking metal, then a command in Russian. The noise stopped and a different Russian voice replied.

The earlier rain had moved on, but thick clouds still blocked most of the moonlight; at times, it'd peek from a clear space between the overcast. There came a splash of moonlight and John quickly counted the Russians. *Ten, so it's a squad of men, but are they the point for a much larger group?* he thought as he slipped the safety on his weapon to off. *I hope they move by us.*

Suddenly, a Russian officer said something and the squad stopped. Men were seen sniffing the air and John realized they might be smelling them, because all of them had to stink. His last washing had been a month earlier.

He picked up a clacker to a Claymore and waited, anxious and worried that a larger group may be behind this one.

Russian words were exchanged by the group and they seemed to be discussing something. Finally, in a tone that sounded like an order, the group grew quiet, and three men moved toward the alert Americans. The Russians held their guns at the ready, obviously aware someone was in the area, but unsure exactly where.

A claymore was pointed right at the Russian squad and John was waiting for the first man to get just a little closer. While he had absolutely no fear of killing these men, something in the back of his mind warned him other Russians were around. *Other Russians around or not, when this sonofabitch gets three steps closer, I'll send him and most of his squad to hell,* he thought. He felt the small animal gnawing at his belly again and knew fear was starting to eat at him. *We'll deal with the others when we have to do the job.*

CHAPTER 4

Master Sergeant Rusak was pissed. The Americans had his men pinned down, with heavy machine-gun fire and rifle fire, and they were unable to move. Senior Sergeant Turchin was down, a bullet to his shoulder and right arm. He'd taken a number of killed and wounded.

His radio man crawled to him, drawing fire from the Americans and handed him the handset as he said, "Helicopter pilot of a Black Shark."

"Do you need some help, comrade?" the pilot asked.

"We are pinned down and need a few rockets placed north of our position, say a hundred meters."

"What of the tanks?" the pilot asked.

"I do not trust them, but I am out of safe range for using them anyway."

The pilot quickly read off some map coordinates and asked, "Is that your position?"

"Yes, but hurry. We have a number of dead and wounded and their fire is continuing to kill us."

The firing from the American's suddenly stopped, as if turned off by the mighty hand of God.

A wounded Russian near the point yelled, "They are pulling back, and fast too."

Lieutenant Markov said, "They are smart, these Americans."

"Helicopter is two kilometers out and starting their approach!" the radio man said.

"Tell him to hit 200 meters further from us, because the Americans are running."

"He said he'll do that."

"Everyone get down, now!" the lieutenant yelled.

The familiar "whop-whop" of the chopper blades were heard and when Rusak glanced at the aircraft, it seemed off course. It suddenly dawned on him that the chopper was going to attack them and not the Americans.

"Give me headset and now!" the Master Sergeant yelled.

Just as he took the headset, he saw four puffs of smoke and knew rockets were heading for his position. "Break, break, you are firing on Russian troops, break!" he yelled in the headset and then lowered his head, waiting for explosions.

The four explosions were so close together they almost sounded like one. Men and body parts were thrown high into the air and then fell to the swamp. Screams were heard and one man walked back down the trail, his left arm off at the shoulder, and a trail of bright crimson marking his movements.

Picking up the headset, he spoke again, "I have an unknown number of dead and wounded. Your intended target is approximately 400 yards north. I repeat, your intended target is approximately 400 yards north." The radio man had his back to him as he spoke.

"I understand, 400 yard north of our last target."

"Base, this is Badger, I have numerous casualties and dead at my current position, all due to friendly fire, do you copy?" As Rusak spoke he heard the chopper approaching again, but this time closer to their real target. Explosions and screams were heard, but they were American screams this time.

"Understand you have taken friendly fire and have dead and wounded. Can you continue your mission?"

"Unknown at this time. Let me get a count of dead and wounded."

"We are sending four Ka-60 helicopters to assist."

"I understand and we will be waiting. Out."

"Corporal Elout, get me a count on our dead and wounded."

"Yes, Master Sergeant."

How in the hell did that dumb sonofabitch screw up and hit us, he thought, and then asked the radio man, "Did you call in our position last night?"

Silence.

Reaching with his left hand, he rolled the soldier onto his back and saw a wide piece of metal stuck in the man's forehead. A puddle of blood was forming under his head.

"Damn, Lieutenant?"

"Yes, Master Sergeant?"

"Do you know if our position was called in last night?"

"I had the radio man call in our position when we stopped last night for a break, but that was about 300 meters back. We finally stopped here to spend the night, why?"

"I do not think our radio man called our night position in and when the pilot read off the coordinates to me, well, they sounded correct. As far as the two pilots knew, we were 300 meters further south. It was our mistake."

"Discipline will be rough on the radio man. I want him arrested now and he can return by helicopter."

Rusak gave a dry laugh and said, "Sir, he is dead, so we had best pray the commander does not come looking for a scapegoat, or we are both in trouble. It was, sir, both of our responsibilities to see it was done and we failed."

Elout returned, his hands and clothing bloody, and said, "We have ten dead and fewer injured than I suspected, but fifteen out of a hundred. I have two men missing. From the fifteen injured only five will need medical care at a hospital. The other ten can still walk and fight."

The smell of cordite filled the air, smoke was still rising from the impact points of the rockets, and the gators were chewing on bloody bodies in the water. The sweet coppery smell of blood was growing stronger.

The radio came alive with chatter, so Rusak raised the handset to his ear. He listened and then replied, "We will be ready."

"Helicopters?" Lieutenant Markov asked and the Master Sergeant nodded.

"Sergeant Bluska!" Rusak yelled.

"Yes?"

"Prepare our dead and wounded for removal. The helicopters will be here in about five minutes. Have Corporal Babin toss a smoke grenade when the helicopters arrive."

"They will be ready to move, and Babin will wait for your order to toss the smoke."

The radio came alive again and Rusak listened and then said, "The Colonel wants to speak with you, Lieutenant." He handed the radio to the young officer, knowing a good ass chewing was about to be delivered.

"Yes, sir. No, sir. I can explain, sir." the Lieutenant was heard to say. A minute later he handed the handset back to Rusak and said, "No charges will be filed this time, since I am just a stupid Lieutenant, but he warned me."

"Pissed off, was he?"

"He threatened to either shoot me or send me to a gulag in Siberia if this ever happened again."

"Listen well to the man, because he meant every word, sir."

"Oh, I will never make this mistake again, never. Prepare the men to move after the Americans, which we will do just as soon as the helicopters leave."

The wounded and dead were soon gone and the group started down the narrow trail again. The point man was nervous, having already marked a number of booby-traps and mines. When they neared the spot where the rockets had struck, they only found two bodies.

Rusak counted over fifteen bloody spots in the grasses so he suspected at least that many were injured, but he knew from experience, it was likely many more.

He reported his finding to the Lieutenant and watched as the man called the base. "This is Badger, and we have seventeen confirmed dead Americans. Yes, sir. Thank you, sir." The young Lieutenant handed the handset to the new radio man.

It was then a loud explosion filled the air and those not knocked down by the blast fell seeking cover. Men immediately began to scream and yell.

Elout ran to the bunch and looking over his shoulder said, "A grenade was left under a body that was face down. When a man rolled the body over to see the dead man's face, the grenade went off."

Master Sergeant Rusak counted five men bleeding hard and two stunned. Hearing a noise in the water near him, he glanced to see gators fighting over the remains of another man. *Damn me, one grenade took out eight men,* he thought and shook his head.

"Three of the five will not make it, massive injuries. The remaining two will lose their arms. Hell, one already has, it is just hanging on by some thin flesh." the Medic reported.

The Lieutenant was already on the radio explaining what had happened. He shook his head and argued for a moment and then said, "Yes, sir." He tossed the handset back to the radio man.

"The base wants us to continue moving, and due to a weather front moving in, our wounded will not be picked up until in the morning, weather permitting. We are in for some rough rains."

Private Elout gazed into the eyes of the Master Sergeant, saw the older man nod, and fully understood what had to be done. He pulled his syringes and prepared morphine for the three most seriously injured. He doubled the morphine doses, so the men would not die in pain, and said a silent prayer as he killed each man.

"Th. . . the three most seriously wounded just died, Lieutenant."

"Leave the bodies. According to Base, they'll send out a graves and registration team in the morning, after the weather breaks." Lieutenant Markov said as he pulled a map from his pocket.

"That will be a waste of time, sir."

"What is that Master Sergeant?" the young officer looked up from the map he had in the hands.

"The bodies will be gone within ten minutes of us leaving, or did you forget about the alligators, sir? Once we leave, we can forget about burying these men."

"They are dead anyway, so it matters little." the Lieutenant replied, and then went back to studying his map.

It matters a hell of a lot to their families, Rusak thought, but kept his mouth shut. As the senior enlisted man, it was his job to help see that orders were carried out smoothly and the enlisted men were cared for, as well as keeping the Commander aware of any problems with the men. He always performed his tasks well, but it was times like this that pissed him off.

"What of the wounded that cannot walk?" Elout asked.

"Rig some stretchers using shirts and bring them with us." Rusak said and then glanced overhead, out of habit, to check the weather. He saw dark, almost black, clouds turning into each other. *Rain will visit us shortly,* he thought.

Once the stretchers were complete, Rusak stood and said, "We will all take a turn carrying stretchers, so I don't want to hear any bitching about the job. Senior Sergeant Turchin, get your point man to moving and let us move men. We have a date with some Yankees in a bit."

Four hours later, the rains came. At first they were gentle and soft, but minutes later, just as the point man stepped from the swamp, the winds picked up and thumbnail size hail began to fall.

"Get the men into the trees and do it now!" Markov yelled to be heard.

Men were heard cursing as they broke and ran for the relative safety the trees offered. Shelter halves came out of packs and men quickly tried to get a shelter up. Master Sergeant Rusak didn't even bother, because with the wind gusting to 70 KPH, it was a wasted effort. He sat in the mud, leaned against a large Pine, and closed his eyes. His helmet would keep him from being knocked senseless and his pack went on his lap to protect his balls. Other than that, he'd wait the storm out.

It was dark and still raining slightly two hours later, but the wind had disappeared and all the men had shelters up. A small community fire burned near the Lieutenant's shelter and the men took turns heating up a supper meal. Few had portable stoves for cooking and none, he knew, had the heating tablets for warming the food. Rusak didn't bother to heat his food and ate his meal cold, knowing ahead of time the food would give him indigestion. He pulled a flask, one of three he carried, and took a long pull of vodka. He wiped his mouth off with the back of his hand.

"Radio man, call in our exact position." Lieutenant Markov said to his new radio operator.

"Yes, sir."

The radio man was heard giving the coordinates and then said, "Sir, Colonel Sokol wants to speak with you." He held the handset out so the Lieutenant could take it.

"Yes, sir. Yes, we will be ready, sir. Out." The officer then handed the handset back to his radio man and said, "Master Sergeant Rusak, we will be picked up by helicopters tomorrow morning, weather permitting, but we will not be returning to base. Intelligence has a spy working with the Americans and has learned there is a larger number of partisans south of Edwards. The helicopters will drop us off there. Our mission is to kill or capture anyone we find in the area."

"We will be ready, sir." Rusak replied. It was nothing new to him and he was used to being flown here or there and ordered to make contact with the enemy. *It is probable,* he thought, *that all we will find are booby-traps, mines, and snipers, but I will not say a word. This Lieutenant is a fast learner, and I hope he lasts longer than the ones before him.*

The Colonel sat in the metal chair, as Colonel Alvang picked up the gas can and neared. The Russian wore an evil smile, because the sadist he was, he enjoyed hurting and killing others. He especially enjoyed torturing women, who he always abused sexually before putting them to death. If Satan had a human equal, it was Colonel Alvang.

"Colonel, I will ask you once more, who else knows of this organization you have inside the gulag? Who else knew of the escape plans? I want names, or you will die a most horrible death."

"Go to hell, you Russian bastard. You'll kill me anyway." While the Colonel was a brave man, burning to death scared the hell out of him and this man was crazy enough to do the job.

"I give you my word, as a fellow officer, if you name the people involved, I will spare your life."

I can't give him the real names or we'll fail as a unit. Damn me, I don't want to die by fire. If I give innocent names, then I'll have to live with the deaths of a half dozen people hanging over me the rest of my life. This is the hardest decision I've ever made, the Colonel thought as he watched Alvang remove the lid to the gas can.

Giving the Colonel a questioning look, Alvang asked, "What is your final answer? Your life for a handful of useless Americans? Perhaps I can get your attention by giving you a sample of death by fire."

"Private Budian, bring another metal chair out here and then get a prisoner from one of the cells. It matters little which one, but a woman would be best."

As they waited, the chair was brought out and positioned near the metal fence that ran around the perimeter of the camp. The Private then left to bring a prisoner.

"I noticed the look in your eyes when I asked for a female prisoner, Colonel; does it bother you that you will cause her death? I understand it's a very painful death, too."

"Her death will be on your hands, you Russian sonofabitch, not mine."

"On the contrary, Colonel, because all you have to do is give me names."

"Go to hell!"

"Oh, I imagine I will Colonel, but you will be there years before I arrive."

The Colonel glared at the Russian, knowing he would burn a guiltless person alive, just to scare him into talking. *Lord, God, please forgive me, but I can't talk,* he silently prayed.

Private Budian returned with a woman who'd had the hell beat out of her. He pushed her roughly into the chair and began shackling her in place. From what the Colonel could see, she was in her early fifties, had once been a beautiful woman, but now she was covered in bruises, small cuts and burns.

Alvang glanced at the Colonel and asked, "Well?"

"No!"

The Russian officer took the gas can and doused the woman well with gas. He grinned as he moved away and removed a box of matches. Glancing at his prisoner, he asked, "Do you have any final words to say, my dear?"

The woman met the Russians eyes and shouted, "United we stand!"

"Tsk, it is such a shame to believe in such foolishness." Alvang removed a single match, struck the head against the side of the box and when it flared, he tossed it to the gas puddled under the chair.

A loud "*swoosh*" was heard and the gas burned clear. Almost immediately the woman began to give a hideous scream and shake her head from side-to-side as the fire consumed her. The sweet smell of burning flesh filled the air, causing the Colonel to puke. Her screams grew louder and louder, until suddenly they stopped, her head fell forward, and she was dead.

Alvang neared the Colonel and said, "You, sir, are next if you still refuse to give me names. What will it be Colonel, your life or the lives of people who mean nothing to you?"

"I . . . I'll talk, but only on the condition I live."

"I'll do better than that, Colonel, I'll let you go free."

"Free? Do you mean to leave the camp?"

"I mean exactly that. Just give me the names and I can have you out of here within the hour." Alvang said, knowing full well he'd not ever let this man live.

The Colonel quickly gave the names of six people he knew that were strongly against escapes and that had liberal views. By no means would he give the names of those really involved, and if killing these six would help the organization, so much the better.

"As soon as the prisoners are locked in cells, you'll be a free man, Colonel." Then, turning to Budian, he said, "Private, when the six are locked up, take the Colonel to the main gate, open it and allow him to leave."

Coming to attention, the Private replied, "Yes, sir."

"Now, Colonel, if you'll excuse me, I have some new guests arriving soon and must prepare for them, especially the two ladies you named." Colonel Alvang then walked back inside the building.

The Colonel could not believe the Russians would set him free, but Alvang had promised he would walk from the gate a free man. Unknowingly he smiled.

56

CHAPTER 5

Mark, Lewis, and May were lost. While May knew the area, it was dark and she was hopelessly turned around. In their effort to get as far away from Edwards as fast as they could, they'd continued walking after dark and now a storm was brewing. They were standing deep in woods and Mark said, "This is silly. With the skies overcast, we have no idea what direction we're walking. I think we'd be smart to spend the night here, because if we keep moving in the dark one of us is eventually going to fall and get hurt. In another hour or so it'll be daylight."

"That's fine with me," May said, "I'm tired anyway."

"Move to the big oaks off our left."

"No fires, huh?"

"Lewis, I can't believe you'd even ask that question. No, no fires."

"We need to get a shelter up and I think by using two ponchos from the Russian gear we can get one up pretty fast." May said.

A long bright line of lightning filled the western horizon, followed by a loud crack of thunder, and rain began to fall. It was a light rain, but all suspected heavier rains were coming.

Earlier in the evening they'd opened the Russian packs and inventoried what was available. Each had a canteen, poncho, two rations, a long blade knife in a sheath, extra ammo, two blankets and a crude foam sleeping mat to keep them dry when sleeping on the ground. They'd been sucking on hard candies from the rations, but now they needed a meal, once a shelter was constructed.

It only took them a few minutes to make a simple 'A' frame shelter and then they opened a tin that looked like a sardine can, using the small opener from the rations. As the tins opened, they could smell the beef, spices and flavorings. While in the prison they'd eaten poorly, a cup of soup twice a day, and now with real food in front of them, the aroma was overpowering.

"There isn't a fork or spoon in my ration." Lewis said in surprise.

"I don't need one." May said and scooped out some meat with her finger. She stuck her finger in her mouth and then said, "Not too good and tastes mostly like fat or grease."

"We'd better go easy eating this, because if we don't, we'll get the squirts. I can't remember the last time I ate anything with fat in it, can you?"

"Nothing in the last six months. Watered down soup has been the main course, twice a day." May replied and then gagged.

"You sick?"

"No, I can't eat this nasty ass stuff. It's like eating lard or fat. I'll puke if forced to eat it."

Lewis said, "Hand it to me then. I'm starving."

Mark tasted the meat and said, "Awful, ain't it? I ate U.S. military rations years ago and they were better than these."

May said, "I almost threw up. How in the hell can a soldier live on those things and fight?"

"I imagine it's around 2,500 calories and from the taste, most of the calories are from fat.""Here," Lewis said, "have my crackers."

"What I'd love to have, is a cup of coff—"

"Hush!" Mark said.

Off in the distance a chopper was heard.

"Do you think the aircraft has Infrared gear?" Lewis asked.

"How in the hell am I do know? I do know we're lucky it's raining because we'll be harder to detect if they do have the gear on board."

"Huh?" May asked.

"Infrared gear sees the heat released by the human body, allowing someone with a screen to see us, or rather our heat. Falling rain plays hell with the gear and most of the time, from what I heard, they shut the system down. Rain is our ally in this case."

"Oh, I see."

"I can't tell where it's at, can you?"

"Off our left as near as I can make out. The rain is messing up my hearing a little."

May said, "The chopper is getting louder."

"I don't see any running lights." Lewis said and then crawled out of the shelter.

"I don't think they'd use lights in a war zone. I know damned good and well I'd not want to use them."

Lewis said, "It's getting closer."

The sound of the chopper passed overhead and then move away from them. Then, three more choppers flew over them within the next hour.

May said, "I know there are some helicopters posted at Edwards."

"If so, it's likely they're returning to base. I can't imagine them going out in weather like this, when we know it's gonna get worst before it gets better." Lewis said as he stood in the rain, his hands on his hips.

"Get back in here and out of the rain. There's nothing we can do about choppers."

Lewis crawled into the shelter and said, "We know the path Russian choppers use to approach the base and that might come in handy some day."

"Maybe, but first we have to find the resistance." Mark said.

"The hardest part," May said, "will be finding food to stay alive long enough to reach them."

"Like I said, maybe, only I don't think so." Mark said.

"Let's get some rest," Lewis said, "because in four hours we need to be moving again."

"What about a guard?" asked Mark.

"We should have a guard, so let's say you, me, and then May. How does that sound?"

"It'll do." Mark said and then sat up and leaned against the trunk of an old oak. He placed his gun in his lap, had two grenades beside him and an extra magazine was beside the explosives.

It became harder for him to stay awake and with daylight the sun broke his fatigue. At some point on his shift the rains stopped and the clouds moved on, but he'd not noticed it. He was just about to awaken Lewis when he spotted movement. He tapped both of his partners on their legs and when they opened their eyes, they saw him with his index finger extended and against his lips. Both sat up slowly, as if yet drugged from sleep and May rubbed her eyes.

Out of the blue a man dressed in a mixture of Russian and civilian clothing walked into view.

He was of average size, carried a Bison and Mark could see three grenades hanging from his belt.

Mark said, "Stop where you are, and I mean now."

The man froze and his eyes scanned the countryside, while his head remained still. "We're off your left side and you'd better be part of the resistance or you're a dead sonofabitch."

"My name is Tom and I am part of the resistance. Who are you?" Tom turned his head to meet the eyes of Mark.

After speaking with all three of the gulag escapees, John said, "If I had the men, I'd hit the damned concentration camp tonight. Feed the escapees and make sure they've all the gear they'll need to stay with us." As it was, he was thankful to still be alive. The Russians, who'd almost walked into their camp the night before, had suddenly turned and moved off in a different direction. All the while his shaking hands were holding the clacker to a Claymore mine.

"They pretty much have what they need, but we did give them additional ammo, more grenades, and fed them some MRE's. While they had some Russian rations, none of them liked the taste."

"The fat content is too high for them, or it was for me at first. But, after the cold weather hits, they'll start to like them, because our bodies crave fat in cold weather. Now, get everyone saddled up and let's move."

Mark and his small group had a difficult time keeping up with the resistance members, because they'd gone two nights with little sleep. They were constantly reminded of the need to keep moving and while exhausted, they just managed to remain with the group. Near dark they entered an abandoned farm house to spend the night.

"I want all the wood we'll need for the night gathered up now and after full dark, no one goes outside. Some of the choppers the Russians have can see at night, using infrared gear, so we'll stay under cover after dark. It you have go to the bathroom later, do it upstairs, or you guys can pee out a window. The infrared gear picks up body heat, so stay inside."

As everyone settled in for the night, John sat in a corner of the living room, petting Dolly absentmindedly. His thoughts were on the traitor and who it could be. His mind began to see the faces of all of them, one-at-a-time, as he evaluated each. When he finished, the only people he was sure about were those in his cell and Willy. Everyone else was suspect.

Then again, he thought, *how well do I know the members of this cell? Even Tom and Sandra were gone long enough to have been captured and persuaded to work for the Russians. Right after we attacked the Russian Air Base the two of them were left for dead. But, I'm sure it couldn't be one of them. I've known Tom longer than I have Sandra and I'm positive they're not the ones. All I really know is it's someone within Willy's inner circle.*

Sandra neared, tossed an MRE to him and said, "Eat."

He opened it, pulled out the entree, and began eating. When he was half finished, he pulled a knife and sliced the pouch open, placing it beside Dolly. While she didn't care much for the meals, she ate them when given no choice. John always shared his meals with his dog and she was the last of many dogs he used to own, the rest killed a while back.

Esom appeared and said, "Margie, who's outside, claims all is quiet."

"Is she under the blankets?"

"She is, and bitchin' about the heat, too. I told her it beat being dead and that's what would happen if a chopper flew over and picked up her body heat on IR." He squatted beside John.

"She'll do the job. I suggest anyone that has guard duty later to get some sleep now. The new people will be allowed to sleep this whole night, because they've gone over 50 hours with no sleep."

"They'll be lucky if they sleep four hours. I've been without sleep for long stretches and when I was able to sleep, I couldn't. They'll likely sleep, wake up, and then do it all over again."

"I've been there, but right now, I need some rest. Wake me if anything happens I need to know about."

"I've already briefed each guard. G'night and sleep well." Esom said, stood and then moved to the far corner where he had his gear.

It was right at dawn, as they cooked breakfast that Tom entered and said, "I just watched what looks like a company of Russian troops unloaded in a field, oh, maybe a half mile from here. Most arrived by truck, but others came by helicopter. They are to the North of us and it looked to me like they were heading this way."

John stood and said, "Alright, y'all heard the man. Let's get ready to move. Esom, booby-trap the front door and the stairs. Once you're done, move south and catch up with us. Saddle up, we're moving."

"What about my breakfast?" May asked.

"Eat on the move or go hungry. You for sure don't want to return to the gulag, do you?"

"No, of course not." She then lifted her Russian pack and prepared to leave. As she moved toward the back door, she was seen spooning stew into her mouth.

"Tom, plant a few toe poppers and mines near the steps and then haul ass to meet us. I don't like this sudden appearance of Russian Troops."

"I hear you, and I don't like it either. It's almost as if they know where we're goin' as soon as we do."

John moved his cell South and had Margie on point and Sandra on drag. They were moving through a thick forest of oaks, when Tom and Esom returned. Tom said, "I hung back just long enough to verify it was a company of men."

A loud explosion was heard, then what sounded like two shotgun blasts, and John said, "We just killed a few or injured them. Now, I want both of you to drop back behind Sandra and plant a few toe-poppers and mines. Don't use very many, but as Tom plants them, Esom, you provide security for him."

"We can do this. Let's go, Esom." Tom replied and then moved toward the rear.

The men had just left when Margie stopped, turned and returned to the group. She said, "I spotted movement about fifty yards in front of us."

"How in the hell could they know which direction we're moving? Margie, swing east for a while. It may be they got lucky and guessed."

After walking east for about a mile, Esom and Tom returned. Tom said "Russians all over the place back there and they're hot on our tail."

"Now, you mean?"

"Yes, now. It's like they know which direction you're moving."

"That's not possible, or is it?"

"Not unless they have a bird in the air that is monitoring us some way or one of us has a plant."

"Plant?" Esom asked.

"A tracking device, something like they used to do with bear and deer before the fall. They'd tag 'em and then attach a collar with a signaling device so they could tell where the animal went."

"Sumbitch, John, that means one of us is a traitor."

"But, which one?"

"Shit." Tom said.

"What's the matter?"

Tom bent over and from the grasses he picked up a small container about the size of marble. It had a very small flashing red light and rest of the case was fully inclosed, making it waterproof. The bug was an olive drab in color. "Here is your bug."

John slipped it in his shirt pocket and then asked, "How many people have moved ahead of us?"

"All, including Sandra, so any one of us could have dropped the bug, if that's what you're thinking, including you."

"Valid point. There's a river about a half a mile from here and I'll dump the bug there. Let's catch up with our people, but keep an eye on everyone." As they began to move, he said, "The only people I trust right now are the new people we picked up."

"Why not suspect them too?"

"Because the Russians knew we were at the Mansion in the swamp. I don't think they could tell exactly where we were, but they sure as hell moved to the swamp fast enough. In the past, as I think back, I can see where the Russians popped up without a good reason. Take the time I shot down the first chopper with a LAW. There was no way in hell they should have arrived in a remote spot like that when they did."

"I don't know and haven't given it much thought. In the swamp, it may be that, once in the old place, the signal was too weak. But, you're right. There have been times the Russians have turned up when they shouldn't have. I just figured they got lucky." Tom said.

"Tom, that doesn't matter. When we find this traitor, they'll die and I don't give a shit who it is or the reason they sold out to the Russians."

"You need to think on what you're saying closely, John. I ain't got an idea who it is, but it could be any one of us. Do you honestly think you could execute me, Mollie, or Sandra?" Tom asked as he gazed into John's eyes.

"I'd not like doing it, Tom, and you know that, but I would, yes." John never blinked as he spoke more, "After all the dead folks we left in the swamp alone, it would justify the execution, but death is the only option. Hell, we don't have a prison."

"There's the river and our group is already on the other side." Esom pointed out.

"Go on across. I'm going to tie this bug onto a log and let it move with the current. This should really mess the Russians up."

Once on the other side of the river, John switched directions and they moved north the rest of the day, seeing no sign of Russians.

That evening over supper, John didn't bring up the bug. He did scan each face and found it hard to believe one of them was a traitor. Supper was a mix of MRE's and Russian rations, which the old timers didn't mind at all, but he made sure May got an MRE. Dolly lay at John's side and he stroked her ear.

It was just after supper, with the fire out, when Dolly began to growl and her hackles came up. John looked, saw nothing in the darkness, but finally said, "Tom, take Esom and circle camp and check for security. Take Dolly too, she'll be a big help."

"Sure, we can check the area." Tom said and took Dolly's leash.

"Go with Tom, Dolly."

Esom smiled and the two men with the dog walked into the darkness.

"Everyone awake and alert until they get back and that means lock and load."

Suddenly, the night air lit up with green and red tracers from all directions. Screams were heard, followed by a loud explosion. Gunshots filled the night air and then four small explosions were heard—then silence.

"John, I need your help! Esom has taken a round. I'm at your one o'clock position, so just walk out now. The way is clear and the Russians dead, or soon will be."

John moved to the two men and asked, "What in the hell did you run into out here?"

"Looked like a squad of Spetsnaz to me. All are wearing NVG's, so we'll gather up their gear in a minute." Dolly, still on the leash, wagged her tail when John neared.

They packed Esom, who'd taken a single round through both legs at the calves, to camp and turned him over to Sandra. As a prior nurse, she was as close as they came to a real doctor.

John, Tom, and Margie moved toward the downed Russians. As they walked, John said, "Take everything they have of any use. Remember, Esom still needs a good pair of boots, size 11. I hope the NVG's are in good shape, and take any spare batteries they may have, too. Take anything we can use."

The first dead man they found had died from a bullet to the throat, so John removed his NVG's and was surprised when they worked. He put them on and said, "When we get two more, you'll both be able to see in the dark as well. Off to the left is another man."

The man must have taken the full blast from a grenade, because his intestines were blown from his stomach. Tom removed the dead man's NVG's and they moved to another Russian, who was also stripped of his night vision goggles.

Tom said, "Now that we can see in the dark, check every man and make sure all are dead. Oh, I think the man on the right has a large pair of boots, so I'll take them for Esom."

A single shot rang out and Margie said, "He was trying to lift a pistol."

"All are Spetsnaz, see the tee-shirts with the blue and white stripes?"

"We've not seen many of them around, so why suddenly do we start to run into them?"

"I have no idea, but whoever has them under his orders, screwed up by using them like conventional soldiers. Whoa, what's this?" John asked.

He picked up a small receiver, about twice the size of a pack of cigarettes, looked it over and said, "By God, this is how they found us." He removed the headset from the dead Russian.

Tom said, "That means the traitor is still sending signals. Turn it on or is it on?"

John turned it on and the compass on the face indicated the signals were coming from their camp. Damn me, that means the traitor is either Sandra, Mollie, or Esom, he thought. He turned 360 degrees, hoping there was a mistake and to check both Tom and Margie. Both were clean.

He continued to walk and when he entered camp, he followed the directions on the compass and it led him right to Sandra.

CHAPTER 6

Master Sergeant Rusak was tired and when the choppers landed to take them south of Edwards, he groaned. *I am too damned old for this shit. My back hurts, I have only one flask of vodka left, and headquarters has no idea what in the hell they are doing,* he thought and then yelled, "Line up, Turchin, by squads and have one squad per bird. Move, people, and let's not keep the pilots waiting." He then walked to the nearest aircraft and climbed inside.

As soon as the men were inside, the engines became louder as the pilot lifted into the air, lowered the nose and began to move forward. A couple of minutes later they were flying in formation toward Edwards. The aircraft were close enough he could see the gunners of other choppers as they flew beside his. The Master Sergeant closed his eyes and leaned back to get a few minutes of rest.

A few minutes later a *'ca-ching'* sounded followed almost instantly by a loud 'zing' and he knew they were taking small arms fire from the ground. One soldier began screaming and when Rusak looked in the direction of the noise, part of the man's lower jaw was missing. The helicopter began to wobble and shake, which made him wonder if serious damage had been sustained by the aircraft. Smoke began to slowly fill the passenger compartment.

"Shit, not good." Rusak said to himself. As the aircraft slowly made its way to the ground, two others followed it down. The last three feet the aircraft fell, when a loud whine replace the straining engine noise. They hit hard, the aircraft rocked violently, but came to rest on its skids. He watched the crew up front switching knobs and buttons off. As soon as the aircraft quit moving the door-gunners helped everyone off the chopper.

Standing in the tall grasses, he saw other troops unloading their chopper, and the injured man was carried to a good bird. The chopper with the wounded man on it lifted and flew away, most likely to the hospital in Edwards.

As the man in charge, Rusak yelled to be heard over the engines of the last helicopter, "Form a perimeter and do it now. Where is a radio man?"

A hand came up and an unknown voice replied, "Here, Master Sergeant!"

"Get your young ass over here, son, and from now on you stay as close to me as my shadow. Do you understand?"

"Yes, Master Sergeant."

The chopper he'd abandoned suddenly started burning and the crew of four made their way to the last working aircraft and left.

"Move everyone about a half a mile west and move into those trees. We do not want to be around when the munitions start to cook off in the burning helicopter. Form on me!"

Moving at a trot, the men fell in behind the Master Sergeant and moved toward the woods. He'd just reached the trees when a huge explosion filled the air and looking over his shoulder he saw a big black and red fireball moving toward the sky. Then came lesser explosions, as munitions cooked off from the heat, and he even saw a rocket fly at an awkward angle into the air.

"Dig in and make a home, boys, we will be here a spell. Radio man?"

"Behind you, Sergeant."

"Get base on the line and tell them we have been shot down and have moved west of the crash site. Then, asked them what they want us to do."

Kneeling on one leg, Rusak pulled the shovel from his pack and began to dig into the dirt. He didn't figure they'd be pick up this day.

"Master Sergeant Rusak, base said for us to remain in the woods and they'll send a helicopter out for us in the morning."

"Tell them thanks and give them our exact map location. If shit hits the barn door tonight, we may need some help."

The radio man listened to the handset and said, "Out." Then turning to the Master Sergeant he added, "They claim we will have a quiet night, because intelligence says we are in a pacified area."

"*Pacified my ass!* Did you remind them our helicopter was shot down flying over a damned pacified area? They can mark the whole map pacified, but it changes nothing."

Seeing Junior Sergeant Shubin, he said, "Shubin, I want you to establish guards for the night, and I want 4 on at a time. You've got close to 30 men to choose from, but from this moment until we are picked up, we will have guards posted."

As Shubin established the guard roster, Rusak walked among the men looking them over. Many he knew, because they were in Turchin's platoon, others he'd never seen before.

"If you men want to eat, do it during the daylight hours. There will be no fires this evening and Corporal Babin, get some mines out and around us that can be command detonated. I want this place as safe as we can get it before dark and that means each of you will have a deep hole to spend the night in. I suggest you buddy up to save on the amount of digging you have to do."

The day passed slowly, but the men had taken all precautions that could be taken under their current conditions. After establishing security, they'd designated a latrine, cleaned their weapons, played grab-ass most of the day, and had just finished supper, but Rusak was concerned. This was not his first time in combat and he'd learned in previous guerrilla wars there were no front lines, so a pacified area this afternoon, could be crawling with enemy tonight. The partisans recognized they'd destroyed a chopper and they'd come to see what they could salvage from the wreckage. How did he know? Because it was exactly what he'd do if their roles were reversed.

"Shubin, make sure the guards know not to shoot at all movement tonight and resist firing unless they discover a direct threat to us. I am not positive, but I suspect partisans will come to look the downed helicopter over."

"I've been worried about that Master Sergeant, because they must have seen the helicopters descend with these troops. But, they have no way of knowing, unless they had a man near, if we unloaded or just picked up the air crew of the disabled aircraft. And, we have no idea which direction they will come from when they approach the helicopter."

"Pass that information on to all troops and, besides the guards, I want fifty percent alert all night."

Fifty percent alert meant in theory half of the men would be awake at all times, but in the past it was really closer to thirty percent that would be awake. Some will try to stay awake, but fatigue will claim them, while others won't even bother to try. The Master Sergeant also tried to smell alcohol on the breath of his men and he know some had flasks of vodka. While he carried his three flasks, his rank gave him that privilege, but not private soldiers. Private soldiers are forbidden any alcohol in the field, unless given by the commander.

"I will see it is done, Master Sergeant."

He is a good Junior Sergeant, but he has a lot to learn about life before he is an excellent Junior Sergeant, Rusak thought and then sat in his hole.

He pulled a flask of vodka, took a long pull and then thought, *I want to see my Esfir, take her out to the theater and watch a musical. Then, a nice supper in a good restaurant, followed by a few drinks on the balcony of our apartment.*

They lived in a small apartment in Moscow and on his income they rented a better than average place. They had good meals and even had enough left over to enjoy a movie or theater once a month. While in America, he was drawing additional pay, due to his access to classified information, assignment to the United States, and dangerous duty, which when combined was close to a 100% increase in his base pay. Esfir was instructed to bank the extra income so they'd have it when he retired. Many Russians discussed the rubles fluctuating value, but Rusak figured he'd never leave the country so it's exchange rate didn't bother him at all.

It was full dark now with the night sounds starting. First the crickets, then the whippoorwills and finally the tree frogs, were heard. Rusak glance upward and saw a million stars sparkling overhead, as if someone had take a handful of diamonds and threw them into the air. The temperature was in the mid-sixties, but he suspected over night it would get cool, and by morning he'd not be surprised to see frost.

All went well until close to midnight, when one of the unit's machine-guns opened up on the left side. Jumping from his hole he ran for the gunner, still half asleep, with his mind functioning poorly. Before he could get to the gun, a loud explosion erupted and the blast knocked Rusak on his ass.

Damn, that was not a grenade but a LAW, he thought as he moved to a foxhole that held a single soldier. His soldiers opened fire and different colored tracers zipped through the air, just above his head, as the Americans returned fire. He glanced at the sky, saw the clouds were gone and yelled, "Radio man!"

The man ran to him, lay outside the hole and handed the handset to the Sergeant. As he spoke with Base, they seemed irritated that he needed assistance. "Look Corporal, I need some flares out here, so I can see what I am up against, and I want them now! Also, standby for a request for artillery fire. Give me some light, numb-nuts, or the next time I return to the base I will beat your ass! I don't care who in the hell you have to ask!"

A minute later the voice on the other end changed, "This is Colonel Sokol. What sort of assistance do you need, Master Sergeant? The Corporal lacks the authority to give orders for fire missions."

The Sergeant once again explained his needs and said, "I need the light now, sir, because I hear them moving toward us."

"The light is on the way, Rusak, and the artillery is here if you need it. Be sure to get me a full body count."

Your damned body count might be of Russians, Colonel, he thought but said, "Yes, sir."

There came three loud pops and then the darkness turned as bright as day. It took a minute for the eyes of the Russians to adjust to the brightness, but once able to see clearly, a huge mass of men were moving toward them.

"Base," Rusak said, "I need some artillery mixed with white phosphorous 100 meters North of my position. Do you require me to resend my location?"

"Have you moved since you called it in last?"

"No, and I need the help now."

"On the way." Colonel Sokol said.

A few seconds later a loud whistling sound was heard and the first two rounds struck in the middle of the Americans with a boom. Bodies flew apart or were thrown high into the air and screams were heard. Men were knocked over like bowling pins.

"You're on target, keep it up!" Rusak yelled to be heard.

Then white phosphorous started exploding, sending long white twisting fingers high into the air that reminded Rusak of a peacock's tail. Horrific screams were heard as the white phosphorous caused burns and fires.

Bullets kicked dirt high into the air in many places around the Russians, bringing an occasional scream of "Medic!"

Rusak now stood and walked among the men yelling, "Pick your targets, squeeze your triggers, and put your man down. Those we do not kill now, we will fight later." While Rusak was scared too, he had to appear unafraid to his men to avoid panic.

Suddenly from the right side, Americans moved from the tree-line straight for the Russians, most of whom were watching the artillery land. The first indication that something was wrong was when Master Sergeant Rusak fell, a bullet to his shoulder.

One man, yelled, "From the right—Americans!"

The Americans moved forward, shooting down into the holes or impaling the unlucky with bayonets on their rifles. Screams were heard and Rusak moved to some brush, which offered his only protection. Pulling his pistol, he fired until empty, and then reloaded with a fresh magazine. The Americans under the artillery fire ran to the Russian position and began their killing spree. Rusak, seeing his position could no longer be held, crawled to the woods, hoping to escape the slaughter. A minute later the artillery fire stopped, most likely because the radio operator was dead.

Willy, the overall commander of the partisans picked up the handset and in Russian said, "Your men are dead now, every single one. You will find your senior man dead, with the Ace of Spades in his mouth. Do you understand?"

Colonel Sokol asked, "Who are you, because your Russian is excellent. I am Colonel Sokol, the man who hunts you and kills Americans. I will eventually kill all of you."

Willy laughed and replied, "Bring it on, you Russian bastard. My name is of no importance, but the fact I will personally kill you one day is something you should remember."

"You toy with me, huh, Yankee?"

"No, I do not toy with you. I speak the truth. One day you will be found with an ace of spades card in your big mouth, comrade."

Switching radio frequencies, Sokol said, "Scramble two jets with napalm. Once airborne they are to drop their canisters on the coordinates I give them. Now, damn you, get them in the air!"

Master Sergeant Rusak reached the tree line, stood, and then ran as fast as he could deeper in the trees. It was standard Russian policy to viciously attack any position that was taken by the enemy. He knew in a bit, either artillery, helicopters or planes would strike hard. Obviously the Americans knew it as well, because they gathered up Russian arms, gear, and ammo and then ran North.

Ten minutes later, as wounded Russians looked to the sky, two jets dived at their position. At the last moment, the jets pulled up and two aluminum cylinders tumbled toward the injured men. There came a loud bang as the containers struck the ground and ruptured, sending a huge wave of fire over the Russian foxholes. Seconds later, Rusak saw men moving around inside the flames, with some jerking, as they performed a comical dance as they burned to death. He turned his head away, vomited, and then moved further into the woods.

About a mile later, he heard a voice say in Russian, "Stop."

He stopped, flipped the safety off on his Bison and waited.

"Is that you, Master Sergeant Rusak?"

"It is me. Who are you?"

"Corporal Babin, and I have two other men with me; both are Privates. We were all slightly wounded but none are life threatening."

"Did you bandage the injuries?"

"Yes; now, Master Sergeant, I have no idea where we are and do not know which direction to walk."

"Edwards is due north as a crow flies. In the morning, I will take a look a the map I have and determine our position."

"Do you think any other men survived the attack?"

"It is possible, but no, son, I do not think so. I was knocked on my ass by a LAW and took a bullet, which I need to fix."

"Where did the bullet strike you?"

"In my shoulder, and it passed through me. Can one of you bandage me?"

Babin said, "Sit in the grass and I will bandage you. I will throw a poncho over the top of us to keep the light from being seen. I have a flashlight."

Ten minutes later, the small group headed west, away from the Americans and the scene of the battle. Rusak was on edge, concerned about the number of dead he'd experienced. He had too few men to stop the Americans, who must have numbered into the hundreds, and his count was conservative. *They must have had someone watching us all day, because they knew exactly where we were in the woods,* he thought and then killed the vodka in one flask and opened another. After taking a second gulp, he passed it around to the other men, because they were hurting too.

Just before daylight they came to macadam road. Staying in the bushes, Rusak pulled the map from his shirt and knew where they were within a few seconds. Placing the map on the ground, he said, "This road runs north, straight into Edwards."

"Then," one of the Privates said, "all we have to do is walk the road into town, right?"

"Wrong. We'll stay in the woods and walk beside the road. The road may be mined or there may be partisans out looking for us. We will not walk in the open if we can help it."

"Is it not safe to walk during daylight hours?" Babin asked.

"Hell, I do not know, not really, but most of the time partisans move at night. I think we will be safe enough, if we move slowly and keep the noise down. I want no talking from now on, unless it is an emergency."

They moved north and in less than a mile, one of the privates tapped Rusak on the shoulder. When the Sergeant Major turned, the man was pointing a brass wire tied to a tree. Following it out a ways, he saw it was stretched across the roadway. He knew if a man on a motorcycle struck the wire, he'd be decapitated, or seriously injured. Pulling his sheath knife, he cut the wire.

Two miles later, Babin, who was in front stopped and motioned the Sergeant forward. Without speaking a word, he pointed at four Americans digging a hole beside the highway. About ten feet away, laying in the grasses, was a Russian 113 *Kilogram* bomb. The Sergeant Major motioned for the men to get down lower in the bushes.

Taking an old SKS rifle from one Private, he waited for the partisans to pick up the bomb. Then, he thought, *It is not like a bullet will cause the bomb to blow up, so I will toss a couple of grenades when they are near the hole. If a grenade does not cause it to explode at least I will get the partisans.*

An hour later, the hole was completed and the men walked to the bomb. They'd secured the explosive with two green oak limbs, making it easier to pack, and each man picked up an extension of the limbs and lifted. When they neared the hole, Rusak threw the first grenade and it landed right under the bomb and then the second grenade landed within a foot of the other. The Americans seemed confused for a second and then one yelled what must have been a warning. The first grenade exploded and then the second, follow by a huge explosion that knocked leaves and small limbs from trees. Dust, smoke and debris filled the air.

Minutes later, after the dust cleared, there was a fine red mist in the air, which the Sergeant knew was blood. There was no sign of the four men or the bomb and all that remained was a smoking hole, with blood in scattered pools on the ground.

"Let us move and do the job fast. We have no idea who heard that noise and may come to investigate." Rusak said as he handed the SKS back and took his Bison. As they moved his ears were ringing from the explosion.

Colonel Alvang had the American Colonel released as soon as the prisoners he'd named were confined. He'd not been allowed to return to the gulag and a private soldier escorted him to the gate. He kept thinking it was all a trick, but when he actually stepped from the Gulag, he knew he was free.

Unknown to the Colonel, his interrogator was in a tower near the gate with a sniper. The Colonel stopped about six feet from the gate, looked over his shoulder and saw the guard was gone. He checked the towers and saw no one looking at him, so he started down the road. *Even if they shoot me in the back, it's a better death than burning alive,* he thought. *I'd not put it past the bastards to shoot me either. If nothing else, the six names I gave them will rid the gulag of those we didn't trust and some who are known thieves.*

A hundred yards later, just a few feet from the forest a shot rang out and the Colonel collapsed to the ground.

CHAPTER 7

John walked into camp, turned the directional indicator on and then moved right to Sandra, *Good God, no*, his mind screamed.

"What are you doing?" Sandra asked and then added, "What is that beeping?" Her face was scarlet.

"Baby, I can't believe you're the traitor." John said as he moved the device up and down her body. Finally he stopped, moved to her, and pulled a bug, identical to the one he'd found earlier, from her left coat pocket. He held it in front of her eyes and asked, "What in the hell is this?"

"I found it on the trail, John, and that's the truth."

"Sonofabitch! Do you take me for an idiot?" he screamed and Dolly sat watching the conversation closely, unsure why John had raised his voice.

Tom moved to his friend, placed a hand on his shoulder and said, "She might be telling the truth. Think about this, John."

"Don't talk to me like I'm a damned fool, Tom, because we both know that didn't happen. All this time when our hiding places were found, good people died, and I now discover my wife, my damned *wife*, is the traitor!"

"I want to know why, Sandra!" he moved toward her, but Tom stepped between them.

Tom raised both hands and said, "She'll get a chance to tell her side to Willy."

John pulled his pistol and said, "Why wait? I'm torn apart by this, Tom. She's my damned wife and how many deaths is this bitch responsible for? Huh? How many? I love her, but I don't want anything to do with her from this day forward. Keep her away from me, or I'll kill her!"

Tom shook his head and said, "Margie, tie Sandra's legs and hands. Tie her hands behind her back and I want everyone to listen up. Right now, Sandra is suspected of aiding the Russians, but she has not had her day in a court of law. Until that time, she's to be guarded well, fed and in no way mistreated. Nonetheless, if she tries to escape," and he met her eyes as he said, "kill her."

John was sitting on a stump crying, with Dolly's head in his lap, and he was unaware he was petting her. The last person he loved on earth was a damned spy for the Russians. He'd trusted her, loved her, and thought they'd spend their lives together, but now she was likely to be executed for being a traitor.

His mind was going a thousand miles an hour, when Tom walked to his side and said, "John, I think she's telling the truth about finding the device. I'm sure Willy will decide fairly when he hears both sides."

At the mention of Willy, John's head snapped around hard and he gazed into his friends eyes as he said, "I won't talk about this. I want nothing, and I mean absolutely nothing, to do with her. From this second on, I wash my hands of her. Y'all can feed her, beat her ass up, or even kill her and I won't try to stop you. She did this, knowing full well our people would die. How—could—she—do—this?"

"I don't have an answer. Hopefully, we'll turn her over to Willy in a day or two and he can deal with the issue. The truth will come out then."

John turned to face Tom, his face wet with tears and his red-rimmed eyes reflecting his anguish. Tears flowed from his eyes and down his cheeks as he said, "She . . . was my . . . wife and I love her. I . . . I'm . . . alone now." He sniffled and then continued, "All I have . . . left now is . . . Dolly. I'm alone . . . Tom, completely . . . alone. How could any American . . . do this to others? How!"

Tom said, "That's enough of this feeling sorry for yourself bullshit. I can fully understand your grief, as well as your shock. Remember, I had to deal with death too, but we haven't heard her side of the story yet. Besides, we don't even know if she's guilty. Now, find something to keep your ass busy for a while."

John, pushed his fears and grief aside as he asked, "Don't you think we should be moving? This is the last known position the Russians have of us and when the squad we killed fails to radio in, they'll come looking." He then wiped his running nose with the back of his hand.

"Good point. Margie, rig a stretcher for Esom, because we'll have to pack his ass out."

"What about Sandra?" Mollie asked.

"Untie her feet and run a rope around her neck and keep the other end in your hand. Keep her hands tied, but put her pack on her and tie her hands in front of her. Make the rope around her neck a slip-knot, so it'll be easier to control her. I don't want her mistreated, in no form, but like I said before, if she runs, kill her."

Twenty minutes later, they were moving through the woods, with Tom on point and Margie on drag. Each wore NVG's, except Sandra, and seeing in the dark was easy now. Tom spotted a huge buck standing on the edge of a field and appreciated the beautiful animal, even seeing it with the green tint of the goggles.

As they moved, Margie planted mines and set traps for anyone who would follow them. Often the Russians would send a dog handler and his animal to follow partisans. Some dogs, but not many, would identify mines by smell, so she only planted a couple of explosives. Her primary goal was to make anyone following them slow down and use extra caution, thus giving her group more time.

They moved throughout the night, stopping every hour for a few minutes of rest. While Esom wasn't a huge man, his weight grew heavy when carried by two people, so John had Sandra's hands untied and gave her a shift of packing the litter.

An hour before daylight, Tom stopped and then after a few minutes he returned to the group and said, "I have a crossroads about a hundred yards in front of us and it's manned by a Russian T-90. I saw no other troops in the area."

"We can go around it easily enough." John said.

"True, but isolated like it is, I would really hate to pass up a good target like this."

"It only has a crew of three, right?"

"Yep and it's very likely all three are inside asleep." Tom said.

"Let's you and me move to the tank and drop a grenade down the hatch. I've yet to see a crew sleep with a hatch closed. I just hope they're really alone or we'll end up dead meat."

"We'll circle the thing first, but we need to hurry, because it'll be daylight within an hour."

"Let's go, and you take the left and I'll take the right side. We'll approach the tank from the rear. Once on top, we drop two grenades down the hatch and then haul ass."

As he moved, John scanned the countryside with his goggles, but saw no additional troops. It was when he was beside the tank that he saw a track was off and broken. Behind the tank he spotted a blast hole, and most likely a mine had exploded, damaging the track. He soon met with Tom.

"I saw nothing." Tom whispered.

"Clean on my side too."

Pulling two grenades, Tom handed one to John and said, "Move quickly and quietly. At the hatch, do not hesitate and drop your grenade as soon as possible. It's likely the munitions will cook off the fuel, so be moving fast before the grenades explode."

"Don't worry about me, I'll be getting the hell out of Dodge. I've seen a few tanks go up and I don't want to be anywhere near when it blows. Now, let's move."

At the rear of the Tank they each moved to a different side and then climbed up. Moving slowly and placing their feet quietly, they were soon near the hatch. John could hear one man snoring in the tank, as he pulled the pin and waited for Tom.

Once ready, both men held the their grenades side by side and then dropped them. When they struck the floor, a loud clang-clang was heard. As they jumped from the tank, a Russian was heard screaming. The drivers hatch flew open but before the crew could move, there came two explosions, one a second later than the other. Glancing over his shoulder as the first grenade exploded, John saw flames shooting out the drivers hatch and the top hatch. Beyond any doubt, the men inside were dead. He broke into a faster run, knowing the gas and munitions were going to explode next, and soon too.

John had just reached the treeline when the tank blew, sending a huge fireball into the dark sky. The turret tilted on it's side and then fell to the grasses beside the tank. At this point, the munitions began to cook off. Not waiting around, the group began to move south, and only the injured Esom kept them from running. The Russians would be pissed to discover they'd lost another tank to partisans.

Glancing back at the general location of the tank, John saw a large band of dense black smoke twisting into the sky. He knew if any Russian aircraft were in the area, they'd be attracted to the site.

Two hours later, as they neared the spot to meet with Willy, John turned the Russian directional finder on and almost fell over when it indicated multiple readings. One reading was off in front to them, but a louder one was coming from his own group.

He called Tom to him and said, "Look at this shit."

Tom turned to the his group and said, "Every damned one of you stand still." When John approached the group his loudest reading came from Mollie. He had the others step aside and noticed no reading from them once away from her.

"So, the traitor is really you, isn't it, Mollie?" Tom asked.

Mollie lowered her head and began to cry. After a minute or so, she raised her head and said, "They have my parents, both of them, in a gulag. They threatened to kill them if I refused to work with them. They're all I have of my family still living. When I was found by y'all in the outhouse hiding with my son, I was already carrying a beeper for the Russians."

"Mollie, how did Sandra get a beeper in her pocket?" John asked in a soft voice, but inside he was livid.

"When Sandra turned her head, I slipped the transmitter in her coat pocket."

"So, you acted alone?"

"Yes, but don't you see, I have to keep my parents alive, no matter what."

Tom exploded this time, "Damn you, you cost the lives of men and women fighting for our freedom! If John hadn't turned the directional finder on just now, you would have allowed Sandra to be executed, just to save your own ass. John, tie her hands behind her back and untie Sandra."

When John untied Sandra, she fell into his arms and said, "John, I was scared and didn't want you thinking I'd do something like this. It broke my heart."

"This is not the proper time or place to discuss this, but I was terribly wrong. Please, forgive me."

She gave him a warm kiss and said, "You're forgiven."

"All right, we still have one live bug in front of us and I suspect it's someone in Willy's group." Tom said.

"Saddle up and let's move. I want to show Willy our new toy and find his traitor, too." John said as he lifted his pack and adjusted the straps.

They moved forward about 200 feet, when a voice said, "That's close enough, who are you?"

"Is that you, Wilson?" John asked.

A man stood, looked the group over and said, "Sorry about that, didn't recognize y'all. Willy is holding a meeting in a bit, so if you hurry you can catch it."

Willy was sitting beside a small fire, sipping on coffee when John's cell entered. As the leader, John moved to Willy's side and whispered, "I've caught one spy and you have one within your ranks, too."

Willy's head came up and he asked, "Who is it?"

"Let me show you." He pulled the directional device from his pack, turned it on and immediately heard it beeping. He turned 360 degrees and then moved right for a group of men eating.

Once among the men, he turned until he was facing a man standing beside Top.

"Move away, Top." John said.

"I don't think I know you." the man said as his eyes reflected fear.

"I'm Captain to you, and what's your name?"

"I'm Alexander Hall, why, sir?"

Raising the directional device, John said, "You're bugged and sending our location to the Russians. Why are you doing this, Alex?"

"The Russians threatened to kill my wife and kids, that's why." He lowered his head.

"Give me the bug and now."

Alex reached inside his shirt, but instead of pulling a bug, he jerked out a pistol. There came a loud shot and Alex collapsed to the ground, shot between his eyes. Parts of the man's skull, brain, and gore flew from the back of his head, splattering a big oak tree behind him.

While the man's body twisted and jerked, as his system shut down, John looked in the direction of the shot. Esom, still laying on the stretcher, had a big grin on his face. His sniper rifle was held in his hands.

"Thanks, Esom." John said as he squatted. He started going through Alex's clothing and found a bug in the dead man's shirt pocket. He handed it to Willy, grinned and said, "I think we need to be moving, because just one airstrike would kill us all and they do know where we are right now."

"Tom! Get everyone up and ready to leave. Keep the other spy secured and we'll deal with her later. Let's move, people!"

They moved until midnight and then pulled in tight, and ringed the perimeter with Claymores, mines, and toe-poppers.

"No fires. If you want to eat, eat your meal cold. We'll have a fire in the morning long enough to have some tea or heat some food, then out it goes." Willy said, then walked to a log and sat down.

John, knowing something was on Willy's mind asked, "What are you thinking about?"

"The other spy. I dread killing her, but she admitted to the crime and must be made an example of, or others will do it too."

Willy lowered his head to his hands and then ran his finger through his hair.

"What about a trial of sorts?"

"That would be a waste of time, because she's admitted to spying and planting a bug on Sandra. Your wife almost died for Mollie's crimes."

John walked to the log, sat and Dolly immediately stuck her head in his lap, wanting her ears scratched. "So, how do we execute her?" He began playing with her ears.

"By hanging, and we'll leave her body twisting in the wind, with an ace of spades in her mouth. We'll plant the bug you found in her pocket, turned on of course, so they'll find her. I just hate killing a woman, only she brought this on herself. The Russians have probably killed her parents already, we both realize that, except how's she to know? A lot of good lives were lost due to her."

"I know, and at first I was mad enough to shoot Sandra, my own wife, without hesitation. Of all types of people in the world today, I hate a traitor the most, because they deceive people."

"She won't much betray anyone any longer, because the hanging will happen at dawn."

"How do we do the job? We don't have a horse or anything for her to stand on."

"Sorry, but she'll not die clean with a broken neck. We'll pull her about three of four feet into the air and leave her ass. Eventually she'll strangle to death."

John started to say something, but didn't. He would not argue for a quick or clean death for Mollie; too many had died, not to mention Sandra was suspect once. He stood, nodded to Willy, and headed to his blanket.

He'd just wrapped up in a blanket when Sandra asked, "How is she to die?"

"Hanging, but she'll be made to choke to death."

"That's so terrible."

"Just remember, it could be you instead of her. If I'd not turned the directional finder on again, you'd be facing death. I feel horrible that I didn't believe you, but it was hard to accept at the time."

"Trust me, I can see your side of things, but I'd never put your life in jeopardy for any reason on this earth, none. I was heart broken that you didn't defend me, but looking back now, I can say I understand. I was actually caught red-handed."

Pulling her close, John said, "I'll never assume anything about you in the future and I'm very sorry I let you down. I should have trusted you and defended you, but I was so angry." He kissed her cheek and trembled when he realized just how close he'd come to losing her.

"Baby, I looked guilty and even at the time, I could see why you'd not believe me. I really could. I'm just glad it all worked out well in the end."

"At dawn tomorrow, Mollie hangs, so it won't work out well for her."

"Let's try to sleep, because we'll be moving at first light. Mollie made her bed when she agreed to help the Russians, now she'll have eternity to sleep in it."

An hour before dawn, all were awake and a very frightened Mollie stood in front of Willy. Willy read the charges and said, "Since you admitted spying for the Russians to both Tom and John, to protect your family, is there anything you want to add before I pass sentence?"

Mollie, her head lowered, said, "My act was selfish, but my goal was never to harm other Americans, but to keep my family alive. After the first attack on us, well, I wanted to quit, but I knew the Russians would kill my family."

"Mark, I understand you have something to say to Mollie."

"Not long ago, Lewis, May, and myself escaped from the Edwards gulag. I was imprisoned the longest and once knew your family. A while back, after these partisans attacked a staff car on the freeway, killed some officers, and then downed a few choppers during the same attack, the Russians shot over a thousand prisoners in retaliation. Your family died in those shootings. You've been used and your family is long dead."

"That can't be." Mollie said.

"I swear to you it is the truth and I saw the executions myself, all of us did."

"No! They promised to keep them alive and feed them better than anyone else."

Willy said, "Top, bring me a rope."

CHAPTER 8

The bullet had only grazed the Colonel's shoulder, but he didn't move, knowing any movement would instantly bring another shot. He was unsure how long he'd have to wait, but suspected an hour would be long enough. *I hope I do not bleed to death before I can safely move,* he thought as he looked at the grasses near his nose. Off in the distance, birds were chirping.

Alvang and the sniper sat in chairs, high in a tower and watched the Colonel. After half an hour with no movement, then the Lieutenant Colonel said, "The Senior Sergeant will have a quart of vodka for you today when your duty ends. I am very pleased with your shooting skills this morning, Corporal, and I will mention your name in my message to Moscow about how you downed an escapee. Come, let us leave the tower so the regular guard can continue his duties."

At the end of an hour, the Colonel crawled slowly into the woods. Once in the trees, he quickly moved south, where he suspected the partisans were hiding. As he moved, he ripped his shirt and made a crude bandage for his injury. He was weak from hunger; he'd not been fed while a guest of Lieutenant Colonel Alvang, and blood loss. However, he knew his only chance of survival was to connect with the partisans. Due to his condition, he stumbled through the woods like a drunk, bouncing off trees and falling over rocks.

After covering almost a mile, he had to rest, so he crawled under a huge pine and closed his eyes. A few minutes later, hearing Russian spoken, his heart began to pound hard in his chest. He'd been one of the earlier prisoners and over time he'd picked up some Russian words, but he was no way fluent in the language.

"How much further, Master Sergeant?" an unknown voice asked.

"About two kilometers, why? Do you have a date or meeting you must attend?"

The unknown voice laughed and replied, "I wish I did have a date, but no, I dislike being out here with just the four of us. If we run into partisans, we'll not be able to fight long."

"We are too close to the gulag to encounter the resistance, or so I think. There is no one out here." the Master Sergeant said.

A third voice said, "I see blood on the grass here."

The Colonel's heart began to beat loud and hard. He knew if they got any nearer to him they'd hear it pounding in his chest.

"It is likely someone escaped the gulag or a wounded partisan came this way. We are infantry soldiers, not camp guards, so the blood is no business of ours." the Master Sergeant said.

"There is more blood here, moving away from camp."

"Corporal Babin, we are not paid to search for runaway prisoners. We are soldiers in the infantry and we fight partisans."

Lowering his head, Babin replied, "I was just thinking we would return heroes if we brought back a prisoner."

"Forget it and continue moving toward the camp. Intelligence needs to know about the partisans attacking us in a large group and the killing of my men. Let the guards worry about prisoners."

"As you wish, Master Sergeant."

Damn me, that was too close, the Colonel thought as he heard the Russians moving away from his position. After about twenty minutes he stood and began to move south again.

The gate guard at the gulag looked at Master Sergeant Rusak as if he were a ghost and said, "We heard you and all your troops were killed."

"Open the gate, Private, because I am tired, hungry and need a strong drink. As you can see, the four of us are very much alive, but all are injured."

The guard quickly unlocked the padlock, pulled the chain and said, "All of you need to come with me to the duty officer. I am not sure how to handle this."

"Lead the way, so I can get some medical treatment and then rest." Rusak replied.

Finally, after two long hours with intelligence going over the attack, he was issued a quart of vodka by his doctor and sent to his quarters. He had a long shower, ate a hot meal in the mess hall, and then returned to his room where he now sipped his strong drink. *This war is much like the war in Vietnam that the Americans fought so many years ago. I do not understand why Moscow cannot see we will never win this conflict. The people all look alike, the general population supports the resistance, and each time we kill an innocent person the people are greatly angered. I do not think our intelligence ever considered the number of guns all Americans owned before we invaded. I read, where was that, I can not re-member, but there were two guns for every person. Only a foolish country would invade a well armed nation. I think since the American government collapsed, our intelligence suspected they would be easy to bring under control, but it will never happen. I miss you, Esfir,* he thought. He then knocked a half glass of vodka down and stretched out on his bed. He was asleep in minutes.

He awoke a couple of hours later, still tired and with his shoulder wound throbbing. He took a pain pill the doctor had given him and washed it down with a sip of vodka, which the doctor had warned him not to do. Almost immediately he grew sleepy and before he was aware of it, he was asleep again.

Near the end of the day he awoke, but felt drugged from the pill, so he remained in his room and nibbled at a ration he had in his wall locker. When his pain grew too intense, he put the pills in a drawer and poured four fingers of Vodka in a water glass. He knocked the drink back and then smiled as the potent alcohol burned all the way to his stomach. With a couple more drinks, his pain dulled and he grew sleepy again. Intending to only rest his eyes, he was soon asleep.

Morning arrived with Rusak starved and since his vodka was low, he popped a pain pill and headed to the chow hall. As a ranking NCO, he sat at a table reserved for other Master Sergeants and Senior Sergeants. This morning the table was empty, so he ate alone. He was enjoying a cup of hot tea, spiked with vodka, when Colonel Dubow made his way to the table. Rusak stood and assumed the position of attention for the Colonel.

"Sergeant, please be seated and we need to talk."

Shit, it is about all the troops that were killed, he thought and then said, "Yes sir. What can I do for you?"

"I need you for a mission, but I see you are on our injured list for wounds sustained in battle against the Americans."

"It is a flesh wound only, sir."

"Can you carry a pack and lead men in your current condition?"

"Sir, I am using vodka to kill the pain, so I'm a little drunk, but I can lead men when I am falling down drunk. I am nowhere close to that condition right now."

"I cannot order you to take this mission, but if you take it and it is successful, I will see you get a case of vodka, a week's leave to enjoy it, immediate reassignment to Moscow, and a medal. A medal can do a lot for you, if it is for bravery."

"Sir, I have been in the army a long time. I know if you are offering me all of these things, it is either dangerous as hell or illegal, or maybe both."

Colonel Dubow laughed and said, "It is not illegal, but I am really not sure if it is dangerous or not. See, we had some spies with the partisans and they carried tracking devices. Now, suddenly, both have stopped transmitting. We have two spies with the Americans, Alex and Mollie. One of our patrols found Alex's body yesterday and he was very dead, along with an ace of Spades card in his mouth. The bug was still in his pocket and working fine. It was left on and when our troops rolled Alex over—"

"Let me guess, sir, he was booby-trapped?"

"Yes, and the resulting explosion killed four men. Moscow is wanting scalps, Master Sergeant, because a squad of expensive Spetsnaz were killed last week. I need a man with your experience to find the Americans, communicate their location, and I will call in an airstrike on them."

"Sir, what of your other spy?"

"We have had no contact with her in over a week. Her beeper suddenly stopped working and we lost contact. Intelligence thinks she has been eliminated, but so far we have found no body. It may be the battery in her beeper has died."

"May I choose my own men, sir?"

"Anything you want, from men to gear, is available. What are you thinking?"

"Immediately reduce all flights where you think the Americans are, sir. Five mornings from now I will take five men and we will fly over the area at high altitude and we will make a high altitude low opening parachute jump. It will still be dark and they will have no reason to suspect we are in the area. I will need the latest in intelligence to even get close to the partisans. One of my men will be an aircraft combat controller and he will communicate directly with any overhead aircraft. It is important the aircraft stay high enough that they are not seen by anyone on the ground, until we need them."

"This sounds like it will work and it is the best idea I have heard yet."

"For recovery, we will need a single Ka-60, with a couple of Black Sharks to provide cover fire, if needed, sir."

"You sound pretty sure of yourself, so it is a go, and not a word of this is to be spoken to anyone."

"Yes, sir, I hear you well and as the Americans say, 'This ain't my first rodeo.'"

Colonel Dubow said, "I do not really understand what that means, but good luck, Master Sergeant."

Five mornings later, the men stood on the flight-line loaded for bear and packing a good one hundred pounds of gear, most of which would be discarded once on the ground. The rear ramp of an Ilyushin Il-76 was down and the five paratroopers walked up the ramp and took a seat in the cargo cabin. The load-master came by and said, "The Pilot said you will be leaving the aircraft at 10668 meters and once the ramp is down, you need to be on oxygen. He will blink the red light for you to get ready and you are to jump the second the green light comes on. If you do not, he will not make another pass. His orders come from Colonel Dubow."

"We will leave the aircraft at the proper time. You just get us there."

The ramp began to close and more engine power was being applied. Each of the men with the Master Sergeant wore a camouflage crash helmet with earphones, an oxygen mask with a microphone, and a transmitter receiver so they could communicate as they fell to 304.80 meters, where they'd open their parachutes. They wanted a low opening so they'd not be hanging in a parachute and presenting a nice target to the partisans on the ground. If all worked well, they'd land and be on their way and the Americans would be no wiser.

Under a clear visor and mask, each man wore camouflage makeup and their uniforms as well as tight gloves, were camouflage as well. All of the men, including Rusak had a minimum of fifty High Altitude Low Opening (HALO) jumps behind them. Each had a bag on their right side filled with ammo, explosives, and other gear they'd need. This bag was attached to a lanyard they would release once the parachute opened. The bag would then hang from the man as he dropped and would be attached to the individual by the lanyard. It would remove much of the weight on him when he landed, thus in theory make his landing easier and softer.

Fifteen minutes into the flight, the load-master walked by and was wearing a mask and had an oxygen bottle attached to his waist. He pointed to his mask, so the five soldiers, pulled a small green knob hanging on their parachute harnesses and began to breath pure oxygen. The ramp began to lower.

When the jump indicator light flickered on and off in red, the load-master helped each man stand by offering him a hand to grasp. They then waddled like pregnant ducks toward the ramp. All five stood lined up ready for the green light. When the light turned solid green, they moved forward and stepped out into space.

Each man spread his legs and arms out to stabilize him as he fell and to keep from tumbling. All five were in one tight circle. An altimeter was mounted on the reserve parachute carried on their chests. A quick glance would be all that was needed to see how high they were as they fell toward earth at terminal velocity.

Rusak's gear was working fine and he had no oxygen or breathing problems. When he passed what he thought was 304.80 meters the parachutes automatically opened, or at least four of them did. The Aircraft Combat Controller continued to fall. After his parachute deployed and he released his equipment bag hanging on the lanyard, the Master Sergeant could only count four parachutes. *Looks like the Corporal rode his to the ground and most likely from fixation with the ground, but it should have automatically opened,* he thought.

Sometimes during the free-fall, the jumper would almost be hypnotized by the drop, with his eyes fixated on the ground. If the chute failed to open properly at 304.80 meters the jumper only had seconds to deploy his reserve or he was dead.

A few short minutes later, the four men landed on the ground close together. They quickly gathered up their parachutes and carried them to the a stream, where they collapsed dirt off a bank onto the nylon. Using short handled shovels, they covered it completely.

"Now, let us find the Corporal's body and hide his chute and remains."

Thirty minutes later they found the dead man and no effort had been made on his part to open his reserve parachute. Most of his gear was destroyed on impact, but they salvaged what they could and then buried the man in some bushes. They even went so far as to place pulled up bushes on the grave to help mask the final resting spot of the Corporal from the eyes of others.

Pulling his compass, Rusak said, "Take a heading due north and remember there is zero magnetic deviation on the heading. I will walk point until we find the partisans. If something happens to me, then Sergeant Bluska, you take charge. At all costs, we must radio the location of the Americans to the Colonel. After doing that, our mission is half over, because we must coordinate the air attack too."

"Who is on drag?" Bluska asked.

"We do not have enough men for a drag man; now, let us move, and no noise."

They walked for hours and saw no sign of the partisans. They broke for a ten minute rest and after a few minutes, Bluska said, "I smell shit."

"No cleaner than you are, I'm not surprised." Rusak said, grinned, and then asked, "From what direction?"

"Up wind."

"Spread out and let's look."

A few minutes later, one of the Privates raised his hand and when the Master Sergeant moved to the man he spotted a slit-trench that had been used as a latrine. A group of people had used it and someone screwed up by not burying the waste. Rusak said, "Spread out and look for tracks. Look for ration cans, dropped paper, anything that will give us a hint of who was here."

Ten minutes later, they'd found nothing, but boot prints and most of them were Russian, which meant little. The partisans often struck trains, convoys, and even base warehouses to take what they needed to stay in the fight.

Pulling his men in close, Rusak said, "None of our troops are in this area, so the tracks belong to Americans. In about three hours, we will pull into some woods and sleep back to back, with one man on guard at all times. Be sure to call in our night position." He looked at the radio man and then continued, "or we might end up getting shot up by our own helicopters. I know the Colonel will have all helicopters with infrared sensing devices in the air tonight."

"What now?"

"I will follow in their tracks, but we will move slowly, because the trail is sure to be mined or have booby-traps. We are in no hurry and they have no idea we are behind them, but they always mine or booby-trap their back trails. If I find anything, I will mark the trip line, mine, or trap with a stick so step over it and all will be fine. Any questions? Okay, let's move."

For two miles all went well and then Rusak abruptly stopped. The soil on the trail was slightly different in color in one small spot and he suspected a mine. Pulling his sheath knife, he reached up and pulled a limb down. He cut a section from the limb, inserted the stick in the dirt near the spot, and moved forward.

At dusk, he walked from the trail and moved into some dense oak trees. He pulled the men in close and whispered, "Back to back, no talking and if you eat, you eat cold food. We have already discussed guard duty, but I will be on guard last. Now, get comfortable."

The troops sat, back to back, and each removed a ration. It was dusk, with full darkness just minutes away when Bluska whispered, "I smell smoke."

Rusak sniffed the air like a dog and said, "I smell it too. We will wait until half past midnight, and then move up wind. They must feel safe if a fire is burning."

An hour later, all meals finished, three tried to sleep as Bluska pulled guard duty. He could still smell the smoke and thought, *They must feel very secure if they have a fire burning, but tonight we will bring hell from the skies to visit them. Many will die and it is a good thing. If we can kill enough of them, this war will end and I can return home. Maybe I will get lucky and be promoted to Senior Sergeant before I return. A promotion will make my parents proud of me.*

The Sergeant allowed his mind to wander and he spent his two hours of guard duty doing a whole lot of thinking about nonsense or women. Finally, he elbowed a Private and said, "Your shift now. Are you awake?"

"Yes and you may sleep."

Rusak was awaken by the Private an hour before midnight. He quickly checked his gear, not needing light to see. All were trained well enough that they could easily check their gear in full darkness and not miss a thing.

Whispering, the Master Sergeant said, "We are not here to fight, but to be Colonel Dubow's eyes. We will call in the location of the partisans and then moved back out of the way. We will coordinate the attack and communicate corrections during the battle. Shoot only if necessary to save our lives, and ideally we will never be seen."

The men all nodded in understanding.

"I will take point and let us go see who has a fire this time of the night in the woods." He stood, adjusted his pack and then walked toward the smoke.

A quarter of a mile later, as he moved around the edge of a large field, he saw the flames of a burning fire. Using his hand, he motioned for the men to remain in position. He then moved forward, hoping he didn't trip a mine or booby-trap.

My God, he thought ten minutes later, *there must be two hundred Americans here. Why so many? Then he realized, They must be gathering for a mass attack against us. I will call this in about an hour before dawn.*

Rusak moved slowly back to his men and slowly moved toward a hill he'd spotted off his left side. Once in place he took the handset and said, "Base, Badger 1."

"Go, Badger 1."

"Give me the Colonel."

"Have you located your target?" Colonel Dubow asked after a few seconds.

"Yes, sir. The target is a large one."

After reading off the coordinates, Rusak asked for a confirmation of the location, and added, "We are located on the hill, approximately 200 meters from the target. We will remain in place and correct the attack as needed. The Americans are sleeping, so make your attack an hour before dawn. Yes, I will do that. Out." He handed the radio back to his radio man.

"Well?" Bluska asked.

"Fast movers will hit the place with napalm in about two hours."

The Sergeant nodded and then broke into a grin.

An hour before dawn, the loud whine of a diving jet aircraft was heard, it's black shape seen against the clouds, and something tumbled from it.

"Lower your heads, now!" Rusak said.

The canister hit just before the wooded area the Americans were camped in, but a wave of flames a hundred yards long shot from the impact point. Screams were heard before the fire landed on anyone, because the enemy knew they were under attack. A second aircraft dropped another canister and the whole wooded area was now burning brightly. Figures in flames ran from the woods, but only to fall just outside the fireball, still burning. Dozens of men were seen inside the fire, their deaths assured.

Rusak took the handset and said, "Use guns on your next pass, on the outside edges of the fire."

"Copy." a pilot replied.

The two aircraft lined up in wingtip to wingtip formation, with a straight approach and machine-gun and cannon fire was heard. At the bottom of their dive they broke off, with one going left and the other going right.

"Badger 1, we will circle above you while you assess the damage."

"Copy."

"Did any large groups of Americans escape that you saw?" Rusak asked.

"None." Sergeant Bluska said, "God, what a horrible way to die."

"All ways to die are bad." a Private said.

"Look at those flames and tell me some ways are not more painful than others. What a terrible smell, too. Most of those that escaped the flames will suffocate, because the immense fire removes the air around it while burning."

"I cannot do a body count, due to the flames, but my conservative estimate is 200 dead Yankees. I repeat, my body count estimate is 200 souls." Rusak said into the handset.

"Copy, 200 dead, and the Colonel will be pleased. Base wants you to move to your pick up point. You will be brought out at first light, copy?"

"Copy, we are moving to our pick up point now. Out."

"Let us move." Rusak said as he stood and it was then he spotted movement coming toward them.

CHAPTER 9

The Colonel first smelled smoke and walking toward it, he saw a small fire burning. It was about an hour before dawn and the weather was chilly, with few clouds overhead. He knew better than to just move toward the camp and called out, "I'm looking for American patriots!"

"Who are you?" a voice asked.

"I am a Colonel, a prior partisan, who was captured about a year ago by the Russians."

"Move toward me, until I tell you to stop."

The Colonel moved and then stopped when told to do so.

Two partisans neared and one moved behind him. The Colonel knew the man behind him had a gun pointed at him.

"Move to the fire. Once there, stop and we'll check you for arms."

"Son, you can check me, but I'm clean. I just escaped from the gulag at Edwards."

"So you say."

The Colonel smiled, enjoying the conversation and knowing the men he'd encountered were security smart. He found himself smiling because he was back among friends, only they didn't know it yet. He was frisked and the man said, "Sandra, come over here and check this guy out. He has a bullet wound and he's lost a lot of blood. He's clean."

Sandra moved to the Colonel's side and a man with a big dog joined her.

"Can you remove your shirt?"

"I don't think so, because I can hardly move my left arm."

She looked at the man with the dog and said, "Get a spare shirt of yours for this man. I'm going to have to cut the shirt off." She then pulled a knife.

Slicing the shirt up the back and unbuttoning the front, she pulled the two pieces of material down each arm. Seeing his upper torso, Sandra said, "My God, he's malnourished! Didn't they feed you at the gulag?"

"Two cups of watered down soup a day and that was it."

"That's hardly enough to keep a person alive. They must know that's a starvation diet."

The Colonel met her eyes, shook his head and said, "Like they give a shit. They don't care and we were only there as bodies to shoot for reprisals. Listen a few days back, I sent three people out by tunnel. There was a Mark, Lewis, and a woman named May. Have you ran into them, by chance?"

Mark stepped from the shadows and said, "How are you doing, sir?"

"Oh, Mark, I'm so glad to see you, son; did the other two make it as well?"

"Yes, all three of us are safe and with this bunch. I think George was killed coming out of the tunnel." Then looking at the others near the fire, Mark said, "The Colonel was the senior man at the gulag and the brains behind our escape. He's a good man and I vouch for him."

"George was killed and the damned Russians hung him up by his heels as a warning to all of us who might want to escape. He was shot to ribbons."

"I'd hoped he'd live, but suspected they'd shoot him dead."

"They did, and where are the other two?"

"Resting; we've been moving a great deal lately."

"Here," Sandra said, "eat this as I fix your wound. Now, there isn't much there, but if I give you too much too quickly, it might kill you. I'll feed you off and on all day. Tomorrow you can start on three meals a day."

Smelling the stew from an MRE, the Colonel said, "It smells heavenly to me, but I've had nothing this rich in over six months."

Sandra replied, "You wouldn't have lasted another six months. I think you would have starved to death within a month, two at the most."

"Looking thin, Colonel." Tom said from beside the fire.

She handed him the MRE entree and watched as he took the first bite. He smiled and said, "This food even feels good in my mouth. So many things involved with eating that we don't consider. The scent, texture of the food, and even the juices come to mind. I've almost forgotten what real food tastes like."

John said, "Hell, I guess so. Did I hear you say you were called Colonel?"

"I am retired Army, thirty years, full Colonel, and have command experience. My real name is Larry W. Tate, but just call me Colonel."

Willy stepped forward, offered his hand and said, "I'm Colonel Willy Williams, John and Tom are both Captains, as well as Sandra, the woman working on you. She's the closest thing we have to a doctor. The ugly black man by the fire is Top and as you may guess, he'd my top enlisted Sergeant. Welcome to our group. Eventually, you'll be the second in command, but right now, I want you to eat, rest and try to recov—".

The loud whine of a jet engine in a dive was heard and then a huge fireball erupted just north of Willy's group. It was followed almost immediately by a second fireball.

"Grant's group was just hit with Napalm!" Top yelled as he stood.

"Either they've a traitor with them or the Russians have a team on the ground. I've heard no choppers moving in the area, so no infrared images were taken. Top, get our people up and ready to move." Willy said as he watched the big fireball roll into its self. Black smoke was rising to the sky as the second jet hit. The aircraft then came back around and shot up the ground, a short distance from the sides of the flames, to kill anyone attempting to escape.

As Top moved among the partisans, questions were being asked, but he had no answers. The top Sergeant suspected the

Russians had a group on the ground, only he wasn't sure, and without real knowledge, he'd learned years ago to say nothing.

"How large a group did Grant have?" the Colonel asked.

"Close to 250 people would be my guess. Usually we aren't bunched up like we are now, but we'd planned to strike the gulag in a day or two. Now I'm not sure what to do." Willy replied.

"I'd suggest you break your people into small cells and disperse them for a few days. In the meantime, you can try to determine how badly Grant was hit."

Turning to John, Willy said, "Release our people into their protective cells. Six days from today we'll meet back at the old junk yard where you took on the tank that day, remember? Take Mollie with you and once safely away, see justice is served. She is to die for spying for the Russians and betraying her country."

"Oh, yeah, I remember the junk yard. As for Mollie, I'll see it's done."

"Colonel, you go with John and his cell. While we're gone, I want you to think a lot about the gulag. Try to remember the strong and weak points, security wise, about the prison. Think of anything that may help us attack the place. I will not sit on my ass and allow Americans to die of starvation."

"I'll do my best." the Colonel replied.

Minutes later, as the groups dispersing, John returned and said, "While you're the second in command, sir, I run this cell. While you are in my cell, I give the orders and you will obey them. Any questions?"

"No, that's typical. You'll have no trouble with me, Captain."

"Saddle up, we're leaving." John said, and then added, "Bring Mollie with us. Once out of danger, we're to see justice is served, by order of Colonel Willy Williams. Tom, take the point and Margie, you bring up our rear."

Unknowingly, they moved straight toward Master Sergeant Rusak and his men. Just as Rusak was about to detonate a series of mines, John said, "Tom, swing to the north and I'll tell you when to head west again."

Tom waved in understanding, but didn't reply.

Master Sergeant Rusak gave a loud sigh a few minutes after Margie brought up the rear. Ten minutes later, Rusak said, "Gather the mines and gear, and lets get to the pickup point."

A mile from Rusak, John stopped and called Tom to him. Once they were together, John said, "Did you see those Russians back there?"

"I saw two, but unsure how many were there. I was one happy bastard when you told me to move west. They had a team on the ground and if one had not been wearing a silver watchband, I'd have not seen them. The morning sun gave the man's position away."

"I'm sure they had defenses in position, so I wanted to avoid a fight." Pulling a map from his shirt pocket, John said, "I expect them to be picked up either here or here, since both are wide open areas."

Tom studied the map and then said, "The first place is more likely, due to poor hiding places for an ambush. If you notice it's on flat land and trees are a good quarter of a mile off. I suggest we get in the center of the field and see what happens."

"Lead the way and watch your ass, because there's a good chance we'll run into the Russian team that's on the ground."

As John and his team moved for the field, Rusak was having radio problems. Each time he attempted to discuss his pick up with base, static would fill the radio, and he'd have to break off the conversation. Finally, he looked at his watch, estimated a good pick up time and said, "Ten hundred."

Base, obviously having the same problem said, "Copy."

"It is the atmosphere." the radio man said and then added, "At times it happens everywhere, but not usually this bad."

"They will be here in less than an hour. Let us move to the first field and get ready for pick up."

John and his people threw Mollie in the waist high grasses and covered her up with brush they cut with knives. They then camouflaged their positions and settled in to wait. John had a LAW extended and ready to use.

"The team." Tom said in a whisper and pointed at the approaching Russians. He counted only four of them.

John whispered, "Wait until the chopper nears."

Minutes later the chopper was heard nearing and John became concerned, because he heard three aircraft. Glancing in the direction of the sound, he spotted a Ka-60 rescue bird and two Black Sharks, which concerned him. The Sharks were equal to the old American gunship helicopters and they'd cause a lot of damage if they started shooting. *Maybe I can down the Ka-60 and we can escape,* John thought, *but suspected a fight. We'll not stand much of a chance against these birds, if they locate us.*

A smoke grenade was popped by one of the Russians on the ground and the big chopper began an approach.

The Colonel, who was beside John nodded, as if he was reading his mind. Then whispering he said, "To down a chopper is worth all our lives."

While John nodded, he strongly disagreed about the worth of a chopper in lives, but he would try to knock the Ka-60 out of the sky.

I'll wait until the chopper is almost on the ground or loading and then fire, he thought as he rose from the grasses and sighted the big chopper in well.

A crew member on the big chopper stuck his upper torso out and motioned with his arm for the four Russian troops to hurry. Just as the second soldier entered the aircraft, John fired the LAW. The aircraft was sideways and he struck the aft section of the aircraft, knocking the tail rotor off. The chopper began to rotate 360 degrees, because the tail rotor kept it stationary. One trooper jumped from the out of control chopper, then a second, and John yelled, "Fire!"

With all his cell firing, it didn't take the Russians long to spot where the danger was located and John prayed the radio was damaged or destroyed. If the Russians on the ground contacted the Black Sharks the party was over. Dolly sat patiently as they fired at the aircraft.

The Ka-60 began to smoke as round after round struck the engines and a few minutes later the main rotor blades struck the ground when the aircraft tilted at an awkward angle. The blade disintegrated, sending pieces in all directions. The chopper fell to it's side and lay still for many long minutes. Suddenly a loud *whoosh* was heard and the aircraft burst into flames. Screams were immediately heard coming from the downed aircraft. Dolly's ears pointed straight up when the yells sounded and it was obvious to John that she heard it all.

A man climbed from the rear door all in flames. Once on the ground, he began dancing madly, until John sent a bullet into the man's chest, and a short time later, a loud explosion was heard. Lowering his head, John waited long enough for anything blown into the air to land and then took a quick glance. A fireball was ascending to the sky; black oily smoke was mixed with the flames.

The Black Sharks, unsure what had happened suddenly lined up and made an approach toward the downed aircraft. Obviously someone on the ground had a radio because, as the aircraft cleared the burning chopper, two rockets were released. The rockets went over John's people, but the resulting explosions were loud.

"Into the grasses! Burrow in deep, so they don't see us." John yelled. He suspected the surviving Russians on the ground had no clear idea from where the LAW had been fired. What concerned him was the attack helicopters might have seen the blast of the LAW firing.

On the next pass the Black Sharks fired Gatling guns, throwing clumps of soil a good ten feet into the air. An explosion was heard of the other side of the field, causing the ground to shake. The attack helicopters must have been confused, because they'd overshot the target and then attacked the other side of the field. The only explanation was the Russians on the ground must think the partisans were fleeing.

Most attackers would flee, but by staying in place, this time, we may have saved our asses, John thought. *In a few minutes, we'll move back into the trees and then make tracks north. I need to get to the old garage in a couple more days.*

Across the field, now in the trees, Master Sergeant Rusak was in pain, as were the other two men. All three had sustained burns and the man John had shot earlier, after he climbed from the rear door of the burning helicopter, was the Master Sergeant's radio man. Rusak was afraid to move, because he had no communications with the Black Sharks and suspected they'd fire on anyone on the ground.

His burns were to his hands and legs, but a portion of the main blade had slammed into his right foot and he felt blood in his boot. The boot was cut and twisted, but he'd look it over once they were safe. Sergeant Bluska was burned badly on the left arm and the same side of his face, with the flesh black. The Private was the worst burned of the three, with a good 80 percent of his body badly burned and still smoking.

Whispering, the Master Sergeant said, "Give the Private a shot of morphine. It should be in the medical supplies you have."

"What about us?"

"Hell, no, do not give us any. We need to have our shit together if we want to survive this. Now, one of two things will happen. The Colonel will either send a team out to recover the bodies and look for us, or he will just write all of us off as a combat loss."

"W . . . what do you think will happen? I am hurting pretty badly."

"I suspect he will come for the bodies and hopefully look for us. We are the only witnesses to the killing of all the Americans with the napalm. And, if you will listen, the Black Sharks have not left the area yet. We have no idea what hit the helicopter, unless one of the attacking Black Sharks knows."

"Partisans were shooting at us, because I saw the helicopter take hits just before it crashed."

"I did too, and suspect they downed the helicopter as well. We will remain in place for 24 hours, if need be, and see what the Colonel does."

"Damn, I do not know if I can take this pain for that long."

"Bad, huh?"

"Worst I've ever felt."

"Wait until the Black Sharks leave or a helicopter arrives and then use the morphine. If the partisans attack us, I cannot protect all of us by myself."

"I will do what it takes, Master Sergeant."

"Good lad."

An hour later, suspecting the partisans were gone, Rusak said, "Sergeant Bluska, give yourself a shot of morphine, because I suspect the risk of being attacked is low now. If they wanted us, we would be dead already."

"T . . . thank you. I . . . hurt . . . so . . . much now." Sergeant Bluska managed to get out as he pulled a syringe of the strong pain killer from his medical pouch.

It was then Rusak picked up the sound of an approaching helicopter and as he concentrated, he heard a number of aircraft headed toward him. He wanted to dance for joy, but instead, he scanned the area and glanced at Sergeant Bluska. The Sergeant was sitting against a tree, his eyes glassy and dilated. *At least he is out of pain; my foot is killing me, but I will wait and let the medics treat me. I do not think it will be long now,* Rusak thought.

Ten minutes later, a Ka-60 landed and Russian troops dispersed. Rusak and his men were quickly found, morphine was given to the Master Sergeant, and he was whisked away by a medic to a chopper. He glanced around and counted eight the of the big choppers and knew they were sending a team after the partisans. As the chopper lifted off, a medic was cutting his shoe off and another was treating his hands. He closed his eyes briefly, because they felt heavy, and before he knew it, he was asleep.

The next Rusak knew, someone was calling his name. He opened his eyes to find Colonel Dubow and Colonel Sokol in his room. Sokol was calling his name, as a doctor protested, "This man has been seriously injured and needs his rest, Colonel."

"It is important that this man answer a few questions about his mission, doctor."

"Talk then, but make it a short conversation."

"We will not take much of his time, doctor, but it is important and could save lives."

As he walked away, clipboard in hand, the doctor was mumbling to himself about rude people.

Colonel Sokol asked, "Master Sergeant Rusak, can you understand me?"

"Yes, sir. I am just so sleepy."

"Try to stay awake for a few minutes." Colonel Dubow said and then asked, "Can you do this, Sergeant?"

"I will try— sir."

Dubow asked, "How many Americans were killed in the early morning attack?"

"At least 200, but maybe more. Too much fire and smoke, but many were killed, so many."

"How many attacked you at the helicopter?"

"F . . . few, sir, maybe, uh, a dozen or less." His mind was starting to clear a little.

"You had two men missing, do you remember what happened to them?"

"One died on the jump in, when his parachute failed to open. The other was in the helicopter when it blew. I had a badly injured private, did he make it?"

"No, Master Sergeant, he did not survive his burns. Can you think of anything else we should know?"

"I think there are a hell of a lot more partisans than your intelligence people are telling you. Right after the jets left, the woods became alive with Americans, and they were still moving when we left."

"What would you estimate their numbers to be?"

"In that one area alone, I think there were well over a thousand left, after the bombing."

"I find that hard to believe, and they were this close to Edwards?"

"My thoughts, sir," Rusak said, "is they were massing to attack something."

Sokol locked his hands behind his back and walked in a circle as he thought, *The partisans are known to attack the trains at times, fire at the base and even at an occasional guard at the gulag, but why the massing of so many? What target here could they seriously feel they could overrun or damage severely?*

"It must be the air base." Dubow said.

Sokol thought for a few minutes and then said, "That is the only target in the area that would be worth the lives of so many men."

"What of the gulag?" Master Sergeant Rusak asked.

Colonel Sokol laughed and once sober, he said, "Surely you jest, Rusak; why risk lives to free criminals?"

"Maybe they do not see them as criminals, sir." the Master Sergeant said.

Dubow said, "I agree with you, Colonel, and I want to increase security at the base. If you run short of men, take them from the gulag. Sergeant, how the partisans see the prisoners does not interest me in the least. You are not aware of the big picture."

"Colonel Popoff will shit when you start taking his men, but you know that, right, sir?" Sokol said.

"I do not care what he does, personally or professionally, because the airbase is of greater importance than his gulag. In the past, the partisans have taken over airbases, so we have to treat the threat as very real. Move the men to the base this morning, and I want more teams out looking for the partisans."

CHAPTER 10

"This is far enough," John said as he and Dolly sat in the thick grasses beneath a huge oak tree and caught their breaths. They'd been moving at a much faster rate than usual and the effort had paid off; as far as they knew no Russians were still on their tails. Tom was still a good half a mile behind them, bringing up the rear.

"When are we going to do something about Mollie?" the Colonel asked and then continued, "I'm not much for killing folks, not that she ain't deserving of death; it's just she's a chore to guard and whatever is goin' to be done, needs done now—today."

"We'll do it as soon as Tom gets here, after we talk."

"Talk? What in the hell is there to talk about?"

"Colonel, no disrespect intended here, but this is my cell and I give the orders. If you have a bitch with how I run things, take it up with Willy the next time you see him. But until then, I run things."

"I'm not challenging your position, not at all; just reminding you that she's been sentenced to death and while she's alive we have to watch her and pull guard. I'm pretty damned tired too, so take that into consideration."

"We'll do the nasty deed today."

Mollies eyes grew large in fear.

An hour later, Tom walked into camp and said, "All quiet behind us, and I think we lost them when we moved over the loose shale."

John motioned Tom to his side and said, "We need to execute Mollie and do the job today. Colonel Tate brought up the fact she's been sentenced to death and it's hard on the guards to watch us and her, too, and he's got a point."

"She'll choke to death, but you know this, right?"

"Of course, or we can wait and hang her in the garage, where I think the fall will break her neck."

"I don't really cotton to see anyone choke to death, so let me get the Colonel and let's hear what he's got to say."

"Colonel, would you come here a moment, sir?" Tom asked.

Once the Colonel was with them, he listened patiently and then said, "I'm not a cruel man, not at all, but how close is this garage of yours?"

"Another day of travel and we'll be there." John said.

"Let her live today then. I know she has caused horrible pain and suffering to her own people, but if we strangle her to death, we're no better than she is. When I brought up guarding her, I was thinking how much easier guard duty would be if we didn't have to watch her, and I'm beat. I don't have the strength or endurance all of you have. I don't think any of us will complain of watching her another night, if it means a more humane death for her. I know I certainly won't mind."

"Sandra?" John asked, because he knew she heard the conversation.

"I agree, so let her live today."

"Margie?"

"I'll guard her, only I don't like it. Not much I hate in this world, but a damned traitor I ain't got much use for. She did what she did for her own selfish reasons. Not a one of us here that hasn't had members of their families killed either by trash running the streets or the Russians. I think our country comes before our families, but she spied on us to save hers. I feel her kind deserve a real slow death and I'll even do the job for you."

"Okay, you can do the job tomorrow, at the garage. Do you honestly think you can kill someone who is unarmed in such a cold manner?" John asked.

Margie stood and replied, "No, I don't think I can kill her, I *know* I can kill her. I look forward to tomorrow, so I can send the bitch to where she belongs—to hell."

The three men exchanged looks, and not a man doubted Margie meant what she said.

"Let's get some mines and toe-poppers out and settle in for the night. If you want to eat, do it now because at dark the fire will go out." John said as scratched Dolly's ears, still thinking of Margie's cold words. *It's a shame when a good woman like Margie volunteers to kill another, instead of being allowed a life of peace. She should be having tea with friends, but instead she'll become an executioner.*

The night was typical with the fire going out before dark, the coals drenched with water, and as folks lay on their blankets, the guard sat under an oak away from the camp. Talking was done in a whisper and there was little of that. Mollie, hogtied securely, was covered with a blanket, after consuming a complete MRE, and made comfortable. She may be destined to die, but all, except Margie, felt there was no need to mistreat her.

One by one folks drifted off to sleep. John fell asleep with Sandra in his arms and Dolly's head in his lap. At some point in the middle of the night, the dog gave a low growl of warning and a minute later, Tom touched his ankle.

"Someone is out there. The night sounds are gone and I heard movement." Tom whispered.

"Wake the others."

The sound of metal striking something hard was heard and then a low laugh. A few seconds later a fire was burning, not fifty feet from John's group. Russian voices were heard and as John watched, sleeping bags were opened and placed on the ground.

A voice was heard on a radio and a soldier picked up the handset and spoke. A minute later, he handed it back to the radio man and said something to the others.

John kept petting Dolly, hoping she'd not growl. As he waited, he counted the men in the group. It looked like a squad of ten men. He glanced at Tom and saw him mimic squeezing a clacker of a Claymore mine. John nodded and slipped the safety off his Bison.

Tom waited until one man pulled a map from his pocket and the Russians moved close to the fire to see. Once they were all in place, except for a lone guard, he squeezed the clacker and exploded the Claymore. The noise was earth shattering as the ball-bearing size pellets ripped through trees, leaves, and men. John noticed a wall of blood explode from the targets and a fine mist of crimson remained in the air long after the men fell to the grasses. Screams were heard, along with a few of them mumbling what John thought were rote memorized prayers.

The guard stood, which was the worst thing he could have done and Sandra fired once, her shot dropping the man. Long minutes passed.

"Stay in position. No one move." John ordered.

Over the next twenty minutes the screams ceased, the prayers stopped, and no movement was heard. Slowly standing, John said, "Tom, bring your flashlight and let's see what we killed. You shine the light and I'll check them out."

"Okay, just like the old days, huh?"

"Sure, I guess. Are you ready?"

A light came on and Tom said, "Let's get this over with. I think we'll need to move in a few minutes."

The men hit by the Claymore were torn to ribbons and John was surprised any of them had survived long enough to pray or scream. A huge puddle of blood was where the men lay, knocked over like bowling pins. To make sure the men were dead, John cut each throat.

"Let's check the last one, the guard." Tom said.

"Use some caution here, because he might just be slightly wounded."

"I'll hold the light off to the side. There he is, straight in front of you. See him?"

"Looks like a bullet to the chest."

"Watch him, he just moved."

John neared the man and said, "Twitching because it's a fatal injury. I'll finish him off with my knife."

"Move to the side, because if he resists, I'm shooting his ass."

John squatted beside the Russian and knocked his helmet off. Grasping his hair he raised the man's head and with a quick flash of his knife blade a fountain of blood shot from the injury. The

Russian began choking on his own blood as his fingers clawed at the dirt. His eyes moved from side to side, rapidly, showing fear and pain. A couple of minutes later, his movements stopped and he gave a blank stare—he was dead.

"Take all the gear we can use. Even the packs, because they might have NVG's and batteries. Since we have some NVG's now, the batteries are a premium. As a matter of fact, when we move in a few minutes, we need to wear them. I suspect the Russians are pissed about the downed chopper."

"I think it's just business as usual, and they've teams out looking for us."

"Most likely." John replied and as he neared his camp he said, "Get saddled up, we're moving. We'll continue to move until we reach the garage today."

"Good, I'm looking forward to hanging this bitch." Margie said.

"That's enough of that kind of talk, right now. You'll do the job, so no reason to rub it in her face that she'll die today. I don't want another word spoken about her death, understood?"

"I understand, completely." Margie replied shaking her head.

"Wear NVG's tonight. We have no idea if other Russian teams are near or not. Tom, what was on the bodies?"

"Guns, ammo, grenades, mines, a sniper rifle with scope, some explosive that looks like C-4, with some fuses. There was this ugly-assed thing, a 40mm grenade launcher."

"It's a Russian *RG-6* and it's a real bad ass in a fight, carrying 6 rounds. Was the man wearing a vest with ammo?"

"Yep, and here it is," Tom handed the vest to him and continued, "if you don't mind a little blood on it."

"When the bullets start flying, I'm not one to care about a little blood on something. Let's get them moving." John said and then added, "Sandra, you take point and Margie, you're drag. Colonel, you handle the rope on Mollie's neck and try to help her moving in the darkness."

Ten minutes later, they were deep in the woods, with Sandra using a compass to maintain their course, as John counted the steps.

At mid morning, Tom stopped at the edge of the woods and whispered, "The garage is off to the left. It looks quiet."

"Let's watch for a while and make sure it's safe. Then, you and I will check the place out." John replied.

An hour passed, then John said, "Y'all wait here, while Tom and I check the place out. If it's safe, one of us will return. If you see one of us attempting to wave you in, it's a trap, okay? We will return here for you."

"Got it." Sandra said and then asked, "Are you taking Dolly?"

"I thought I would, because she's good with booby-traps and mines. Unless you want to keep her with you?"

"No, I agree with you taking her."

"Come, girl, let's go for a walk. Tom let us lead the way." John said and then moved forward.

The garage looked about the same, except a tank had blown part of the front of the structure off with a cannon and the walls were pock marked with holes from machine-gun and rifle fire. The damage was done over a year prior and the Russians had sent a dog team after John and his cell. Dolly had been injured in a fight with the Russian dog. Eventually the dog and the soldiers were killed.

They moved to the front of the garage and instead of opening the door, a classic place to place a booby-trap, John and Dolly entered through a huge hole in the wall. Then, carefully checking the door and allowing Dolly to smell it, John opened the entrance way and Tom entered. Dust and debris covered the inside of the facility and the old wood burning stove with pipe was still in place. Nothing looked disturbed since their last visit, but they went out the back door and checked as well, finding nothing out of place.

"Return for the others." John said.

As Tom walked away, John began moving things around inside the garage to allow for sleeping and preparing meals. An old aluminum table was in the corner, cigarette butts littered the office area, and the walls were pitted with metal hand grenade fragments from a booby-trap that had exploded. Looking at the table, John thought, *It's been so long since I ate at a table, I may have to try it tonight. I guess formal dining is out, since I lack the appropriate clothing.*

When Tom and the rest joined him in the garage, Sandra said, "I don't like this place and didn't like it the first time we were here."

"I saw tank tracks in the in the grass and they're fresh, too. I'd guess a day or two ago." John said. "They come from the west, so we didn't see them before."

"Most likely a scouting party of Russians," Colonel Tate said and continued, "and they do it all the time. Usually, if a place has a road, they use armor to check it out."

"Margie, you go outside and keep your ears and eyes open." John ordered, as he looked at Mollie.

Tom said, "You can't put the execution off much longer. Let's take a walk around and see what we can find that'll work. I suspect a four foot drop will be enough, but I'm no expert on hangings."

"I saw an old crane out back that's rusted to hell and back, so we can use it. Tie a rope to the main hook block, have her stand on the operators cab and then push her off. The hook is pretty high up, so it should work."

"We might want to add some weight to her feet, because she's like the rest of us, thin. We want her neck to break."

"Listen, once we push her from the cab, she dies. I want her neck to break, but if that doesn't happen, then she'll choke to death. Willy found her guilty of spying and she admitted to us she was doing it. She must be made an example of and we'll put a note on her that will state her crime. She will be left hanging, too. I figure it's a hundred yards to the garage, so we'll be gone before the stink gets too bad."

"Sandra can stand watch, while we see if Margie can be an executioner or not." Tom said.

"You gather up some wheels without tires, while I go and get everyone except Sandra."

The small group returned, with Mollie suddenly looking apprehensive, and Tom said, "I rigged a rope and have three tires we can attach to her legs. I don't know how to make a hangman's noose, but I have a good tight slipknot in place."

"Everyone, follow me to the crane. Once there, Mollie, Margie, and I will climb to the top of the operators cab. Margie will attach the rope and then push Mollie from the cab."

"Don't . . . don't kill me, please. Please don't do this. I promise I won't do it again, please! Oh, God, help me!"

"Colonel, gag the prisoner." Tom said.

Mollie resisted, but a few minutes later they were standing by the crane, with the prisoner's eyes huge in fear.

Moving to Mollie, John tied a rope around her neck and said, "You can either climb up and onto the cab, or we'll pull you up by the neck. If you'll climb, nod."

She quickly nodded.

John pulled his knife and cut the rope holding her hands behind her back, she'd need her hands to climb. Mollie quickly climbed on top of the operators cab, John following her, pistol in hand.

Once on top, her hands were quickly bound behind her back, her feet tied together, and the hanging rope placed around her neck. She was crying now, realizing she would die in just a few minutes, but her tears were wasted on her captors. Once John had three tire rims tied to her feet, he removed her gag and said, "You have two minutes to pray, because two and half minutes from now, you'll be standing in front of God."

"Don't do this to me! I beg you, please! I only wanted to keep my family alive and I meant no harm!" She rambled on and on, making little sense.

"You have one minute left, so I suggest you pray, because you *will* die. If you don't believe in God, that's okay too, only I'd take no chances if I were you. You'll know in a minute if God's real or not."

Exactly one minute passed and then John said, "Margie, push her from the cab, but watch the rims or they'll knock your ass off as well."

"No! You can't do this to me, no! Please, please, I —"

Margie was smiling an evil smile as she pushed Mollie from the cab and then moved to the side as the three rims followed the doomed woman.

Mollie fell with a scream, reached the end of the rope, the noose tightened, the extra weight pulled on the body, and her head separated from her torso. The head, eyes blinking, fell to land near Tom, who took a step back. The body fell to the ground and began to quiver and jerk violently. Blood spurted high into the air from her severed neck and her hands were opening and closing into fists. Finally, the fingers stopped moving, except for a thumb that quivered.

"Sonofabitch," Tom said, "too much weight."

Margie was still on the cab, giggling at the horrific scene.

John turned his back to Mollie and said, "Once she's bled out, well hang her by her feet and place the sign on her chest. She was sentenced to hang and by God, we saw the job done."

Margie said, "Did you see that bitches head fly off? I loved it! She got *exactly* what she deserved!"

John's eyes narrowed and his voice was firm as he said, "That's enough of that bullshit. We just hanged one of our own and I don't care much for the job. If you think it was cute or fun, that's fine, but by God, keep your mouth shut!"

Margie started to speak, but must have thought otherwise, because she closed her mouth. She then nodded and climbed from the cab. John moved to the head and placed the ace of spades card in her bloody mouth.

"Once back at the garage, Margie relieve Sandra as the guard."

Margie moved to the guard position and Sandra soon joined the others inside the garage. She could tell by John's face that something bad had happened.

"How'd it go?" Sandra asked.

"We added too much weight to her body and it pulled her head off."

"My God, John, you didn't?"

"Yep," Tom said and then added, "and I'm sorry to say the weight idea was all mine."

"Look, she's dead and she died quickly. Our mission is complete, so let it go." the Colonel said. He then pulled an old wooden chair from the wall and took it to the table. Sitting he continued, "We did the best we could, but I've never hanged anyone before.

I've seen a few shot, so this was a first for all of us. The next time we catch a spy or traitor, and there *will* be a next time, we know how to do the job right."

"The next time." John said in a voice just above a whisper.

CHAPTER 11

The Russian medivac helicopters made a straight in approach to the air base and landed beside the base hospital, where Master Sergeant Rusak and his men were attempting to recover from their injuries. Medics were working hard to save the one badly burned Private that had lived long enough to be airlifted out, but the other had burned to death with a flaming helicopter on his back. Then, in another unit, a Corporal had stepped on a mine, which exploded a large container filled with oil and gasoline, and the explosion killed five and injured seven men. As far as the medics on the choppers were concerned, it was just another day in America.

Master Sergeant Rusak was in a private room, by order of Colonel Dubow and his medical attention was superior. Thanks to the Sergeant, the Colonel had reported the largest number of Americans killed so far in the conflict. He'd been immediately added to the promotion list for General, Rusak was now a Major, and Bluska a Master Sergeant. The Private was a Senior Sergeant, but it was unlikely he'd live long enough to enjoy the pay. Rarely, if ever, did a man survive being burned as badly as he was, so it didn't look good. All five would be awarded some medal or the other, only none of them cared and two were dead. The cost was easily justified in Rusak's mind; two or three men for over two hundred Americans.

"I see you are awake, Major." a doctor said as he entered, clipboard in hand.

"Major?" Rusak asked, unaware of his promotion into the officers ranks.

"Uh, yes sir, that is what your chart reads."

"My name is Rusak, Captain, and I am a Master Sergeant."

"Not any longer." Colonel Dubow said and entered the room, "You have been promoted, as all of you have been. Our number of kills is a new record and all of Russia is talking about our unit, but since your mission was classified, all they know is we killed over two hundred Americans."

"Sir, I cannot be an officer, I lack the education."

"Seems Russia does not require an education in your case, Rusak. Once returned to Russia, you will be sent to a school where experts teach men to become officers. Our country needs men like you, and we have been assured you will graduate. You will learn language, protocol, customs, dining, and writing. I am sure you will do just fine."

"I . . . I am not sure what to say."

"Then be a good officer, and say nothing, Major. Now, once you are up and moving, you will take command of the infantry unit Lieutenant Markov is currently commanding. We were short of good officers, but your promotion will fix our shortage, in one unit anyway. We have line units being commanded by Lieutenants and Captains, when we should have Majors and Captains."

Rusak was feeling sleepy and had no idea he'd been in the hospital for almost a week. He'd lost one toe, had a mangled foot, and his burns, while painful, were not life-threatening. He gazed into the Colonel's eyes and said, "Yes, sir."

Dubow tossed a quart of vodka to the new Major and said, "Celebrate in moderation, since you are on medication."

"Sir, what of my men?"

"So, you are thinking of your men already? See, you will make a fine officer. Of the three of you, you are the least injured. Bluska has some serious burns to his face and left side, which means he will be returning home for more advanced medical care. The burned Private is hanging to life by a thread, and the doctors tell me it is only a matter of time before he dies. He experienced over eighty percent of his body burned and has developed pneumonia, so forget about him."

I cannot forget about him, he is one of my men. I am not sure I can be an officer, if they write men off and forget about them so easily, the new Major thought.

"Are you okay, Major, you look as if your mind is wandering?" Colonel Dubow asked.

"It is the drugs, sir. The medication makes it hard for me to concentrate or keep my thoughts lined up properly. I apologize for my lack of attentiveness, Colonel."

Patting Rusak's shoulder, Dubow said, "After your combat injury, I have no problem understanding how the drugs can affect you. You are on painkillers, medicines to make you relax, and medication to help you sleep. I want you to rest until the doctors say you are fit for release, and worry about nothing. Once you are released, you will need to move to our officers quarters and start eating at the officers mess. Your promotion was a big one, Rusak, and now your thinking will have to change. You need to consider the big picture of combat and not just the small window you were looking out in the past. Men will die, but it is your job to make sure we kill more of them than they do of us. Attrition will end this war, as it has all wars in the past. Mother Russia will be victorious in the end, as we always have been."

What of Afghanistan and our mess there, Colonel? We damned sure did not win there, Rusak thought as he opened the vodka and took a short snort.

Over the next month, few Americans were killed, but mines, booby-traps and ambushes racked up the number of Russian maimed and dead to the point Moscow was wanting answers. Colonel Sokol was under a great deal of pressure and was drinking far more than usual. More than one staff meeting was canceled because the man was unable to function due to strong drink. He was terrified of failure and knew anything other than complete success would be frowned upon. He walked around his office now, hair uncombed, breath reeking of alcohol, and his nerves shot. He needed a shave desperately, except his hands were shaking so badly it wouldn't happen today.

"Falin, I want you to select fifty prisoners and take them into Edwards and hang them."

"Oh, and why fifty, sir?" the Major asked, knowing full well the Colonel's mind was not working as it should.

Suddenly grinning, Sokol said, "Because I just ordered it done. I may be drinking a bit more than usual, Major, but I am still the boss here and what I order, you will do."

"Yes, sir. I will see them killed within the hour." Major Falin replied, suspecting he would do like the last time and simply forget the order. Sokol no longer followed up on his orders and usually forgot them anyway. The constant consumption of alcohol had deadened his mind to the point that other officers joked about him now. He no longer attended interrogations or watched executions as he once did. All he did these days was stay in his quarters and drink.

"I cannot figure out," Sokol took a long swig of vodka and then continued, "why the Americans are so damned, uh, —"

"Determined to beat us?" Falin asked. It was typical of Sokol to forget words these days and others often finished his sentences for him.

"Exactly."

"Sir, these people have a history of being determined. I would like to remind you that these are the same people who carved a once great nation out of woods and wilderness. There is very little quit in Americans over all, especially when it comes to fighting for their country. My guess is we are no closer to conquering this country today than we were when we first arrived."

"They must have a weakness we can use to bring them under our control."

"Death usually works, but not always. The last bunch we hanged were still praying for their country when the truck they were standing on drove out from under them. Colonel, they died praying for America and not themselves."

"I believe in no God!" Sokol screamed and then guzzled more vodka.

"What you and I believe is not important. It is something most Americans believe and that is what we are battling."

"You stand there and expect me to believe the Americans are all Christians and we are fighting a holy war of some sort? Bull-shit."

"No, sir, this is not about religion, as you know. Americans are complex people, sir, and while they might come to blows over politics with each other, they will not tolerate being invaded by anyone. They see America as blessed by God and a special country. Most are willing to die to regain their country and that spirit is the very essence of what we are fighting."

Cocking his head to one side and glaring at Falin, Sokol said, "With their country torn to hell and back, do you mean patriotism is the reason for their fighting us? Hell, they have no country!"

Knowing arguing with a drunk was a waste of time, Falin said, "I must leave, sir, and see to the executions you ordered."

"Executions? Who is to be killed now, Falin?"

"You requested fifty American's be hanged, sir."

"Yes, yes, I guess I did at that. Major, if you had my job, what would you do to bring the partisans under control?"

"So, do you want my honest opinion, sir?"

"Yes, uh, please." Sokol moved to his bed, sat on a corner and met the Major's eyes.

"I would break our troops down to squad size groups, train them better on mines and booby-traps, and then send them out. I would keep them out a month at a time, resupplying them with helicopters, and evacuating their dead and wounded. I would fly in replacements for those killed and hospitalized and keep them in the field."

"Surely there must be more to your plan." The Colonel took a long swig of his drink and then pushed the cork deep into the neck of the bottle.

"I would have everything that flies working with the troops on the ground. They would allow the men to stay out in the field a long time, provide assistance in fights, feed the troops and keep them supplied. The infrared aircraft I would have out every night the weather would allow. The key, or so I see it, is to work smarter with what we have, sir."

"What else, Major?"

"Sir, this is none of my business, but I have heard rumor that Colonel Dubow is considering relieving you of duty if your drinking does not slow down or stop. I cannot validate the information and am only telling you what I have heard."

"You are right, Major, it is none of your damned business. Now, I want what you suggested implemented immediately and want you to present our new tactics at the staff meeting this week."

"Sir, the staff meeting was yesterday and you missed it. I covered it for you. I am sure you were so busy it had slipped your mind."

"Well, by God, prepare another meeting, and I want you to explain what you just told me to everyone. I want all forces to work closely together and help end this damned war, understood?"

"Yes, sir, I will call for a meeting later this afternoon."

"Good, good, and let me know how it goes." Sokol stood, with the bottle in his hand and raised it to his lips. Instead of taking a drink, he tossed the half empty bottle to his bed.

The Major saluted, turned and left the Colonel's quarters.

Major Rusak was back in the saddle again and leading troops, but as an officer, he found his role much safer. His job was to run things and not personally go into the field. Additionally, with his promotion and Sergeant Bluska's, the other men in his old unit had been promoted as well. He had a tent set up in the woods and he was surrounded by a hundred men. They were all dug in and for the first time in his career he slept well at night. He liked the idea of Colonel Sokol's and agreed that smaller units with air support would do well. He currently had twenty units of ten men each out in the field and most of each day he'd sat by the radio drinking hot tea. This was the second day of the insertion by chopper, so he was tense and a bit nervous. So far, all was quiet.

He'd just raised his cup to his lips when the radio exploded with excited chatter.

The radio operator began to talk and Rusak could hear gunfire and explosions in the background as the men in the field began requesting assistance. A huge explosion was heard on the radio speaker and then complete silence.

"Bravo 6, do you read, over?" the headquarters radio man asked continuously.

A few minutes later, an accented voice, speaking Russian said, "My name is Colonel Williams and your men are all dead. This is the third squad we have killed today. Come for me and you will discover Americans are hard to kill, comrade. I do enjoy fighting your squad size units, because they are like children in the woods."

Rusak took the microphone from his radio operator and asked, "Who are you?"

"I am the leader of the partisans and a prior Special Operations man, a Green Beret, which I am sure you Russians know. And, what is your name?"

"My name is Major Rusak and one day, Yankee, you will die."

"Of course I will die, because all things eventually die, Major. You think you are safe, surrounded with a hundred men, but I can kill all of you with a single order. I know exactly where your tent is located, Major. I also know you are a prior enlisted man, a Master Sergeant, so I do not take you lightly. You, sir, are a threat to my people and will soon die."

"Come for me, Yankee dog."

"Name calling, eh? It means I must have pissed you off, which is good. When we visit, I will personally, if possible, kill you, but you *will* die. Enjoy your evening, comrade, and give our coming fight some thought."

Handing the microphone back to his radio man, Rusak thought, *There is something unnerving about speaking with an enemy and having him threaten to kill me. I must double and triple check our defenses and get the men dug in deep. I must take his threat to kill as real, and I do believe he will try.*

Razor wire was flown in, a tank was placed in the middle of camp, and a man with a flamethrower was added. The foxholes the men dug were now deeper and each had a small shelf carved in the soil where hand grenades were stored. Rusak had the men positioned two to a hole, so one could sleep while the other stood guard.

The tank crew had orders to sleep in the tank, which brought a round of cursing because it was cramped and uncomfortable. Finally, the three man crew accepted their orders and he'd not seen them since. The only time one of the crew was allowed to leave their armored beast was to use the latrine or gather supplies from the choppers. Thousands of ration meals were flown in, as well as drinking water and more ammunition.

Rusak still suffered from pain but most was located in his shoulder, where he'd been injured first. Some mornings, right after waking up, he'd down a long pull of vodka to ease his discomfort. This morning, right after brushing his teeth, he downed about a half pint of the strong drink, and made his way to the radio operator's tent.

The senior radio operator was at the desk and said, "The body of the last informer has been found and fairly close to here, at an old automobile junk yard. The medic said it was a woman, but she had been left to hang and was in pretty sad shape when found. She was hanging from her ankles, with her head on the ground, and a sign reading "Traitor" pinned to her chest and the usual card in her mouth."

Rusak waved the man's comments away, because informers were not his responsibility. He picked up the log of messages received and sent, scanned the list and then asked, "I notice where some infrared Ka-60's discovered some heat sources last night. Why were the targets not attacked?"

"Mainly because they were too close to our location. According to a pilot named, Paley, a Warrant Officer, we were surrounded by people moving in close to our position. He seemed to think they were massing for an attack, but nothing happened."

Rusak remembered the words of Colonel Williams, *When we visit, I will personally, if possible, kill you, but you will die.* He felt a shudder go through his body.

The day was a good one, with one Russian ambush killing twenty Americans and another killing two and injuring many more, but they escaped. Dogs were trailing the injured men now.

Just as the sun when down, the radio came alive with chatter. Rusak moved close to the speaker and listened as a half a dozen teams reported contact. *Strange,* he thought, *all of the contact happened at the exact same time.*

"Major, Lieutenant Markov is under attack by a large force and is barely holding his own."

"Have him contact air support and they will clear the way."

"Master Sergeant Turchin reports he needs support or he will be overrun shortly."

"Tell him to contact air support as well. What in the hell does he think I can do? There is nothing any of us can do for him or his men; we are a headquarters, for God's sake, and have no guns."

"Well, besides the request for help, he said he has never seen so many Americans out in the bush in his life. They encountered hundreds of mines, booby-traps and avoided at least two ambushes. You know Turchin well, and the man does not panic easily, sir."

"Get the air base on the phone and tell them to get anything that can fly into the air and do the job now. Colonel Dubow gave me any assets I need to do this job, and right now I need aircraft."

Thirty minutes later a flight of three jets flew low overhead and continued moving north. It was full dark now, with the little camp pitch black. No one spoke, everyone was awake, and no one moved.

Near 2200 hours, the listening post outside the wire reported a lot of movement.

"Ears one to base. Movement all around us. Request permission to pull back into the wire."

Rusak nodded to the radio man and said, "Tell them to come in and do it now."

A minute later, the radio man said, "They are coming in now, sir."

Abruptly guns sounded as red and green tracers flew through the air. Some of the green, which was Russian, was being shot into the wire, at the camp, and all of the red was. Sticking his head out of the tent, Rusak said, "Call the base and tell them we are under heavy attack."

When the radio man did not reply, the Major turned and saw the man was on the ground, kicking as blood spurted between his fingers from a bullet to the face. He is dead, Rusak thought as he moved to the radio.

CHAPTER 12

John and his group were joined by the others at the old garage, and Willy was pissed that the Russians had killed over 250 partisans with just two jets many weeks back. He paced around inside the garage as he listened to the almost fully recovered Esom.

"I'd estimate the number of Russians in the woods to be around 100 to 120 and they're dug in well, with razor wire and a few dogs. We can take the place, but why should we?"

"Because we can, and to show the Russians we'll hit them when and where we can."

"But the cost in lives will be high for us."

"I think a lot depends on when we strike and how many of us attack. I plan to hit them around 2200, when most will least expect an attack. Additionally, at the same time, I want the Russian Squads looking for us to be hit as well. I want to do the most damage with the least losses to our side."

"Colonel," Esom said, "like I said, we can take the place, if you want to pay the price."

"Good, let's move."

The night was early, just a bit past 1900 hours, but the walk, barring any problems, would take an hour and a half. The moon was not out yet, but most of the partisans wore NVG's for ease of movement in the darkness. The wind was light, and it reminded Willy to position his men downwind from the Russians. By doing so, the dogs would have a harder time discovering their scent.

The Colonel was the only one of the group not packing a pack and it was due to his physical condition, not his age. The gulag had robbed him of most of his strength and power, because of a poor diet, and he was not capable of carry a load this night. He did carry a Russian pistol and four grenades; he knew how to use both.

An hour later, shots were heard to the north and then to the east of them, followed by explosions, so the other groups were ambushing Russians right on time. John knew the Russian commander would be swamped with calls for artillery or air support. So far, he'd seen few big guns in action, only that didn't mean the enemy wouldn't use them. He knew the closest airbase was at Edwards and the number of aircraft they had was limited to a dozen or less, depending on what maintenance had ready to fly on any given day. However, John also knew it didn't take more than just a couple of aircraft to raise hell with troops on the ground. Their only hope was the aircraft would overlook protecting the headquarters in the field and try to take care of the squad sized units in the field instead.

Esom dropped back from second in line to say to Willy, "Only about a quarter of a mile left and we'll be there."

There came the loud scream of a jet passing low overhead and a few seconds later it was gone. Off in the distance booms were heard from explosions, but what caused the noise was unknown, only the jet was suspect. They continued to move toward the Russians.

"We'll hit them on the side with the tents and communications gear. If we knock all communications out, we'll have a field day. Place two Claymore mines pointed toward the tents, and when they go off, we'll attack. Kill every man."

No one said anything, because it was a pretty typical attack for them. Usually, they'd attack after tossing grenades, shooting a LAW, or using mines. It shocked the enemy deeply and once dazed, they were easier to kill or injure.

Once in position at the Russian field headquarters, the men quickly placed the mines, as Willy viewed the camp with his NVG's. It was a quarter to 2200 and he'd wait an additional fifteen minutes to blow the mines. His timing was important, so his units attacking the small groups of Russians would all strike at the same time. He wanted air support confused by what was happening and make them choose which to defend. If communications were knocked out here, the jets and choppers would assist the small units— maybe. Like living, it was a gamble.

Finally, at 2200, Willy whispered, "Blow the mines."

Two loud explosions filled the night air and warbling screams were heard in the camp. As one, the partisans ran toward the Russian headquarters, shooting anything that moved. John moved to the first tent, entered and found two radio operators on the ground jerking due to injuries from the mine. He shot both men and then shot the radios to pieces, the parts flying through the air as bullets struck. Satisfied, he moved to the next tent.

Pulling the flap open, he saw no one and it looked to be the personal tent of an officer, most likely the commander. Quickly searching for anything of use, but finding little, he ignited some papers on a folding desk and piled some blankets close to the fire. Within a minute the tent was filling with flames and smoke.

He'd just left the tent when he heard a loud, "swoosh" and when he looked in the direction of the noise, he spotted flames shooting into a small group of partisans. *Flamethrower,* he thought and pulled a grenade. He tossed the explosive and while his grenade landed close to the deadly weapon, the flamethrower continued to squirt liquid hell in different directions. By the light of the flames, he saw five men stumbling and on fire, their bodies human torches.

All gun fire concentrated on the flamethrower and three grenades exploded near the man. Someone must have struck the fuel tank on the man's back, because it exploded with a loud, *kaboom.* A huge ball of flames shot high into the air, and the man instantly faltered around in flames. Bullets struck him and he fell, the area around him covered in fire. The fire lighted the area well, making it easier for both sides to find targets.

John, with Dolly at his side, moved toward a row of foxholes and sent bullets flying into the men in the holes. At one point, he stopped firing as Dolly rushed a man crawling from his protective hole and watched as the big German Shepherd clamped her teeth down on the Russians throat. Then the dog began shaking her head from side-to-side, until blood suddenly spurted from the soldiers neck, and his body grew limp. Dolly released her grip on the man and watched him closely as his left hand twitched.

The tank crew opened fire with a machine-gun and slowly began to back out of the camp. John heard a scream and when he glanced in the direction of the noise, the tank was backing over a man's body. Once in the darkness, the tank sped toward the nearest road, the three man crew thankful to have survived the attack.

A small number of Russians, maybe five, broke for the relative safety of the woods, but were gunned down before they'd covered half the distance. While the flames were still burning, the intensity was not as great, and John suspected that when the fire died, any surviving soldiers would try to escape. *The smart ones will wait,* he thought as he heard Willy's whistle blowing, which was the order to retreat and take anything of value that could be used. John quickly searched the men he'd killed and removed all ammunition and gear. He also gathered up rations, guns, and pistols.

Sandra neared him carrying a full load of weapons and said, "I spotted another flamethrower; looks undamaged, in a hole off the left of the communications tent."

"Esom!" John yelled and when the man neared, he continued speaking, "Take this gear I have and let me fetch a flamethrower Sandra found. It's a weapon we don't have yet."

"Sure, but keep away from me with the damned thing. After seeing the way the other man went up in flames, I want nothing to do with it." Esom shook his head.

Glancing around, men and women were leaving, each with their hands full of something useful. John found the flamethrower beside a dead Russian and after cutting the man's throat to make sure he was dead, he slipped the weapon on his back. He then walked toward Willy. When he neared, he watched the Colonel place an Ace of spades card in a dead Russian Lieutenant's mouth, the senior man found dead.

"Let's move, people, the enemy will come visiting as soon as they fail to make contact with this camp. Tom, see that mines and booby-traps are placed to welcome our visitors. I want a grenade, with the pin pulled, placed under this Lieutenant."

"Look what I found." John said.

"Good, but I don't want you using that damned thing in battle. I don't want it even near me. It's a terrible weapon, and deadly for the user at times. Now, let's move."

Twenty minutes later, under cover of dense pine and massive oaks, the group heard first the sound of jets overhead and then helicopters. John tried to count the choppers in his mind, but could not, and figured over a half a dozen. A few must have been the Black Sharks and not the Ka-60's, because the whine of their engines were different.

It was then Willy said, "Time to break up into small cells again and meet back at the old garage. If possible, bring what you salvaged from the attack, but take no risks with the gear. If packing the gear and supplies slows you down, discard it, booby-trap it, and move on."

John and his cell broke from the others and changed direction, moving north. They'd covered about four miles, when shooting was heard near and all dropped to the ground. Tom crawled to John and whispered, "Firefight, oh, maybe a hundred meters off."

There came two loud explosions and the firing grew more intense. Screams were heard and orders yelled as well, but John was unable to tell the language used.

"We wait until the firing stops and then check it out. I'll not walk into something I know nothing about." John whispered his reply.

Close to fifteen minutes passed before the firing died down to an occasional pop of a pistol or crack of a rifle. Even at that distance, moans and groans of the injured and dying were heard.

John stood and using his hands, motioned everyone toward the battlefield. He whispered to Tom, "Take point and see what happened. I'll move us forward about seventy-five meters and wait."

John nodded and moved forward. A few seconds later, the foliage seemed to absorb the man completely and he disappeared.

Once stopped, the group had a short wait. John returned in just a few short minutes, and pointed down the path they'd just walked. He then took the point and led the group away from the battle site. He covered about a half mile before he stopped and lowered his pack to the ground.

"Russian special forces from what I could see, and Mark Johnson's cell is dead and I mean every swinging dick in the group. I counted nine American bodies and recognized Mark's face on one of them."

"Spetsnaz?" John asked, surprised to find them in the woods again and so near.

"I'm pretty sure, because the men I saw were wearing the blue and white stripped t-shirts under their camouflage uniforms. One cocky bastard, none were wearing rank, was even wearing a light blue beret on his head. The stripped undershirt and beret means Spetsnaz to me." Tom said and then shrugged.

"We need to take them out, if we can, but I don't want to risk all of us." John said, and then thought, *The flamethrower might work, if grenades are tossed at the same time. I'll shoot the flames, because other than Tom, I'm sure no one else knows how to use a flamethrower.*

"What are we to do?" Margie asked.

"Keep moving north and in about a mile, swing west for about three miles and then move toward the garage. Sandra, you take Dolly with you." John handed his wife the leash to the big dog.

Sandra met his eyes and said, "Be careful and no heroics, okay?"

"Baby, Spetsnaz is a dangerous threat to us and must be eliminated at all costs. Hell, if they get on our asses we'll never have any peace and over time they'll hurt the partisan efforts. Willy has given orders that anytime they're spotted in small groups, we're to kill them."

"I understand, but use some common sense during the attack. You tend to expose yourself needlessly at times and this is not a good time to do that. So, promise me you'll be careful."

He kissed her cheek, met her eyes and said, "I promise I'll take no unnecessary risks. Now, are you happy?"

She smiled, which brought a grin to his face, and then replied, "Not really, because I know you, but we have our orders." Then looking around at the others, she said, "With these two gone, I'm in charge so saddle up and let's move. Esom, you pull drag and

Tate, you take point. Now, when you get tired, Colonel, let me know and Margie will take your place. Let's move, people, we have a mission to complete."

"Stay safe, baby." John whispered to his wife.

She didn't reply, but did give him a big smile and wink.

As soon as the small group walked away, Tom said, "In order for the flamethrower to work, we'll have to catch them bunched up, which might be hard to do. In any case, I'll wait for you to start the dance before I do anything."

"Let's move and see what we can do to these men. I think we can convince them that they need to back off a bit." John then ignited the ignition flame port and grimaced. Death by fire, to him, was horrific.

Tom shrugged and replied, "Okay, but even if they don't leave us alone, we can for sure take a few of them out of the picture—permanently."

The walk to the battlefield was short and when they arrived, the Russians were taking turns being photographed with the American bodies. One, a huge man, pulled Mark's head up by the hair and said something John didn't understand. The soldiers quickly laughed and catcalls followed. Like soldiers the world over, they were proud of their deadly work. Quickly counting the men, John saw ten, with two providing loose security.

Glancing at the flamethrower, he saw the ignition flame was burning and all he had to do was point the nozzle, squeeze the trigger and the pressurized flammable mixture would spurt toward the Russians. He raised the flamethrower, aimed at the middle of the group and squeezed the trigger. A loud "swoosh" was heard, so John moved the weapon from side to side, to make sure his liquid fuel found targets. The heat was intense and the screams of the wounded tore at his heart, but these were his enemies, the same men who'd just killed Mark and his cell. The heat grew intense and he heard three loud explosions from grenades he'd felt, more than seen, Tom toss.

He released the trigger, glanced at his target and saw all the men were in flames, except for the two guards. The smell of the burning human flesh was strong to his nose and at one point he puked.   With his eyes watering, he asked, "What about the guards?"

"One guard is down, but I can't see the other. Let's wait about ten minutes and then we'll check them."

"Hell, it'll take me that long to clear my vision. The smell of people burning has always bothered me."

"It bothers me too, but I rarely puke these days."

John removed the heavy backpack that contained the cylinders of the flamethrower and placed it on the ground. He pulled his Bison sub-machine gun and made it ready for use. He also checked the pistol on a web belt around his waist and looking at his watch said, "Let's move forward and search for both guards. The eight men near the partisan bodies are burnt crisp and black, so they're no longer a threat to anyone in this world."

They stepped from the brush to the small clearing and both moved apart as they neared the first guard. When less than five feet from the man, Tom said, "This one is no threat, because the top of his head is missing. The other guard is on the other side of this clearing." He slipped the ace of spades into the dead guard's mouth.

When they neared where the other guard was seen, all that they found was a pool of blood.

Tom said, "This blood is bright, so it's likely a fatal wound or at least a serious injury to his organs."

"Follow him. I want no one to escape our ambush."

"What about the Flamethrower?"

"Take a compass heading so we can return, and lets move."

Tom pulled a compass from his pocket, took a reading, and then said, "Okay, let's move."

The wounded Russian was good in the woods and John knew if not for the blood, they'd have lost the man. At one point, maybe a quarter mile from the killing spot, they spotted a bloody bandage stuffed into some brush. The man was severely injured, with a lot of blood loss, and it was just a matter of time before he passed out, or so John thought.

"Off to our right, those leaves look unnatural to me. See how they're covering something?"

"Looks like a gun barrel in the dirt sticking out from the leaves. Watch your ass when we near."

When they approached, the first thing John saw was the Russian blink his eyes. *He's alive, but won't last long,* he thought and then said, "He's alive, because I saw him blink his eyes."

Tom pulled his knife and said, "I can fix this and do the job quickly."

"Please . . . American . . . let me . . . die. I . . . am . . . close. So . . . weak." the Russian said is surprisingly good English.

John moved forward, kicked the rifle from the man's hands, and searched him. He collected two grenades, a long bladed knife, a set of NVG's, and pouches of ammo. "Where are you hit?" he asked as he squatted by the unarmed man.

"My . . . stomach . . . and chest."

"Do you not carry a first aid kit?"

"I have one . . . oh, the pain! It is . . . on my . . . belt. Right . . . side." He arched his back and muffled a scream.

"Is morphine in the kit?"

"Yes, all . . . you do is . . . place it against . . . my thigh and then . . . push down."

When John opened the kit, he saw two auto-injectors, so he met Tom's eyes and the man nodded. The first injector worked fine and John threw the empty container into the woods. In just a few seconds the man was lying still and blinking his eyes slowly. When John raised the second injector, the Russian gave a weak smile and managed a slurred, "Thank . . . you."

Once the second container was empty, it joined its mate in the brush and John stood. He gathered up the gear and handed some of it to Tom. "Let's go," He said, "we're finished here."

CHAPTER 13

Rusak was caught completely by surprise when Willy and his group detonated the Claymore mines and he'd been on the opposite side of camp, checking their perimeter when the explosion sounded. Like everyone else, the suddenness of the attack had him bedazzled for many long minutes, minutes that lasted a lifetime for many of the Russian soldiers. Tracers of red and green flew in all directions, screams were heard, and men started dying quickly. Seeing they had no chance to survive the attack against superior numbers, Major Rusak and five of his men blended into the night and were the only survivors.

Finally, after covering about a kilometer, Rusak asked, "Do any of you have a compass? I was on the line checking security when the attack happened and have no gear. And, are any of you injured?"

"I have one, but not sure how to use it." a Private said and then asked, "Will they shoot us for leaving our comrades to die? I'm not injured."

Everyone else was fine, except for the oldest Corporal Rusak had ever seen said, "Light bullet burn on the left arm. It is not much."

Darkness made it difficult to see, but the moon was out and it helped. Knowing some of the men were young and inexperienced, Rusak considered having five men with him a gift from God; he said, "We will survive as long as we do not rush things and avoid the enemy. I know what I am doing and if you listen to me, I will do all I can to get you home safely."

"This is my first battle, sir, and I do not like it much." an unknown voice said from the darkness and Rusak ignored it.

"Give the compass to me and no, they will not shoot us. This is a war and men die." Rusak took the compass, opened it and took a reading. He knew Edwards was slightly to the east but more north than his current position, and he estimated about twenty kilometers. They'd gotten off lightly if only one man had any injuries.

"How many of you are veterans of previous battles?" Rusak asked and one soldier, the old Corporal, replied, "I am a veteran. Actually, I could be called an old war horse."

"How many fights have you been in?"

"I have been in every hell-hole this army has been in over the last twenty years. I know how to fight; uh, maybe too well for the army."

"You are a bit old to be a Corporal, are you not?

"I drink, fight, and lose a stripe. Such is life in this mans army. I made it all the way to Senior Sergeant once, only to lose the stripes over the following months."

"I will tell you what I will do. If you help me get us back to Edwards, I will make you a Senior Sergeant again and keep you at that rank, as long as you break no serious laws. What is your name, Corporal?"

"I am called Koslov, which means—"

"It means goat or goat herder, I know the meaning. I want you on point, with the compass, and it will be dangerous. I will keep track of our paces. We have units out and so do the Americans. By all means, move us deeper into the forest to start and we will continue moving once daylight."

The Corporal took the lead and moved deep into the forest and once locating a small clearing, he turned and asked, "Will this do?"

"Yes, this is fine. We move after first light. When we leave, we will be in no hurry, none at all."

"I like your thinking, sir, but you sound more like an NCO than an officer."

"I was a Master Sergeant until a month or so back and then the army promoted me. Now, no talking and if you want to eat today, do it now. I want everyone back to back, so we can cover the area around us. Do not fire on anything without my approval first."

"I do not like this." the Private who'd surrendered the compass said.

"What is your name, son?" Koslov asked.

"I am Private Abram Orlov, Corporal."

"And the rest of you?"

A tall thin soldier replied, "I am Private Alkaev."

A chubby looking man said, "Private Boris Arent,"

"Private Baskov, Yegor Baskov, Corporal."

"Do what the Major suggested and eat now, because it will be a long day, and we will not stop until darkness. I want the meal done and all of you sitting in a circle, awake, the remainder of the night."

"Can I build a fire?" a voice that sounded like Private Orlov asked.

"No light at all. You will eat in the dark and your food will be cold. If we make a fire out here and our helicopters do not kill us, then the Americans will. We do not want either side to see us right now."

Private Yegor said, "But, we are Russian soldiers. I do not understand why we do not want other Russians to see us."

Shaking his head in frustration, Koslov said, "Just follow orders, Private, and all will go well. Now, eat."

The night passed slowly and it was near 0300, when Rusak heard the sound of people walking. He heard noises, as someone walked through leaves and another person stepped on a stick. He had no mines or anything for defense, except a half-dozen grenades. He heard other sounds and was unsure how large a group was nearing him.

He elbowed all the men and no one said a word. They waited in silence and listened, while hoping for the group to move away from them. Rusak heard a dog growl and a command was given in

English. The group stopped and the dogs growling grew slightly louder.

If he lets the dog off the leash, it will come right to us. Looks like no choice except to fight, The Major thought, as he made his gun ready.

There sounded an unknown number of shots fired quickly and two Privates, Baskov and Arent, fell screaming as they were struck hard. The other four men returned fire and moved to the scant cover offered by nearby bushes. Koslov tossed a grenade and Arent must have been struck again, because his shrieking suddenly stopped, mid-scream. Americans began screaming as soon as the grenade exploded, but the Russians had no idea if the explosive did any serious damage or not. Bullets, fired by the partisans, made zipping sounds as they flew through the foliage and continued on to strike the ground or trees behind the four men.

They are using NVG's, Rusak thought, *which explains how they can see us.*

Soslov neared the Major and said, "They are wearing NVG's and we need to get out of here now. Arent, I think is dead, as all of us will be if we do not move and now."

"Get the two Privates and follow me. We will return to near the old camp and wait for help."

"If they come. They very well might write us off, but move, sir, and we will follow."

The four Russians ran through the woods and more than one had minor injuries from briars, limbs, and falling after tripping. The moon was out, but in the woods, it was pitch dark. Curses were heard, until Rusak ordered the men to keep quiet.

I do not think the partisans will follow us, but they might, the Major thought, but said, "Slow to a fast walk now and for God's sake, avoid any trails. I know the partisans will have them mined or booby-trapped. Are any of you injured?"

"Something slapped me in the back, but it does not hurt, and I can feel a wetness in the area." Private Orlov said.

"Check him out, Senior Sergeant Koslov, and let me know what you find."

The wind picked up a little as Koslov moved to the Private. He pulled a flashlight from his web belt, draped the man and himself with a poncho, and instantly saw a bullet hole. Using his knife, he cut the shirt, gave a low whistle and said, "Bullet to his shoulder and it hit from front to back, shattering bone when it exited. He is in shock now, but will need morphine within the hour, once the shock wears off. I will bandage him and we need to get where we intend to be quickly. Once he has the drug in him, he will be useless to us."

"Okay, as soon as you have bandaged him we will move straight to the spot I have in mind."

Colonel Dubow was livid and paced a circle around his desk as his top officers met with him for a staff meeting. Cigarette smoke filled the small room, and more than one flask of vodka was seen as a quick snort was taken by one of the senior officers. It was very early, or very late, at 0400, and a light rain was falling.

"Major Falin, you mean to sit there and tell me that Major Rusak's position, with over a hundred armed men, was overrun and all were killed?"

"That is what our initial intelligence says, sir, but we have a flight of Ka-60's with two Black Sharks going to the spot as we speak. It will be daylight by the time they arrive."

"Sonofabitch, now, how did this happen? Huh? How did one hundred well trained Russian soldiers get killed by some raggedy-assed country peasants? Colonel Sokol, what are your thoughts on this situation?"

"It is simple, sir, superior numbers. Plus, with all due respect, these are not peasants by any stretch of the imagination. No, sir, many, if not most, of the partisans are prior military, or police, and they have been well trained in fighting. It is to our advantage to remember these men are a well disciplined and a substantially armed group." the Colonel spoke, and then emptied his flask with one long drink.

"Bullshit, Colonel. I want the resistance crushed and I want the job done today! Are not most Americans Christians, Sokol?"

"Yes, sir, but few actually practiced their religion just before the fall. Americans had gotten to the point they no longer needed or followed God, or so I have read. Why do you ask, sir?"

"I want you to take 500 prisoners from the gulag and kill them as an example of what we will do each time a Russian soldier dies. From now on, we kill five of them for each of our loses."

"Sir," Sokol stood, wobbled from his morning drinks, and then said, "I may be a drunken fool, but I strongly suggest, sir, you not do this. Now, I hate Yankees as much as any Russian alive, except all this will do is bring them together, much stronger, against us."

"You are partially correct, Colonel Sokol, you are a drunken fool. Now, carry out my orders immediately, or I will have you shot for being intoxicated while on duty! I am tired of the resistance and demand we put a stop to it, and by God, I mean now, today! And get your worthless ass sober! That will be all, gentlemen."

As Dubow moved for the door, a Master Sergeant yelled, "Ten—hut!"

Chairs screeched as men stood for the commander, but once he was outside the doorway, the talking started right off.

"There is no quick way to stop the resistance." a Colonel said.

"The killings will just unite the Americans in their effort against us. This should not be allowed to happen." Major Falin said.

"Then, sir," Colonel Sokol said, "you run and tell Colonel Dubow he is wrong. This is *his* camp, *we* are his men, and the prisoners in the gulag *belong to him* as well. He can killed every damned one of the prisoners, if he chooses to do so. Hell, he has already threatened to have my ass shot and I believe him, too."

"Well, then, Colonel, you had better run and do your killings, do you not think?" Falin asked.

"I intend to do the job, so if you will excuse me, gentlemen, I have some Christians to kill." As he walked out the door, Sokol yelled, "Master Sergeant Turchin, have the camp guards round up five hundred prisoners from the gulag and have them readied, in batches of twenty, for transportation to an area for execution. Of course, do not let the guards know the nature of the trip, and keep your mouth shut as well. I need to think of a new way to kill this batch so it grabs the eyes of the Americans."

Turchin clicked his heels together and replied, "Yes sir, I will see to it right now."

Waving the Sergeant away, Sokol kept thinking of a way to kill the prisoner's to attract the most attention, thus bringing shock to the Americans. He walked back to his quarters to have a few drinks and to refill his four flasks.

The first batch of prisoners arrived and unloaded smoothly enough. Twenty captives, most were men, stood together near the back of the truck in a misting rain. Fifty Russian soldiers surrounded them and two machine-guns were placed to shoot any who might break and make a run for safety.

"Line them up in a single column." Sokol ordered as he walked from the nearby shelter of a huge oak tree. He had a ciga-rette in his mouth and a pistol in his right hand.

A few minutes later, Master Sergeant Turchin said, "They are ready, sir."

"Sergeant, have the first man brought behind the building."

When Turchin grabbed the first man, the American screamed, "What do you want of me? I have broken no camp rules!"

The man was pulled by two guards to an unseen position be-hind what looked to have been a bakery at some point in the past. Screams were heard and a pounding noise. A few minutes later, Turchin appeared with the two guards, and all three uniforms were spotted with blood.

"Next prisoner!" Turchin yelled.

Two men made a mad dash for the safety of the woods behind them, only to be cut down by the machine-guns. As the smoke rose from the machine-gun barrels, the men were heard screaming in pain as Sokol walked to them. Near the two men, he raised his pistol, the weapon coughed twice and both men instantly grew quiet. The man on the left quivered a little, gave a loud sigh and joined his partner in death.

Turning to face the prisoners and his troops, Sokol yelled, "Hurry and complete the crucifixion of this bunch, because we have many many more to do before this job is done."

When the next man was led behind the building, Sokol walked along, behind the condemned man, to see if his orders were being obeyed to the letter.

"Move to man." a soldier who spoke poor English said, as he pointed to a huge Russian.

The captive, frightened, moved slowly to the big Russian and was quickly grabbed and placed on his back. It took Sokol, with his alcohol dazed mind, a few seconds to see the man was being tied to a crude cross, constructed of tree trunks. Once ropes were wrapped over his arms, chest and legs, he was nailed to the cross. With each strike of the hammer, the man gave horrible screams that echoed between the buildings. Then, before he was moved to be raised on the highest hill, long deep cuts were made in both thighs, so the man would bleed and feel pain. The prisoner's head was moving from side-to-side, in fear, as he suddenly realized what his enemy had in store for him.

"Why are you doing this to me?" the captive screamed as they moved him toward a large flatbed truck. Blood from his injuries ran down the cross and fell to the dirt, leaving a line of crimson to the vehicle.

Sokol replied in English, "I find it appropriate for Christians to die as Jesus died. Do you not agree?"

"God will be the end of you, you murdering animals! What you're doing is wrong and you know it, but God Almighty will judge you. Do not do this to us. Shoot us, if you must kill, but this manner of death is sacred to us."

"What is the matter with you, comrade, do you not see the humor in your own death? What better way for a Christian to die?" Sokol said and then turning to his men he said, "Take this one away. Master Sergeant Turchin, this method of killing takes too much time, so we will have to speed the process up or find another way to kill them. At the rate we are doing this, say ten minutes a man, in an hour we've only crucified six people and after ten hours, only sixty. Way too slow. Finish this batch up and then we will talk some more on this subject."

When the last man was hanging on his crude cross, three hours later, Sokol said, "Of the next bunches we will kill them much faster. We will still hang a hundred on crosses, but the remainder will be burned to death or shot. Find a large building and cram two hundred people in it, especially any children, because most of our men hesitate to shoot children, and then soak it in petrol. Once that has been done, set it on fire. When it is burning well, you may leave. For the shootings, use a large field and the machine-guns. I want no one to escape, do you understand me? If a single person lives, I will shoot you myself."

"I fully understand, Colonel." Master Sergeant Turchin said, but thought, *You are about a ruthless and coldblooded sonofabitch, sir. What have these people done to mother Russia to deserve such a horrendous fate?*

A young child of about ten cried out and when Turchin glanced at the noise, he spotted the child crucified and on a cross with the adults. Blood ran freely down the child's legs, from deep cuts made to speed up the death of the victims. For the first time, in his many years as a soldier, Master Sergeant Turchin bowed his head in shame.

"Get the men ready to return to camp with the trucks. I will be returning with them, since the killing is in such capable hands, Master Sergeant."

"Yes, sir." Turchin replied. As he spoke to the truck drivers, he thought, *More than likely, you need to return for more vodka, Colonel. I can't believe a drunken fool like yourself would leave me to do your nasty work for you. Nonetheless, it is a lawful order and as such, I cannot refuse, but it disgusts me.*

When the next batch arrived, it would take the four trucks three trips to bring 200 prisoners, Turchin had them placed in an old warehouse he'd found. The place had old gas cans, remains of chemicals, and other flammables stored inside. He hoped the resulting fire would kill them quicker, if some explosions occurred as well.

Major Falin arrived and said, "The Colonel sent me along to keep the Americans under better control."

"Do what is needed, sir, because they are scared to death right now."

In excellent English, Falin said, "Ladies and Gentlemen, the gulag was becoming over crowded so we have moved you to this warehouse for a few days. No later than two days from now you will all be moved to a new prison about three miles west of here."

Some women smiled, but the men returned hard looks of distrust, so Falin added, "Once all of you are here, we have a big meal of beef and vegetables we will feed you. The new camp will have much better food and you will all be fed three times a day."

His comments relaxed most, but a few of the men glared at him, which mattered little to the Major, because these Yanks would soon burn to death. Even the cries of small children didn't have any impact on the man, but it did his Sergeants and Private soldiers. A good twenty-five percent of the selected victims were kids.

"Come," Falin said and then added, "we have work to do to prepare for the next batch of prisoners." Once outside the warehouse door, he locked the door and had all windows nailed shut, from the outside. He then had ten men pour petrol around and on the building.

"Now, everyone back away from the warehouse." Falin said, and once all were clear, he struck a match on his boot heel and tossed it to the gasoline.

The flames, fed by the fuel, burned hot and soon the whole structure was ablaze. Screams of fear and pain were heard as smoke filled the facility. The wood was as dry as a desert and soon the roof was burning as well.

"Look below the door!" a private yelled.

Turchin looked in horror as the right arms of two men were extended from the building as they attempted to crawl under the small space under the door. The arms were blackened and dirty. Then the small right arm of a badly burned child popped out from under the door and the Sergeant turned away, sickened by what he was a part of this day.

CHAPTER 14

John cursed that his group had only killed the two Russians that lay dead at his feet. Both were Privates, and he suspected the Commander of the Headquarters had been with the dead men. They'd been lucky that Dolly had smelled them, or it was very likely they would have never discovered them at all. The green camouflage of the Russian uniforms made them hard to see at night, even with NVG's on. Pulling a hand drawn ace of spades card, John placed it in the mouth of the older looking Private and then said, "Let's move. I want to be at the garage before sunup. Same positions as before."

Jets were heard almost constantly moving overhead, their engines whining as they passed from every imaginable compass heading. John wasn't worried about the jets so much as the Black Sharks and Ka-60's, both of which carried special gear to allow them to spot humans on the ground. The earlier mist had turned to rain and the safety of the group had gone up considerably. The infrared technology used to spot targets failed to function at a hundred percent. They needed to move now and do it quickly, while the weather was against the enemy.

When they neared the garage a couple of long hours later, Tom said, "I'll go check it out. We may be the first to return, but I doubt we're even close, not at the speed we moved."

John knew he was hinting that the Colonel slowed them down, and the man did, but there was no safe place to leave him. Just because the former prisoner was weak and malnourished wasn't his fault. *I suspect it'll take him months to gain most of his strength back,* John thought as he saw Tom wave from the door of the building. "Okay, people, let's move to the building."

Inside, a fire burned in the old wood stove and cans of Russian rations were being heated on top. Men and women were laying in all positions on the filthy floor, fatigue obvious in some faces. Willy raised his head, gave a weak grin and said, "You're likely the last ones that will return. We suffered fifty dead and twenty wounded, but we've shown the Russian Bear we can hit them when we have the urge."

"Damn, Willy," Esom said, "I knew it'd cost us in blood to take the place." The black sniper shook his head at the number of fatalities.

"Esom, it cost us more than I thought, only right now dead partisans matter little. John, bring your group to me and let me explain the total cost of our attack."

Once everyone was close to him and seated on the floor, Willy said, "The Russians were so pissed that we killed a hundred of them, they killed over five hundred prisoners from the Edwards gulag."

"Oh, my God." the Colonel said as his eyes met Willy's.

"How do you know this?" John asked and pulled Dolly near. As he waited for a response, he scratched her ears.

"One of our spies in Edwards reports one hundred were crucified, two hundred shot to death, and another two hundred burned up in an old warehouse. It looks as if we need to turn ugly again and start doing the same to prisoners of war we catch."

"Hell," Tom said, "we kill 'em anyway."

"We shoot them, Tom. However, from now on, all prisoners are to die in the same manner as our counterparts in gulags."

"What exactly does that mean?" Sandra asked and then quickly met John's eyes.

"It means, for the next 100 prisoners we catch, we'll crucify them as well."

"I don't like it, because it puts us on the same level as them, and by God, we're different." John said, his voice filled with anger.

"Well, I'm sorry you dislike it so much, John, because your cell will start our revenge tonight. I want the nightly convoy to Jackson hit, and hit hard. Every effort will be made to get prisoners. Once the Russians are captured, we'll take them to a spot along the freeway and then crucify them."

"Damn it, Willy." John said, "I don't think I can crucify a man, because it's not right."

Giving a dry laugh, Tom said, "If I remember correctly, a couple of years back you had no problems torturing a member of the Patton family almost to death in your barn. John, as much as I hate to say it, I agree with Willy. We must show them, no matter how bad a taste it leaves in our mouths, that we can and will do the same to their people. Only then, maybe, will they respect us enough to stop the inhumane killings of innocent prisoners."

Sandra asked, "Any children killed?"

"Over twenty-five of those discovered burned to death were kids, most under the age of ten." Then, pulling out a poster written in Russian, Willy read, "All resistance is to cease immediately. From this day forward five prisoners will be killed for every Russian. You cannot win your war against us, so lay down your arms and we will welcome you as brothers. Come to us and let us stop this fighting. We have food, warm beds and clothing for all. Signed, Boris Dubow, Colonel, Commander of Russian Forces Mississippi."

"Bullshit," the Colonel said, "I got half a cup of watered down soup a day and they liked to killed me during each interrogation. They have a butcher named Sokol, a Colonel, that is one blood-thirsty sonofabitch! He burned me, cut on me, blew an eardrum out, and put my old ass through the most horrible pain in my life. If I ever catch the bastard, I will skin him alive! Do you hear me, Willy?"

"I hear you, Colonel, and I'll give you the man if we ever get our hands on him and that's a promise."

The Colonel didn't reply, but did smile.

"Tonight, I want most of the convoy to pass before you blow up the tanker of gasoline that is always toward the end. The tanker truck is usually the fourth or fifth truck from the end of the convoy, for safety reasons. At that point, we rush in, kill a few and try to snatch some prisoners. I'll take my cell and yours. Now, I realize some of you may dislike what we'll be doing to the prisoners, but I've given this a great deal of thought. I'm in charge and I've made up my mind. When you're in charge, feel free to do things differently. We leave at 1900 hours. I suggest we all get some rest before then."

As they broke up to catch some sleep, Willy said, "Colonel, you'll remain here until I get back. I don't see a valid reason to risk both Colonels on the same mission."

"Smart thinking and I will keep things running smoothly until you return."

Catching John looking at him, Willy winked.

At 2100 hours, both cells lined the south-side of the east and west highway to Jackson, Mississippi. Claymore mines were in place, partisans positioned, and all were ready for the 2200 convoy.

At exactly 2200 hours a lone motorcycle rider passed, then two more motorcycles, and finally an old American car used as a staff car, usually occupied by a Captain or Major. *One thing about the Russians, they always start the dance right on time,* John thought as he petted Dolly.

Tonight's convoy was larger than usual, with twenty-five trucks counted. Usually the trucks were empty on the way to Jackson, because the city had a large airport. More supplies were flown to the capital city than sent up the Mississippi to Vicksburg or other areas.

"Smith says the end of the convoy is coming up and the tanker will be here in no time." Tom said.

"Everyone, get down, now!" Willy yelled and picked up both clackers to the Claymore mines.

John pointed at the approaching tanker and said, "Here it comes!"

As the front bumper passed in front of him, Willy set off the first Claymore and the vehicle continued to move forward by momentum. When the tank was in front of him, he squeezed the second clacker, creating a ball of yellowish-red flames, as the tank was ripped to shreds by the powerful mine. No screams were heard, but John knew the driver of the truck and his security man were burnt toast. Nothing could survive the intense heat and flames of the gasoline truck. The tanker continued to move forward, rocked a few times and then fell on it's side, burning brightly.

The convoy was stunned, those in front doing as they were supposed to do and gunning their engines. Those behind the tanker stopped, mainly because when the big tanker had been blown on it's side, it was blocking the roadway. Partisans ran forward and a firefight quickly started.

Willy stood and yelled "To the trucks!" Suddenly his head snapped back quickly and his skull flew apart and Colonel William "Willy" Williams fell to the ground—dead.

John, seeing Willy fall and realizing he was dead, called out, "Take the trucks, now!"

Grenades were thrown by the partisans and the stunned Russians tried to establish a defense, but they were simply overwhelmed. Rifle fire filled the night for a little less than ten minutes. Finally, four Russians raised their hands in surrender.

"Margie and Tom, move forward and secure those men. Take no chances, and I mean *none*. If one so much as passes gas, kill his ass."

"Come on, Margie." Tom said as he stood and slowly walked to the men, his finger on his trigger.

No resistance was offered and all four were soon hog tied and lying on the highway. Sandra neared and said, "We have two dead, one of which is Colonel Williams. The other is a man from Willy's cell named Benson. Both were killed instantly. We have two flesh wounds and neither are serious."

"Tom, take care of the prisoners and we'll take them to the spot Willy had prepared."

"I hear you." Tom replied.

"Margie on point and Esom, you bring up our rear."

At the arranged spot for the crucifixions of the Russians, all was prepared, except they had two more crosses than needed. More than once John had thought of stopping and shooting the men in the back of their heads, but he felt he owed this final act to Willy and his memory. After all, Willy had ordered this done.

"Who will nail these men to the crosses?" Sandra asked, detesting the whole idea.

"I'm in charge," John said, "so I'll do the nailing. However, Tom, I want you to tie each man securely to his cross before I lift a hammer. I want you to tie their wrists, forearms, chest, knees and ankles securely around the cross. I suspect the screams from the nails entering a hand will make the others hard to control."

"Hell, I'd guess so. I know you'd have a hard time with my ass if you had me as a prisoner. Esom, bring the Russians to me one at a time. Let me gag each of them before you start or they'll raise holy hell screaming."

Each man was tied to a cross and then John picked up the hammer and moved to the first man. Turning his head he said, "Esom hold his arm tightly as I drive a nail through his palm. We'll do this hand first and then the other."

The Russians eyes were huge when he realized what John had in mind and he kept trying to speak as he shook his head violently. Ignoring the man, the first blow of the hammer drove the nail through the man's hand and into the wood. It only took one more hard strike to make the nail head flush with his victims palm. The other hand was more work, because the Russian kept balling his hand into a fist, but a quick blow with the hammer stopped all hand movement. A muffled scream was heard as the second hand was nailed in place. His feet were crossed and a single long nail, driven through both feet, secured him.

"A crucifixion will take days to kill, so how do we speed up the process?" Tom asked. "I mean, if the Russians rescue them in a day or so, all our work is wasted."

"We'll open their bellies. Just slice through the skin and leave the inner organs alone. I think drying out and the resulting septic poisoning will kill these men." John said.

"Damn, John, that's cold!" Sandra said from his side.

"As much as I dislike doing this, I'm following orders."

"Bullshit, because you're in charge now, and *you* decide what is done." She almost yelled at him, obviously pissed.

"Okay, I'm in charge, so Esom do as I ordered. This is being done in Willy's honor, like it or not, Sandra."

She turned and walked away.

The four Russians were soon opened up like Christmas turkeys, with rolls of intestines hanging loosely from their bellies, as John squatted at the ground beneath them, praying for forgiveness. What he'd told Sandra was true, but with the death of Colonel Williams, John discovered a deep hatred for his enemy. He would no longer treat any Russian as human, but as vermin that deserved the most horrific deaths. When Willy died, John lost more than a leader, he'd lost a good friend.

They walked to the hanging Russians and placed a sign on the man on the end. Willy had written in Russian, "For every way an American dies, Russians will die the exact same way. For every American that dies, ten Russians will die. God Bless America!"

Standing, John said, "Okay, Tom take point and get us back to the garage. It looks like the Colonel back at camp is now in charge. Margie, bring up our rear."

Back at the garage, the Colonel listened closely as John explained what had happened, and the old man didn't speak or interrupt. When John finished, the Colonel said, "While I disagree with torture, I think it has a place in our current battle against the Russians. They are a vicious enemy and we must meet force with force and torture with torture. It may be the only way to stop them from torturing more of our people, until we can break them free."

Sandra, who'd been quiet on the walk back, now spoke, "Colonel, I disagree with you and John, about the torture, even though I can understand your thinking. In the future, Russian soldiers will fight to the death, rather than be taken prisoner. If they know they'll be tortured to death and not shot, what have they got to lose?"

"That may be true, my dear, and personally, I don't give a damn what the soldiers do." the Colonel said and then looked at his top Sergeant.

Top shook his head and said, "I dislike torture too, but it has it's place at times, like when you need information to save lives, when you may be facing a serious threat, or in a case like this, where the enemy started it."

"Top," Sandra said, "you sound like a little boy. He started it is a childish response."

"Sandra," Top said, "I'll let your comment go for right now, except to say we must meet our enemy head to head no matter what the Russian bear does next. As Willy said often enough, 'Russians are animals in war. They are brutal and sadistic,' and I agree with him."

"To win this war, we must be more vicious than our enemy." the Colonel added.

"I left Esom positioned in the woods with a Russian sniper rifle to watch who comes for the Russians we crucified. Since the spot is clearly seen from the highway, the next convoy that passes will see the men. He's to kill the senior man that responds and then melt into the trees."

The Colonel laughed and said, "Well, someone is about to have a really bad day. Gentlemen and ladies, I have been looking at the map of the Edwards airfield and I have an idea that might ruin the day for many Russians."

"Oh?" Tom asked with arched eyebrows.

"The Russians have their main fuel tanks on a slight hill. If we can get a man or two to the tanks, open the petcocks, the fuel will flow downhill. Downhill from the tanks is the main camp at Edwards, the flight line, hospital, and all repair hangers."

"Kind of stupid to put the tank of a hill, right?" Sandra asked.

"I know little of petroleum, oils and liquid storage, or POL for short, but suspect they use gravity to speed up the refueling process. Now, the tanks are puncture proof, but they can be punctured, except what it really means is they have a low chance of fire.

The term is used meaning if the tanks take a tracer round, they'll not explode. However, if our men cannot access the petcocks for one reason or the other, they're to blow the tanks with some C-4 explosive."

"They're likely to keep the petcocks padlocked, Colonel." Tom said, and then leaned forward, resting his elbows on his knees.

"We have one pair of bolt cutters and that's it. They'll make short work of the padlocks, if there are any, so don't worry about them. My biggest concern is guards and if they have any security positions near the fuel tanks."

John said, "By God, I'd not want to be placed as a guard anywhere near a damned fuel tank. During an attack you know they'd blow."

The Colonel laughed and after he sobered said, "I don't think the guards have much say about where they guard. However, we may have to take the guards out before we can do anything to the tanks. I want the petcocks opened and left open, then the C-4 placed with a ten minute timer. Within ten minutes the whole camp will have fuel covering it."

Margie said, "The resulting explosion will be something to see, don't you think?"

"It will," John said, but quickly added, "but the important thing is we'll be teaching the Russians that no place is safe for them."

"Exactly," the Colonel said and then quickly added, "and our goal is mainly a psychological one. Make them feel unsafe, even when they are in fact very safe. However, if we can take out an aircraft or two, they'll be an added bonus."

"The only problem with this idea, and I like it, is the simple fact the Russians have doubled the number of guards around the base."

The Colonel grinned and then said, "We'll fake an attack in three areas before we hit the base. Tonight we'll hit their main supply depot, which is located about a half a mile from the base. After that, in a day or two, we'll strike their trains again. Then, a week from now, we'll hit the gulag and we'll hit it hard. My intentions during the prison strike is to actually free some of the prisoners, if we can. I want them thinking we're really after more supplies and wanting to free Americans. They'll, or so I hope, move some men from the gulag to provide additional security to all three areas."

"The key question is, do they have enough men to guard all locations securely?" John asked.

"That's an interesting question and right now, well, I have no answer."

CHAPTER 15

Colonel Popoff was notified by a helicopter that four crucified naked people were on a slight hill near the highway to Jackson. He'd quickly called Sokol and confirmed that no Americans had been killed near the roadway.

Strange, he thought as he placed a call to Colonel Dubow.

"Just a moment, Colonel, and I will let him know you wish to speak with him, sir." a female Sergeant said.

A few moments later, "Good morning, Popoff. What can I do for you?"

"Boris, we have a problem. One of my Ka-60's reported four crosses with bodies hanging from them a mile or so from where our convoy was ambushed. We suffered six missing and two of those were in the fuel tanker, so we know what happened to them."

"Did you check with Sokol to see if he had done the job?"

"He has killed plenty of them, but none near the main highway. He concerns me, because with his heavy drinking, I am not sure he is able to remember much."

"Take a couple of squads with you and check the area out. Keep a Black Shark near and use it if you run into any trouble. Let me know what you find."

"Yes, sir, goodbye."

"Goodbye, and call me if you need my help."

Calling Major Falin, Popoff said, "Meet me at my staff car in ten minutes. I have a strange hunch that four of the six men missing from the partisan attack on our convoy have been found."

Within thirty minutes, two deuce and a half trucks, holding two squads of men and their gear were nearing the site of the crosses. Popoff and Falin were riding in a staff car, between the much larger trucks. Two motorcycles, one in front of the larger vehicles and one at the rear, were providing extra security.

Stopping on the main roadway, Popoff exited his car and stood in the warm morning sun. Falin, as the Junior Officer, was barking orders to the Russian infantry as they lined up for movement toward the hill.

Popoff pulled his pistol from his holster and then said, "Come to me, Major, so we can discuss this after looking it over with binoculars first. We can expect mines and booby-traps, if those are not Americans on the crosses. Be sure to wa—"

As Major Falin was looking at Popoff, a perfectly round circle appeared slightly above the Colonel's right eye and then the back of his head exploded. Bone, blood, brain and gore flew from his head to land on the nearby staff car. Falin attempted to move, but before he'd even realized Popoff had been shot, he felt a hard blow to his back. Falling to the ground, face down, he looked at the early morning dew on individual blades of grass and smiled, because he felt no pain. His world slowly faded from full light to darkness and then Major Falin died.

Sergeant Shubin, the senior man now alive yelled, "Sniper!"

After the men were hidden, one Private asked, "What do we do now, Sergeant?"

"Radio man, come to me." Shubin said, ignoring the man's question.

A man ran to Shubin and fell to the grasses beside him. Taking the handset offered by the man, the Sergeant said, "Black Shark One, this is Camp Three, I have a sniper in the trees approximately two hundred meters west of my position."

"Copy, Camp Three, a sniper in tree line approximately two hundred meters from your position. Get your heads down, I am rolling in hot now."

Raising his head, which brought a shot from the sniper that clipped his left ear lobe, Shubin screamed, "Everyone down now! The Black Shark is attacking the woods!"

The chopper used Gatling guns on the first pass and on the second four rockets were released. The pilot then asked, "Let me speak to Camp One."

"Uh, Black Shark One, both Camp One and Two are down. They are assumed dead at this time."

"Copy, assumed dead. Confirm the status of both and contact Colonel Dubow immediately. He wants a status report. I will remain overhead to assist if you still have problems."

"Copy, Black Shark One. Wait a minute and let me check the condition of both."

Slowly Sergeant Shubin stood and after a few minutes, other men stood. He made his way to the downed form of Colonel Popoff and saw he was dead. The men were all joking and clowning around now, knowing the sniper was dead, but Shubin was not so sure.

"You men get behind some cover and do it now. We have no idea if the snip—"

Esom's shot struck the Sergeant low and in the gut, the force of impact knocking him from his feet. Landing on the hard concrete of the highway, Shubin began screaming as the pain hit him.

A medic moved to him, grabbed his feet, intending to drag him behind a truck, which offered some safety. The Medic's throat exploded, with blood and gore spattering the road and men near him. As the medic bled out, the radio operator said, "Black Shark, that damned sniper has just killed two more of us. Uh, the Sergeant might still be alive, only I am not going out to get him."

Suddenly, Shubin gave a great warbling scream as his feet kicked at the concrete and his back arched in pain.

"Unidentified voice, this is Black Shark One, get your heads down, I have two fast movers with napalm that will light up the woods for you."

"Copy." the radio man replied and then yelled, "Get down, napalm attack on the trees!"

Out of the clear skies came a pair of shiny jet aircraft diving for the woods. Just before the Private thought they would dive into the ground they pulled up and released two oblong containers each. The containers tumbled end over end until they entered the trees and were lost from view. A split second later, a giant wave of flames came from the trees and extended almost to the clearing before falling. Black dense smoke rose to the sky, as a fireball rolled inside itself.

The radio man, impressed by the fire, stood and said, "Thanks for the fire, I think it has cleared the sniper."

"Do you have a condition for the other officer that is down?"

The radio man moved to Major Falin, checked him and said, "Dead. Both officers are dead and the Sergeant will be too, if we do not get a helicopter to remove him and soon."

"Copy you need a medical evacuation for the Sergeant."

Dubow was pissed as he stood beneath the four crosses with the remains of his men. He'd just lost two senior officers and a medic coming to look at the bodies, so his mood was sour. Sergeant Shubin was stabilized and was in an intensive care unit, his future unknown. The Sergeant might live, but the doctors claimed it was too early to know yet. He'd rounded up Sokol, drunk as usual, and made him come to see what his reprisals were doing to the Russian Army.

"Sokol, you will immediately stop killing Americans by any means except a gun. Shoot all the sonsofbitches you want, but no more burnings or crucifixions. Does your drunken mind understand me?"

"Yes, sir, I fully, uh, understand." Sokol replied, his voice slurred.

"Why in the hell did the sniper kill Popoff, when it is you that needs shot? I am ordering you right now, no more drinking on duty at all, none. If I catch you drinking one more time on duty, you will either join the Americans in the gulag or you will simply disappear. Am I making myself clear to you?"

Snapping to attention, Sokol replied, "Clear, sir."

Turning to Master Sergeant Turchin, Dubow yelled, "Move the men forward to recover the bodies of our comrades. Tell the men to watch for mines or booby-traps as they move, Sergeant!"

"Yes, sir. Okay men, you heard the Colonel, move toward the bod—"

At the word move, the men moved and there came a short scream, a wall of fire erupted, and one man fell to the ground. As his body jerked and danced wildly on the ground, Turchin yelled, "Keep your eyes open for mines, men, or you will end up like this man." He pointed at the squirming soldier on the grasses.

A medic quickly looked the injured soldier over and said, "He is still alive, but not for long. His body is mangled to hell and back."

"Kill his pain." Turchin said, which everyone knew meant to put the man to death by injecting morphine.

"Sonofabitch!" Dubow yelled in anger, "How many more will the Americans kill! I grow tired of this damned cat and mouse game they play with me! They need to feel the might of Mother Russia! Sokol, get in my car and we will return to the base." The Colonel turned and then moved toward his car.

Seeing Sokol hesitate, Dubow said, "Get in the damned car and do it *now*, Sokol!"

Sokol staggered forward, his benumbed mind already focusing on his next drink of vodka.

Esom had fired the shot at the Medic and then climbed down the tall oak he'd been shooting from. He picked up his pack and started running toward the clearing. The guns and rockets had missed him and in a typical sniper setup, he'd shot the Sergeant and then waited for others to come to his aid. There had been times in the past, when he'd killed five or six trying to rescue a wounded man. Usually, he ended up killing the wounded man too, but the aircraft were getting too close, so it was time to move.

He was within ten feet of the clearing when he heard high pitched whine of jet engines, looked over his shoulder and saw two jets release Napalm. The two oblong aluminum containers were flipping end over end and he knew he had to cover some distance. Knowing the Russian soldiers would have their heads down, Esom ran as fast as he could over the open field, praying he'd reach the other side before all oxygen close to the fire was sucked into the flames. He made it, but just barely. His heart was beating loud and hard, because it was the closest to death he'd been in a long time, as he entered another patch of woods and made his way toward the garage. The dense black smoke was seen over his shoulders for miles.

As he moved, he thought, *Not a bad day of shooting. I bagged a Full Colonel, a Major, a Sergeant, and a medic. I think the Russians have learned to respect our snipers.* He then broke into a slow trot he could keep up most of the day and smiled.

Back at Camp Edwards, Dubow called an emergency staff meeting with all his senior men, officers and Sergeants. As with all staff meetings, each commander gave a short talk of how his particular unit was doing.

The hospital commander, a Lieutenant Colonel, stood, moved to the front of the room and said, "Since my last briefing, the Private that was horribly burned in the helicopter crash has died. Additionally, Major Rusak was discovered early yesterday morning by one of our ground patrols and recovered with some of his men. All are hospitalized at this moment, with the Major suffering from extreme exhaustion, Senior Sergeant Koslov has a deep cut to his left thigh, and Private Orlov has a shattered shoulder wound as a result of a bullet. Privates Arent, Baskov, Alkaev, are dead, bodies not recovered."

Master Sergeant Turchin asked, "How did Koslov make Senior Sergeant? The last I heard and saw he was a Corporal, sir."

"While working on the Major, he stated Koslov deserved a medal and a promotion for his actions during the initial ground attack and in the events that followed. Rusak said he could not guarantee a medal, but he could promote the man and did. He was—"

Colonel Dubow interrupted and said, "I want my chief of personnel to see if he is worthy of the Hero of the Russian Federation Medal and if so, prepare the paperwork for submission. If not, see he is awarded the medal right below it in importance. While we are losing our asses in this country, we need to show our people that we still have brave men."

"I will see to it as soon as this meeting is over, sir." a thin lanky Captain replied.

"Now, take your seat, doctor, and let me explain the real reason for this meeting. As of today, actually a couple of hours ago, we no longer have Colonel Popoff or Major Falin with us. Both were killed by a sniper less than five miles from this room. Both died almost instantly, but it leaves me with no gulag commander and no executive officer. I want Lieutenant Colonel Bunin to take over as the camp commander until Moscow either approves my recommendation for his promotion to Full Colonel, or sends me a replacement. Captain Taras, you will step up into the executive officers position and I have the authority to make your promotion effective immediately. As of right now, you are promoted to the rank of Major. Are there any questions?"

There were no questions, so Dubow waited a few minutes, took a sip of water from his glass and then said, "Okay, let me switch subjects on all of you and discuss our current problems with the resistance. They are starting to embarrass us greatly and this morning we found some of our men crucified, mocking the crucifixions that were done to 100 prisoners by Colonel Sokol and his men a while back. I will not put up with the resistance any longer. I want my special units to prepare for an active part in our struggle.

Tomorrow morning, if the weather is favorable, I want some type of toxic chemical agent dropped in all unpopulated areas. I do not care how many civilians we kill, but the partisans must be hurt badly by this. Now, we have used gas before, but I now want patrols out, before we drop the gas, but with the gear necessary for them to safely do their jobs. This war is about to turn mean, gentlemen, and ugly."

Looking at his aircraft maintenance commander, Dubow asked, "How many broken aircraft do you have, Colonel?"

Pulling a clipboard open, the man quickly replied, "Sir, as of right now, I have eighteen flyable aircraft, including helicopters and fixed wing, three down for routine maintenance, and two with serious problems, both being engines."

"Sir, just a quick question, if I may?" Colonel Walsky, chief of special units, asked.

"Ask your question, Colonel, and let us get back to aircraft status."

"My troops, as you know, are made up of both men and women. I guess I do not really have a question, so much as wanting to point out, this will be the first possible combat for my female troops. I would like to suggest we milk these missions for all the propaganda we can, sir."

"Fine, Colonel, send a damned cameraman out with them. Is that all?"

Suddenly flushed, Walsky replied, "Uh, yes, sir."

Turning back to his aircraft maintenance officer, Dubow said, "Now, continue with what you are going to do to get as many aircraft into the air tomorrow to deliver our chemical attack."

An hour after sunrise, six large Ilyushin Il-28 medium bombers took off from the old Jackson international airport and flew toward Edwards at low altitudes. At exactly the same time, on Edwards airfield, eight Antonov An-12 aircraft, fitted with tanks holding a chemical agent, took off and moved south, the sun reflecting from their silver wings as they banked. The chemical war against the American resistance was entering a new and deadly stage.

The Antonov An-12 aircraft looked similar to the American version of a C-130 from years gone by and required a much shorter runway than the big bombers. While the Ilyushin Il-28 bombers were classified as medium, they needed a much larger landing surface than the prop driven An-12.

Once airborne, the overall commander, Colonel Dubow, reminded each aircraft of the grid they were assigned to fly. As the aircraft separated and approached their targets, the Colonel was wearing a smile. He was smart enough to know many of his enemies had chemical gear and he'd not kill all of them, but he'd surely catch many of them unprepared and some would die. His goal was to reduce the numbers of the resistance and nothing more.

On the ground below, a woman working her garden looked up at the aircraft and pulled her three children close. She found it strange that rain drops were falling and there wasn't a single cloud in the sky. Suddenly, her youngest fell to the ground and began convulsing violently. Her little body flipped and flopped in all directions, but by now, the other two were also on the ground, mirroring her fatal actions. The woman screamed and realized the Russians had dropped something poisonous on them! She fell to the ground and as her world faded, she was thinking of her children. A few minutes later, all four of them were dead—all huddled together.

Five hours later, with most of the countryside sprayed, the Colonel gave orders for the aircraft to return home. He was hot; wearing the chemical | biological suit was always hot and the protective mask was no cooler. However, he was sure his little surprise visit would kill partisans and that was his only goal.

No sooner had the aircraft touched down and the brakes applied than the Colonel noticed all base personnel in their protective gear. He smiled and said to his co-pilot, "Please take control now, Captain, and taxi us to the our parking spot."

Shortly after arriving at his office there came a knock on his door, so the Colonel opened it and asked, "Yes, Corporal?" He was still in his protective gear and expected to be for at least forty-eight hours.

From the Corporal came a muffled response, "Colonel Bunin to see you, sir."

"Show him in." Dubow moved to his desk and sat.

Colonel Bunin walked into the room, wearing his protective gear, and when about three feet from the commanders desk, stopped, and rendered a near perfect salute, as he said, "I wish to speak with you, sir."

"Misha, pull up a chair and be seated. I would offer you a drink, but it is hard to sip vodka while wearing a mask. Now, what can I do for you?"

"This poisonous gas of yours has killed over half of my prisoners, sir. Now their deaths mean little to me, but I wanted you to know, and by daylight, I expect all of them to be dead."

"How many are still alive?"

"Close to two thousand."

"The late Colonel Popoff," Dubow said with a laugh, "was always complaining about the crowded conditions of the gulag. I do not see that as a problem in the near future, Colonel."

"Okay, but keep that in mind, sir, if you come after prisoners to shoot tomorrow. I fully expect it to be empty by morning."

Standing, Dubow asked, "Anything else, Colonel?"

Bunin said, "No, sir, just wanted you to know what was going on." Seeing his commander standing, the Lieutenant Colonel stood as well.

"Get on the phone to Jackson and let them know your shortage of hostages. Have them send, oh, say a couple thousand next week. I am sure they are crowded and will be pleased to send you all you want, Misha."

Knowing he was being dismissed, Bunin extended a gloved hand and said, "Thanks for the idea on getting more prisoners, sir."

"No problem, and let us hope by morning we have much more than just dead prisoners. I did not spray almost half of the state of Mississippi to end up with *only* dead captives. Enjoy your evening, Colonel." the commander said as he shook hands.

CHAPTER 16

John and his cell were way down in the southern part of the state, almost at the Lousiana border when the chemical attack occurred. Of course, they were not affected by the chemical attack, but John was thankful they were not up north when the attack happened. The last time the Russians used chemicals, it had almost killed Dolly. A dispatch rider, on a captured Russian motorcycle had brought word and it had spread like wildfire to all the partisan camps.

As they sat in the dirt, deep in a swamp, Tom suddenly asked, "Why did the Russians decide to use gas now, knowing good and well that it would kill the prisoners at the gulag and put their own personnel at risk?"

"Willy once told me that Russians don't think like we do and to never assume everything they do has an obvious reason. They place little value on human life and their goal in war is to win, period. They'll do anything to win, even violate the laws of the civilized world, or lose hundreds of thousands of their soldiers."

"Hell," Esom said, scratched his beard and continued, "there ain't a United Nations anymore and no laws to violate. When we fell, the U.N. busted up and scattered in the wind in less than a month. We were footing the biggest percentage of the bills for the whole damn organization. As for them losing soldiers, I'll do my best to kill 'em."

"I'm talking about the moral laws of the world."

"Okay, but it's like a man and honor, some don't have any and never will. What the Russians don't understand is, everytime they use gas or kill a bunch of us, we grow stronger in unity and support. Our uninvited guests are here on borrowed time and eventually we'll kick their asses out."

Tom walked to the group; he'd been off in the distance being briefed by the commander of the Southern part of Mississippi, sat in the dirt beside Dolly and said, "All the gulags in the state will be hit by all partisan forces exactly ten nights from tonight. The overall object is to free prisoners, but we know many will be killed during the attempt, or be unable to survive once released. Our primary goal is to show the Russians we can do what we want, when we want. Also, reports for our neck of the woods shows our losses due to the gas attack at around ten percent, which is low. Or course, all dogs or other animals in the area are dead. Our Colonel states the stink of decaying deer and small game is overwhelming at times and the wind reeks of death. The partisans have taken shovels and gone out to bury dead animals."

"Ten days from now? Damn, we'll have to push to get word back to the Colonel, unless he's been informed another way."

Tom grinned and replied, "The guy on the motorcycle took the word back to him, so our only rush is to get there in time to be part of the attack. I'd suggest we move today, because even moving at thirty miles a day, it'll take us a good four or five days to return."

"Yep, so gather up the supplies we have from this group, pack it all well, and let's leave within the hour."

Three days later, as they traveled overland for the garage, Dolly suddenly alerted and growled.   John, having turned the flamethrower over to Margie whispered, "Down! Tom, do you see anything?"
"No, not yet. Let me move to the far right, which is the direction she was looking, and take a look see."

John nodded.

A few minutes later, Tom returned and whispered, "Russian tank, T-90 and some support troops."

"How many other men?"

"Looked to be around two dozen, but to be honest, I didn't count them. I saw two German Shepherds with handlers, which concerned me with the wind shifting as it has all morning."

"Okay, ideally we'd attack them at night, but that can't be done, or we'll be late getting back to the Colonel. Gather around me and let me explain how we'll do this."

Approximately an hour later, the small partisan group was gathered on the downwind side of the big tank. John had orders from the Colonel, just like Willy, to always try to destroy any armor or heavy vehicles. The heavy vehicles were murderous during encounters with all resistance fighters and at all costs they were to be destroyed where found. They were grouped close on the edge of a small clearing, the tank stopped almost in the center. Esom was positioned high in a tall oak, less than a hundred yards from the more than 47 ton tank.

The tank must have had engine problems, because it kept trying to start, but nothing happened. Two of the crew were standing on the tank and one was yelling at the driver, who sat in his seat with his hatch open. Ground security troops were gathered around and laughing at the crew, as they played grab ass and joked around.

They're like troops the world over, John thought as he tapped Margie on the shoulder.

Margie stepped from the woods and stopped just inside the clearing. She raised the nozzle, pulled the trigger and a wall of flame shot forward, engulfing most of the Russian troops. Loud screams and yells were heard as flames ate at the victims, but not a shot was fired.

"Fire!" John yelled and squeezed the trigger on his Bison.

Men fell, some in flames and some not, but fall they did. Two or three returned fire and a loud grunt sounded and when John glanced in that direction, he saw Tom was down and Sandra was moving to his side.

"Charge!" John screamed and moved forward.

One Russian trooper ran from behind a large boulder, but was cut down before he could reach the relative safety of the forest. It then became quiet.

"Check all downed Russians and if in doubt, shoot the sono-fabitch." John ordered and moved toward the main group of downed soldiers. Flames were still cracking and popping, but the Russians caught by the flamethrower were as good as dead. The driver of the tank was still positioned in his seat, his head now blackened and his eyes wide in horror, as almost clear flames danced in the air on him.

Sandra neared and when John saw her, he knew instantly she had bad news.

"How's Tom?" he asked.

"Dead. He took a bullet to his heart and there was nothing I could do to help him. If is makes you feel better, he never regained consciousness after being hit."

John was in shock. He'd known Tom for years and never expected him to die. He moved to the boulder the Russian had attempted to run from and sat down. Dolly, unsure what was going on, moved to him, and sensing his grief, placed her big head on his thigh. John slowly rubbed her head, but didn't utter a word as tears ran down his dirty cheeks.

Three minutes later, two loud shots were heard and then nothing.

Margie said, "Sounds like Esom caught some Russians."

When John didn't reply, she asked, "How do you want the tank destroyed once the flames die down some?"

"Huh?" John asked.

Margie asked, "How do we destroy this tank?"

"Oh, when were're ready to go I'll puncture the gas tank and then drop two grenades down an open hatch. It'll blow soon after that."

"Are you okay, John?"

"Uh, no I'm not. Tom was just killed."

"Oh, not good. He was with us from the very beginning."

Standing, John didn't reply; instead he looked for the senior man, but found none, due to the fire burning the uniforms. So he moved to the lone soldier shot down near the woods, and intended to place the ace of spades in his mouth.

About three feet from the body he discovered the soldier looked like a woman. Turning, he said, "Margie, come here. I think the Russians are starting to use women in their fight against us."

Margie neared, glanced at the body and said, "Looks like a woman, but only one way to find out." She squatted beside the body and unbuttoned the jacket, then cut the shirt right down the middle. An olive drab bra was discovered, as well as the outline of large breasts being retained by the cotton material. Margie smiled, but did not speak.

"Sandra, fetch Esom and let's move. As y'all move north, I'll tap the gas tanks on the tank and then drop grenades inside. Let's do the job fast, because we have no idea who may have heard our shots."

"I hear you. Margie, help me gather any gear we can use and then we'll get Esom as we head out."

Sandra at least had the sense to gather up things we need, but Tom's death is so unexpected. I never thought he'd be killed in a small operation like this, John thought as he moved toward the big smoking tank. The flamethrower had played hell on the soldiers, but did little actual damage to the tank, other than scorching the side of the turret. Puncturing the diesel tanks, using his sheath knife, he surveyed the battlefield and realized he was lucky to have lost only one man, but what a man he'd lost. Tom was almost like a brother to him.

Giving the fuel tanks about ten minutes to leak, he climbed to the turret and opened the hatch. Pulling the pins from two grenades, he dropped both down the hatch at the same time, hearing the loud clank as both struck the metal floor. He jumped from the metal beast and ran for the woods, knowing the resulting explosion would be tremendous.

He hadn't reached the end of the field, when two loud explosions were heard, followed by a huge blast that sent the turret spinning high into the air. The resulting flames sucked some of the air away from him and his back was hot, but he continued to run. After about a hundred yards, he glanced over his shoulder and saw a dense black cloud from the explosion reaching for the sky. He knew they had to move and move quickly, because the Russians would be pissed—yet again.

Less than an hour after destroying the tank, the small group heard a flight of three choppers fly overhead toward the dead Russians. John and his small group, now smaller than usual, stopped with the first indication of an aircraft approaching.

"They'll send choppers out to look for us." Sandra said as she looked for aircraft through breaks in the leaves overhead.

"Yep, so increase your speed." John said to Esom, who was walking point, and was close enough to hear the conversation. He had no drag security on this trip, because the group was now only four people and all, except the point person, was packing Russian gear and supplies.

Esom nodded and immediately began to move forward at a much quicker pace.

Two hours before dusk, Esom froze and motioned for John to come forward. Once at the sniper's side, he looked where the man now pointed. Straight in front of him was a force of about fifty people and they looked to be civilians. One man was seen with a weapon and it looked to be an old M-1 carbine from World War Two.

For over an hour John watched and finally thought, *They're bedding down for the night and we'd better approach them before full darkness. I have no doubts these people are civilians and the guards look to be partisans, but they're poorly armed.* "I'll make an effort to contact them," he whispered to Esom.

"Watch your ass, because they're wound up tight and are a scared bunch in my mind."

John nodded and then called out, "Hello the group! We're partisans and would like to join your camp for the night."

Heads quickly turned toward John and the man with the gun asked, "What's the capital of Montana?"

"Hell, man, I ain't got no idea and really don't give a shit. I live and fight in Mississippi, not Montana."

The man chuckled and then said, "Approach us, but hold any weapons in the air using your left hand, okay?"

"Sounds fair to me." John said and then stepped from the cover of the brush.

"Nate and Thomas, check 'em out and take the gun from him. Then bring him to the fire."

John was quickly frisked and the thoroughness of the job made him suspect prior grunts or officers of the law. When prodded in the back he moved to the fire and sat. The other two men carried pistols, but the speaker carried the carbine. Not overly concerned, because Esom likely had his back covered, he asked, "Are you part of the partisans? We are, but I wonder about you, since you're so poorly armed."

"I'm a gulag escapee, like every one here, and took the gun from a guy that tried take us prisoner, so he could collect the reward money. The Russians offer five hundred dollars for every escapee turned over to them. Fifty of us would be a hell of a lot of money, so when he made his move to capture us, I knifed the bastard."

John thought for a minute and then asked, "Do any of you have any military experience? And, I'm John." He gazed into the eyes of the man with the carbine.

The man smiled and replied, "The ugly one to your left is Bill, the other is Larry, and my name is John too, but I go by the name of 'Skeeter.' All three of us have Army experience, but I have no idea about the other men and women in our group."

"How in the world did you get away from the Russians? I mean, you're a big group."

Skeeter laughed and said, "One night, oh, about a week back, the Russians were hit by some partisans. The fence was broken in a number of places. I'd guess over 200 of us made a run to freedom, but after the machine-guns grew quiet, you see how many completed the run. Now, others may be free, I really have no idea, but if they are, they're in smaller groups than this one. I saw well over a 100 bodies on the ground just as I entered the woods. That doesn't mean all of them were dead, but I'd guess most were or headed that way."

"What will you do now?"

"We'd thought of joining a partisan group and until you showed up, well, we had no idea how to contact them."

"Do you have any old or ill folks along? A partisan group is always moving and we only need fighters, so kids under 14 years of age aren't needed."

Skeeter laughed and said, "Everyone of us ran from the camp, moving through machine-gun fire and are here today. No, there are no ill or old with us, and not a single kid. I think the youngest man we have is 19 years of age. Thomas! How old are you?"

"I turned 19 last August."

"Satisfied?"

"I have a little food with me and so does my sniper. We can share with you, but it'll not go far with 50 people."

"Some of us are in better shape than others, John, so we'll feed the weaker of the bunch tonight."

"Can I have my weapon back?"

Skeeter nodded and Larry handed the Bison to John. The partisan stood and waved Esom into the camp. If anyone was surprised to see a black man when the sniper stood and moved toward them, no one said anything.

After introductions by the small fire, John said, "The life of a partisan is rough and usually pretty damned short for most folks. Before any of you join us, make sure you're willing to die to free this country. The life of a freedom figher, is not glamorous, nor comfortable, but it is a good cause. Out of the fifty of you, ten might be alive a year from now, maybe."

Skeeter scratched his head and then said, "Well, the odds are bad, for sure, but they're better than the odds of surviving a long stay in a gulag. All of us would have likely been dead within a year. At least dying as a partisan we'll have a fighting chance and that, John, means a great deal to all of us."

"Okay, now understand, we're moving north, near Edwards and that's all any of you need to know right now. We have a few weapons with us, and we'll pass them out shortly. Remember, once you join, you can't quit. It's either freedom or death for each of us."

"Fully understood, and it's expected."

Sitting by the fire, John said, "Esom, go fetch the women. Tell Sandra I want her to look everyone of these people over closely."

"Women?" Skeeter asked, as Esom turned and walked back into the woods.

"My wife, who is also a nurse, and Margie, a prior Air Force survival instructor. Women and men serve as partisans."

Skeeter nodded but didn't say anything.

"We knocked out a Russian tank earlier and killed about two dozen men, so they'll be looking for us. I'm afraid your fire needs to go out. The Russians have infrared gear and can spot any sources of heat. If they happen to fly over us tonight, a group this large is sure to draw attention."

"I know nothing about that sort of thing, but we've been out here a week without any problems." Skeeter replied.

"They'll be looking tonight, be assured, because of the men we killed today."

Once the women were in camp, the fire was put out, and spare weapons were handed out. Even after handing out every spare they'd taken from the Russians, only about ten men were well armed. Most of the Russian guns were left behind at the battlesite, because the flamethrower had damaged them. John only took gear that was completely serviceable and knew it was the only smart way to do business. A bad or poor quality weapon that jammed, or didn't work, was a simply a heavy club. All his guns, even the ones stolen from the Russians, were in top shape and cleaned frequently.

With the fire out, the large group drifted off in ones or twos to sleep. John suspect the couples were married, but it no longer mattered. People were joining others for survival and it was needed these days, because two could survive easier than one.

"What was your rank and specialty in the army?" John asked Skeeter.

"I made Corporal, but then promotions were frozen and I didn't make another stripe before I got out. I worked in the motorpool, caring for vehicles of all sizes, even tanks and personnel carriers."

"And, Larry and Bill?"

"Both were infantry, but not sure where they were stationed. I think Larry made Sergeant, but got out to attend college. Bill I'm not sure of, but he was enlisted."

Standing, John said, "I'm going to bed, but keep two guards on duty at all times. If choppers are heard or any other aircraft, wake me. Any movement around, have your men to sit tight, and wake me as well. We have some other cells operating in this area, so we don't want a firefight with our own people. Make sure the men you have guarding know how to use the Claymore mines we have out."

"I'll let them know and if we have problems, we'll wake you."

John was soon stretched out beside Sandra, with Dolly's big head on his thigh. He looked up at the stars and wished his country knew peace. The loss of Tom almost killed him, but he'd known deep in his mind that all of them were living on borrowed time. *The odds are against any of us living to see America free,* he thought and then drifted off to sleep.

How long he'd been asleep he had no idea, but he heard a voice say, "John, we have visitors overhead and they're circling."

John instantly sat up and asked, "Chopper or plane?"

"Chopper and it's moving slowly."

"The odds are it's reading infrared equipment and spotted us."

One of the guards said, "The chopper is moving right for us!"

CHAPTER 17

Colonel Dubow sat in a chair next to the radio operator chain smoking a rough blend of turkish cigarettes as fast as he could, and drinking coffee. It was 0200 and he'd been awake for over 20 hours now, wondering how the partisans survived the gas he'd sprayed. His choppers and airplanes using infrared gear indicated large numbers of partisans on the ground. So far he'd withheld all attacks, until his intelligence group could get an estimate of the number of partisans in the field.

"From what is being reported throughout the state, by other bases, I would guess well over 5,000 men and women are on the move tonight, sir." Major Taras said.

"Are you fairly sure of the number? That is a hell of a lot of partisans on the ground, Major. And what of around the area when the tank was destroyed?"

"Our aircraft indicate an even dozen groups within ten miles of the tank, but there is no way of knowing which group is responsible for carrying out the attack, sir."

"I want all twelve groups brought under immediate attack, and I mean now."

Looking at the radio man, Major Taras said, "You heard the commander, so give the order."

Warrant Officer Paley was flying one of the Russian choppers, a Ka-60, that was modified to carry machine-guns and rockets. His infrared sensor operator sat in the back, monitoring a computer screen that showed targets as a glowing red image. Paley was an excellent pilot, having been in the business a long time, but he was better known as "The Trader," because he'd wheel and deal anything for the good of his unit and troops. He drank too much, loved to play poker, and was a brave man.

"Mister Paley, I have a large number of glowing targets to our west, maybe a thousand meters."

"Sergeant Titov, I hope this is not like the last time, when we killed a herd of deer."

"Sorry about the last time, but this reading is different. There are so many giving off heat I cannot see the individuals clearly."

"Are you sure of this? I mean *absolutely* sure? Colonel Dubow was so pissed the last time, he threatened to shoot me."

"One hundred percent sure."

"Okay, let me radio the base and see what they want us to do."

"Copy."

Long minutes passed and Titov knew his last error had caused all of them to get a good ass chewing, from him on up, and he'd been required to attend additional training. They'd wiped out a herd of deer, and the ribbing they'd taken was rough.

"Hold onto your seat, Titov," Paley replied a few minutes later, "We are rolling in to attack now."

"Copy and understand, we are attacking."

The aircraft dipped nose down and the Sergeant heard two rockets release from the chopper. Paley then nosed up and banked sharply to come back around. Glancing at his screen, Titov saw the glowing spot separate and then scatter in different directions. He quickly began counting the individuals. "Mister Paley, I counted fifty-four individuals on the ground and about ten are un-moving."

"Copy ten unmoving. Rolling in for a second pass, using the machine-guns this time."

The firing of the guns was loud and the chopper shook violently as they hurled death to those on the ground. Paley fired short burts and a few seconds later, he pulled up again and banked to the right this time.

"Any fast movers near?" Titov heard the co-pilot ask.

"No, they are off to our west and working on targets there." Paley replied.

Glancing at his screen, the glowing people began to go out, as if someone switched a light off in a number of different rooms. However, a good dozen were clearly spotted running over an open field.

"Check the field at your twelve o'clock position, maybe 500 meters in front of us."

Paley flew low over the area and went into a hover to allow Titov to pinpoint targets. He then felt some small arms fire strike the chopper, followed by a loud explosion. Red lights began to come on almost instantly.

"Base, this is Bear 19 and I am heading back to base. My control panel lights are lit up like a Christmas tree and I am declaring an inflight emergency."

"Bear 19, this is Badger 26, I have you visual and your engine is showing some flames."

"Copy, I understand you see flames coming from my engine."

"I suspect you were struck by a LAW or RPG, copy?"

The controls of the big chopper were still responding, but Paley wondered for how much longer. "Uh, copy, Badger 26."

"Badger 26, abort your mission and escort Bear 19 to base." Colonel Dubow said over the radio.

"Understand, Colonel, and will do, over."

Flying close, Badger 26, a Black Shark attack chopper, looked the Ka-60 over closely. The pilot then said, "Bear 19, it looks as if some panels are missing on and near your engine. I suspect a fuel line was cut or ruptured."

Glancing at his fuel gauge, Paley saw he was losing fuel. However, he'd seen what partisans do to captured Russians, so he kept flying toward safety, and would only put it down if all hope to keep moving in the air was lost.

Five minutes later the aircraft began to shake and rattle as it moved and he saw he had just enough fuel to reach Edwards.

"Tower, I am coming straight in when I reach the base."

"All other traffic is currently on hold, Bear 19, and you are expected."

"Fire warning lights are on now, Mister Paley." the co-pilot said.

Glancing at the console, he saw the lights were on, so he made a decision, "Tower this is Bear 19 and I have to put my aircraft on the ground. My fire warning lights are on and I am in danger of blowing up, or so I think."

"Copy, and we have you on radar. Expect ground troops to your location within thirty minutes."

"I will bake them a cake. This is Bear 19, out."

Paley was a bear of a man, well over six feet and about two hundred and twenty pounds, solid muscle. He'd grown up on a farm, attended a local university, but after discovering strong drink and women, he'd washed out of college. He was a better than average looking man, and kept his blond hair cut short.

"Pilot to crew, I am setting us down in the field ahead. Titov, when we exit the aircraft, I want you to grab our survival kit. We should have ground troops with us within thirty minutes."

"I will bring the kit, Mister Paley." Titov replied and glanced at the survival kit.

The lower the aircraft went, the more shaking Paley felt in the control stick and the more dangerous it became. Finally, he placed the chopper in a shallow dive and then pulled the stick back, with help from his co-pilot, when within twenty feet of the ground. He began to lower the aircraft and, when within five feet of the grasses, the engine stopped, and the chopper dropped like a stone to the earth.

As they fell, Paley, switched his agent discharge button to flood the engine with a fire extinguisher foam. His co-pilot turned the main electrical power off, to avoid the danger of electrical sparks upon impact with the ground. They'd practice this thousands of times, but now that he had to do the job, Paley had problems finding the button.

They landed hard and if it'd been daylight, they would have seen a dense cloud of dust surround the chopper. The co-pilot gave a loud scream on impact and Paley was surprised they'd remained on the wheels, which he'd extended, hoping the rubber would absorb some of the impact forces. He'd honestly thought they'd flip over on their side when they struck. They'd tilted hard enough the main rotorblade had flown apart when they struck the ground. All were trained to wait for the aircraft to come to a complete stop before exiting. Looking overhead, he saw about half of the still moving rotorblade was missing.

Titov stuck his head in the crew compartment and asked, "Are you two okay?"

"Lieutenant Koslov has injuries, and I suspect it is his back."

"What is the risk of fire?"

"Little. I managed to flood the engines with extinguisher at the last second, so any flames are out, but I have no idea how hot the engine area is. Heat alone could cause a fire with leaking fuel."

"Can you get out on your own? If so, let me take the survival and first aid kits to safety, then I will return to help get Koslov out of his seat."

"Good, I am fine, but hurry. I do not like being in a freshly crashed helicopter."

The Sergeant laughed, patted Paley on the right shoulder and exited the aircraft. He took the survival and first aid kits to about fifty meters from the left side door, placed them on the ground and then returned to the co-pilot's door.

Opening the door, he said, "Undo his harness and I will take him on my back. Off the left is where the gear is and where I will bring Koslov."

With a quick twist of his hand, Paley released his harness and did the same for his co-pilot. Koslov moaned when the harness released and screamed when Titov pulled him from his seat. All three moved in the direction of the survival gear. The aircraft was smoking, but not a man on the ground saw any fire.

When Titov placed the injured co-pilot on the ground in some trees, the man screamed once more. The Sergeant met Paley's gaze and said, "Either his back is broken or he has hurt it in some way. Do you want me to inject him with morphine to kill his pain?"

"Yes and you have the first aid kit, right?"

"I have it."

"Kill his pain then. If we have to move him, I do not want him screaming all the time."

After giving Koslov morphine, Sergeant Titov returned to the downed aircraft for their individual weapons and ammunition. When he returned, Warrant Officer Paley was on the small survival radio talking to someone.

"One man, my co-pilot, was injured in the crash. We suspect serious back injury and have given him morphine for the pain. How far out are you now? Okay, out." He quickly pushed the telescoping antenna into the radio. He smiled and then said, "Less than ten minutes now. Be sure to have the flares ready, in the event we need them. Once you left, I began having pain in my lower back and legs."

"It may be from the g-forces you experienced when we struck the ground. I had my harness tight and it still rattled me pretty hard. I have to say, Mister Paley, that was one of your smoother landings."

Both men laughed and then Paley said, "Get down. I just saw a man moving near the helicopter."

"Shit," the Sergeant said, "not good."

"Well, I have some more bad news, he looked to be wearing NVG's, and if he is, we will not last long. The question is, do we fight or surrender?"

"Have you ever heard of a partisan group taking prisoners?"

"Well, that answers that question."

A man with a dog moved toward them and Paley whispered, "Let me start the shooting if we need to fight, and then you join in quickly. I do not like that damned dog, so I will try to kill it first."

"Okay," Titov replied in a whisper.

Paley looked behind the man and the dog to see a group of people moving around the downed chopper. *Not good; looks like momma Paley will be short a first born son come morning,* he thought as he aimed at the dog.

John stopped when Dolly gave a loud warning growl and he quickly spotted the three men in the trees, but he was standing in an open field, in a full moon, and with his dog with him. He clearly saw a Russian pointing a pistol at him, so he turned to the right and walk away.

Too damned close, Paley thought as he lowered the pistol. He then placed the sidearm in his shoulder holster and picked up his Bison. He met Titov's eyes and grinned.

The sound of helicopters nearing sent the people at the crash site running for the trees and Paley watched as the man with the dog neared two other men and pointed in his direction. *So, he saw me and moved away. I wonder why?* the Warrant Officer thought.

"Bear 19, this is Rescue 1, over."

"Roger, Rescue 1, I hear you and you are nearing my position. Be advised, there are unfriendly people in the area, about a 100 meters south of my position."

"Get your heads down; I am sending two Black Sharks in to clear the area."

There sounded something that reminded Paley of a big zipper being suddenly pulled opened and a steady light of green tracers flew through the air to strike the woods. *Ricochets* flew through the air and in the trees, the bullets tore into the wood like a chainsaw. Screams were heard, but then it grew quiet.

"Bear 19, I have some rockets coming into the trees, so get down lower this time." the rescue chopper pilot said.

No sooner had Paley and Titov lowered their faces to the grass than two loud explosions were heard, followed by more screams. Spotting movement above him, Paley saw the rescue chopper starting to lower.

"Bear 19, I have two corpsmen and three others coming to get you. Do not move toward us on your own."

"I understand."

"Taking small arms fire." the rescue pilot said as the aircraft touched the grass and the Black Sharks flew toward the trees again.

In just minutes, Koslov was on a liter, and Paley and Titov were being escorted to the rescue aircraft. About a foot from the door, Paley felt a blow to his back and collapsed to the ground. He was picked up, rolled into the aircraft and the other men boarded behind him. One of the medical men began looking Paley over, but the medic's head suddenly snapped back and his helmet exploded into a thousand pieces, sending plastic, fiberglass, brains, bone and blood in all directions. To Paley, the whole thing took place in slow motion, including the look of surprise seen on the medic's face.

"Hang on!" the pilot yelled and applied full throttle and lowered the nose to gather speed.

Bullets started slapping the aircraft with a loud bang and men ducked out of instinct. In the matter of a few minutes, it grew quiet and the only sounds were of the engine. Paley was surprised the engines were running smoothly with no sign of quitting. The dead medic had fallen over him, so he pushed the man away and the other medic neared.

Twenty minutes later they landed at Edwards Air Base, the dead medic was removed and the injured Lieutenant and Paley were taken by ambulance to the base hospital. Sergeant Titov was brought along too, so he'd receive a physical examination to ensure he wasn't injured in the crash and resulting firefight.

Hours later, as he lay in his bed, Paley heard a voice, "Mister Paley, are you okay?"

Opening his eyes, he saw the young Sergeant stood by his bed with a quart of vodka in his hand. Handing it to the pilot, he said, "You are not to have drink in the hospital, but I know you enjoy a snort at times. Hide it after you have your drinks or they will take it away from you."

"Are . . . are you okay?" Paley asked, the painkiller dulling his thoughts.

"I am fine and ready to go flying with you again, but looks like we are grounded as a crew for a long while."

"How is, uh, Lieutenant Koslov?"

"Not good. His back was severely injured when we hit and they think he will never walk again. The last time I spoke with a doctor, he said they were sending him out to the Jackson airport. From there he will return home for treatment."

Paley pulled the cork from the vodka, took a long drink, and then replied, "He is in bad shape if they fly him home, because you have to be almost dead to get out of here."

"Speaking of dead, the recon force that landed the next morning discovered over twenty bodies in the woods."

"Any dogs?"

Sergeant Titov laughed and said, "I asked that question too and the answer was no. While they did find dog tracks and dog shit, no dog. The Senior Sergeant said it was a big dog, too."

"It was a damned German Shepherd, and I know because I saw it."

"Relax, Mister Paley, we are safe and it does not matter now. Hell, have another drink. Colonel Dubow has promoted me to Senior Sergeant and you to Captain, all because of the bodies they recovered."

"No shit?"

"No shit, and he has put us in for one medal or the other. Medals and money will buy me a bottle of vodka, because all they are is metal and ribbon."

"Not true, lad, because with the right medals, the government will see you are always employed and have a pension, so think of your future."

"I had not given that any thought at all. Hell, it is hard to think of a future when you might be dead tomorrow."

Handing the bottle to Senior Sergeant Titov he said, "Take this back with you and enjoy it. Mixing it with these painkillers is not good. I am sleepy now. Congratulations, Sergeant, you are a damn fine soldier." Paley's head dropped to his pillow and the Sergeant saw his pilot was asleep.

Putting the bottle in his coat, he turned and left the room.

Colonel Bunin, his promotion confirmed, stood and said, "We

now have more than 3,000 prisoners, sir. More than enough for any work or other projects you may need done."

"Speaking of work, the word from Moscow is to screen the prisoners and put their skills to work for the good of our motherland." Colonel Dubow said.

"Put them to work? But they sabotage everything they touch."

"You will need a tough quality control center then, made up of soldiers. If one worker keeps messing up, shoot his ass and make the other workers watch the execution."

"That might work. But, really, sir, what kind of skills do you think these people will have?"

"It may surprise you, Colonel. At any rate, discover their skills and develop a plan to put them to work. Workers are to have 1400 calories a day and non-workers, 900."

"I will see to it immediately, sir."

CHAPTER 18

John moved through the trees on point with Dolly at his side, scanning the countryside as he moved. He was pissed. When the chopper had gone down after he'd struck it with a LAW, the group had moved to the fallen bird. Skeeter had tried to control them, but nothing had worked. Now, they were missing about half of the original group, killed by the Black Shark helicopters when they attacked the trees. John had warned the people to move away at right angles, but most ran blindly.

Bill moved to him and asked, "Do you want me to take point a while? You've been out here since we left this morning, and a tired man does none of us any good."

"Sure, take my place for a couple of hours, and thanks." John stepped to the side of the trail and let the younger man take the lead; Dolly stood at his side, her tongue hanging loosely from her mouth. He fell in beside Skeeter.

"What's on your mind?" Skeeter asked.

"As I said earlier this morning, we need to get your people under control or we'll arrive with no escapees except three or four of you."

"John, first these aren't my people and second, they know nothing of the military. I suspect of all the men, maybe ten have served. The rest have no idea what they're doing most of the time. I do know they rushed the chopper last night in hopes it carried food, not realizing it carried death instead."

"Well, we'll feed all of them, once back at camp, but right now they need to follow orders. I want you to pass the word, anyone failing to follow our orders will be shot."

Snapping his head toward John, Skeeter grinned and asked, "Surely you're not serious?"

"Oh, but I am serious. I'm dead serious. We're, to the last person, a very professional acting group and the first thing we all learned is to follow orders. Your people must learn it too, because not listening to orders can place me and others in danger. I demand all orders be followed at all times, or I will shoot their asses. And feel free to quote me on this subject when you speak with them."

Lowering his eyes, Skeeter said, "I know you're serious, but don't you have jobs some of these people can do and keep them out of the fighting? Some want to serve with us, but lack the skills needed to stay alive."

"Where they serve is up to the Colonel, not me, so I have no say in it. However, if we get back, I'll voice your concern to the man." John said and then added, "Now, move to each member of the group in line and tell them what I said."

"Right now?"

"Why not? A minute from now we might be under fire and I'll start shooting people who don't follow orders."

"Okay." Skeeter replied but thought, *This is a rough group I've run to for help.*

The afternoon was uneventful and by dusk they were all seated in the old garage, discussing what to do with Skeeter's people. While they weren't his people officially, that's how they were referred to by everyone.

"We do have some technicians, administration, and medical staff held in reserve, but they move frequently to avoid detection by the Russians. While they're not fighters, not really, we'll use them if push comes to shove in a battle." Colonel Tate said.

"Understood, sir," Skeeter replied, as he handed the man a list written in pencil, and continued, "and I have no problems with that. The list I just handed you contains the names and work experience of most of the folks with me. Ten of the twenty-five have prior military service, two were cops, and the rest have various skills."

"Those experienced with the military will be assigned to cells, the police officers too, but the rest, if possible, will go into none combat positions. While your people are appreciated, we need more fighters than we do those who cannot or will not fight. John, due to the losses you've had recently, you'll get Skeeter, Bill and Larry in your cell."

"Ranks?" John asked.

"Well," the Colonel chuckled and then said, "You are now a Major, Skeeter is a Lieutenant, and the other two are Sergeants. Oh, and Sandra has been promoted to our senior Captain. That means, uh, with the next opening, she'll be a Major."

By opening, all knew he meant death of an officer. It was a cold hard fact of life for each of them, and while the military ranks had no pay, it settled squabbles as to who was in charge.

"Colonel?" a man named Wilson said as he neared the group.

"What do you need, Sergeant?"

"Just before we got here, one of my men was playing with the directional finder and picked up a strong signal coming from this structure."

"Are you positive?" the Colonel asked.

"Oh, there is no doubt, but the batteries in the device are weak and we have no replacements."

"Sonofabitch," John said, and then added, "why all the traitors all of a sudden?"

"Fear, sir, plain old fear." the Colonel said and then thought for a few minutes. Finally, he said, "I know little of electronics, except what I learned as a child, but if I remember correctly, if your batteries are low, and you wait an hour or so, when you turn the item on, you have a little battery time."

"Sure, but only a minute or so, sir, maybe." Wilson replied.

"John and Skeeter, make sure no one leaves this building. Here in about 30 minutes we will line everyone up and check them with the directional finder. Now, I want it understood right now, the penalty for all traitors is death, no matter who it might be."

"Hell, that's why the Russians have discovered us so quickly over the last few weeks." John said and then thought, *Who can it be? I now trust everyone in my cell with my life.*

"Yes, and it's why we will move out of here just as soon as we execute the spy. Unlike the killing of Mollie, we'll shoot this one." Colonel Tate said, remembering the fouled up hanging of the woman.

Thirty minutes later, the Colonel said, "I want everyone to line up, all of you, and do the job now."

There came mumblings of the sleepy, complaints from the tired, but they lined up and then Colonel Tate said, "Turn the locator device on now."

Top held the device now and he flipped a switch and quickly said, "In the middle of the line." He looked up from the machine and said, "One of those three people have a bug planted on them. I can tell no more, because the device battery has died."

"Bill Shaw, Sandra, and Margie, stay where you are, but the rest of you move to the left side of this building right now." Colonel Tate said as he pulled his pistol.

"W . . . what is going on?" Sandra asked.

"I'm no damned traitor! Hell, I killed the last bitch that was!" Margie said brusquely.

"All three of you keep your mouths shut!" Tate ordered and then turning to Esom he said, Undress each of them and check their clothing carefully. The device may very well be sewn into a shirt or even their underwear."

"Yes, sir. Sandra, start by removing your coat."

"By the way, do a cavity search on all three as well. The device may be shoved into an orifice for all we know." the Colonel said.

Sandra said, "Esom, you'll find some rubber gloves in my medical bag, which will make your job easier and cleaner."

Esom put the gloves on and slowly and meticulously searched each item of clothing, discovering nothing. He was embarrassed when he started to do the cavity search and Sandra put him at ease, "Esom, relax, all you have to do it insert your middle finger into each of us. You'll know right off if anything is out of place."

"But, you're John's wife."

"Right now, I'm accused of being a traitor, a name I dislike, and don't deserve. So, check me and let's get this over with. You seem to forget, I am a nurse."

After checking Sandra and not finding anything, he moved to Margie. Margie was clean as well, so that really made everyone assume it was Bill Shaw. Bill had been with the group for about six months and his loyalty had never been questioned. He was a tough fighter, a man of his word, and held the rank of Staff Sergeant.

"Bill, is it you?"

Bill lowered his head and said, "Yes, but the Russians shot my father and when they threatened to kill my mother too, well, I agreed to pack a bug. My mother is all I have left, Colonel."

"For months we trusted you! *Why?* You are responsible for the deaths of your own people, Bill!" John screamed.

Sergeant Wilson stuck his head in the door and said, "I've got two tanks and about a hundred Russian infantrymen moving for this place. My guards report two choppers overhead and at least two jets, sir. If not for the NVG's we wouldn't know about the infantry."

"How far away?" Colonel Tate asked.

"Maybe two hundred yards, but distances are hard to guess with NVG's on, sir."

"Bring the guards in and break up into your cells. Four days from now we'll meet on the Pearl River, down by the freeway. But, you," the Colonel said as he raised his pistol, "will not be with us, Bill. You have thirty seconds to pray and then you'll be standing in front of God."

If Bill prayed, he did it silently, because he stood glaring at the Colonel. Suddenly, a shot rang out, loud in the small room, and a bullet struck Bill in the very center of his chest. He screamed, grabbed his injury and fell to the floor. Colonel Tate walked to the downed man and placed the second shot in his head, spraying the floor under him with bone and blood.

"Now, break into your cells and get the hell out of here. Those of you who were Skeeter's people, stay with me for right now, except for those already assigned to a cell. Good luck to all of you."

There sounded a cannon and the door to the garage flew off it's hinges and a loud explosion was heard just outside.

"My cell, form on me!" John yelled and ran for the rear door, holding Dolly by her leash. Quickly donning his NVG's he said, "If you have NVG's get 'em on now. If you don't, team up with someone who does."

When the six others were behind him, he ran from the building for the security of the dark woods. As he ran with his group behind him, Russian bullets kicked dirt, grass, and rocks high into the air as they struck all around him. Once in the trees he stopped and grinned when he noticed no one had been hit. "Margie, you take point and Sandra, bring up the rear. Get a good pace leaving and we'll slow down at some point later tonight. Until we can find three more pairs of NVG's for the new men, we'll do point and drag at night."

The evening was uneventful and around 2200 a bright light danced across the black sky, followed by a sharp crack. A gentle breeze appeared and all knew it was only a matter of time before rain visited.

"If you have ponchos, now would be a good time to put them on." John said during their break. "It's going to start raining shortly."

Skeeter and his men removed rain gear from their packs and as they were putting it on, Dolly gave a low growl and looked to the north, the direction they'd been traveling. They'd moved off a narrow trail to rest, but John figured someone was near and walking south. Looking in the direction of the trail, he spotted a squad of Russians, well armed, moving south. By the green light of his NVG's he noticed all of them wore the goggles as well.

The man in front stopped, looked down at the trail and said something John did not understand, then he realized they'd found a track. He flipped the safe of his Bison off and stood ready.

Skeeter tapped his shoulder and when John looked at the man, he held two grenades, pins pulled, with spoons held in place. He nodded and the Sergeant threw both grenades, one at time at the Russians. One exploded near the Russian point man and the other near the end of the soldiers. The loud blasts were followed by screams and yells. John opened up with his Bison, shooting low and knowing he was hitting his target by the shrieks.

Once his cell fired a few rounds, John yelled, "Cease fire! Cease fire!"

It grew quiet, except for the moans, groans and cries of the Russian wounded.

Skeeter started to move forward, but John grabbed his shirt sleeve and said, "Give them a few minutes to bleed. Right now adrenaline is all that's keeping some of them alive. We'll check them in about fifteen minutes or so."

The cell all knelt or squatted as they waited. Finally, John said, "Take no chances when we near this group. Keep in mind, we don't know if we killed all of them or even injured all of them. I suspect they had a man on drag and if so, he may be around or he may not. A smart man would run for home. If it moves, put a bullet in 'em again."

As they moved toward the downed Russians, John paid close attention to Dolly, who would alert him to any danger. A man tried to stand on the right, but a blast from Margie's twelve gauge shotgun blew the man off the trail. A pistol shot was heard and then Bill said, "Playing possum, but he ain't now."

Five minutes later, John said, "Skeeter, you and your men go over these Russians and take what gear you need. Be sure to get their NVG's, spare ammo and weapons. Each of you should have a good pistol, sheath knife, and other gear you need. You'll also find Russian rations, which taste like shit, but they'll keep you alive."

Bill said, "I need some new boots and a jacket, if I can find something that'll fit."

"You'll find them, if you don't mind a little blood."

Skeeter said, "The sleeping bags and mats will be good too, so take those as well."

Bill asked, "What's that noise?"

"I don't hear anything." John replied.

"I do." Sandra said and then yelled, "Choppers!"

A long row of machine-gun fire stitched the center of the trail, killing Bill immediately and knocking Larry, Margie, and Skeeter from their feet. Bill's headless body was squirting blood high into the air as Skeeter screamed in pain.

"Sandra, Esom, drag a person into the woods and then cover both of you with a poncho! *Hurry,* because the chopper is coming back around!" John yelled.

The Ka-60 approached the trail again, hovered over the dead, about ten feet above, and sent bullets blindly into the trees, from both open side-doors. The aircraft banked sharply and a side-door gunner sent a row of bullets down the trail again. Bodies danced madly as the big slugs tore into them and at times a bloody limb was knocked high into the air.

Damned infrared detection gear on the chopper, John thought, and then remembered he'd left without getting another LAW or two.

Margie, still packing the flamethrower stood, pointed it at the chopper and pulled the trigger, sending a long flowing stream of bright flames to the windshield of the hovering aircraft. John saw the flames splash on the glass, fly toward the engine cowling and watched, fascinated, as she sent two more squirts toward the big metal bird. The pilot, blinded by the flames, twisted the aircraft to the side and as he started to go up. The Mollies flames struck the left door-gunner, who fell from the aircraft, but remained attached by a wide nylon strap as he burned.

With the fire still burning on his windshield the pilot, now flying by instruments alone, raised his chopper higher into the air. At about 500 feet the nylon strap holding the door-gunner must have burned through, because the man fell from the aircraft, landing someplace in the trees. The chopper then limped home, minus one gunner.

Once the sound of the chopper were gone, John stood and yelled, "Check our injured and do the job now. We need to move and do the job as soon as we can. Those Russian bastards will be back and I don't want to be near this place when they get here."

"Larry is in sad shape, with his left leg needing amputation and his neck spurting blood." Sandra said, as she neared covered in crimson.

"Any chance he'll live?"

"None."

John walked to the unconscious man, pulled his pistol and a single shot echoed through the trees. "How about the others?" he asked.

"I'm fine, just lost my balance." Margie replied.

"I had a bullet graze my thigh, but I have it bandaged and I can move." Skeeter said and moved toward the group. Once there he asked, "What was the purpose of hiding under our ponchos?"

"For a few minutes it blocks our body heat from the infrared on the aircraft screens. After about five minutes, heat is released from the edges and it's no longer effective."

"I see." Skeeter replied and then looking at Margie he asked, "What in the hell made you shoot that thing at a helicopter?"

Margie gave a dry laugh and then said, "He pissed me off."

"Damn," Skeeter said.

"Actually, I wasn't sure it'd work or not, but we didn't have time to resupply at the garage, so I suspected John didn't have any Law's. My goal was to blind the pilot by brightness, but never dreamed the fuel would stick to the chopper so well."

"Well," John said, "you killed a door-gunner too, only we don't have time to look for his body. Saddle up and let's move. Sandra take the point and Skeeter, you're on drag. I want to move fast, almost at a trot for a couple of hours."

"Not a problem." Sandra said and took off at a fast walk. John gave her a minute or so and then started moving.

Esom moved to John and asked, "Why were those Russians out here?"

"Most likely they were placed in position once we scattered from the garage to trap us, only it didn't work out that way, not in our case anyway. I suspect the chopper was pulling infrared duty when it picked up the body heat from the men we'd just killed. From that point on, it was us against them."

"Well, we won." Esom said and then grinned.

"Yep, we surely did, but what about the next time?"

Esom's smile disappeared and he moved back into line.

At the Pearl River, slightly south and east of Jackson, the partisans met under an old overpass from the highway. A guard was positioned to view any traffic moving on the road, moving either east or west.

John had been assigned a second sniper, a young man named Curtis, and another woman named Amy. Both were veterans of years of struggle. As his group mingled and talked, meals were heated on an open fire, and all had their first hot meal in days.

Curtis explained he had over 200 confirmed kills as a sniper, but knew a man in Alabama with over 500. He said, "'Bama is full of Russians and the rednecks are giving those Russian sonsof-bitches pure-Dee hell."

"What you say may be true," John said, "only it's not taken any pressure off of us."

"It's hard to say really, because if 'Bama was pacified, we'd have more Russians on our asses over here, huh?"

"Well, that's true, I guess. Nonetheless, we've more of 'em in Mississippi than we need."

"Gentlemen and ladies, I need all of your cell leaders and Sergeants to meet with me. We've a mission to plan."

"Mission?" Skeeter asked, "What kind of mission?"

"I plan to hit the gulag at Edwards."

John felt the little critter that lived in his stomach come alive, gnawing at his insides. Certain missions scared him and this one did. *How are we going to rescue more than get killed?* he thought.

Colonel Tate said, "Previously we've discussed hitting the camp and what I am about to propose includes the gulag in that attack. We've lost many people over the last month, so we have to slow the Russians down a bit."

"We still hitting the fuel tanks as you once suggested?" John asked, and Dolly lowered her head to his lap.

"That is the key to our overall success. We must reach the fuel tanks, open the petcocks and release the fuel. Once the area is sat-urated good, we do our damage using grenades."

"When?" John asked.

"Tomorrow night. I know it's soon, but the Russians are now screening people for job skills and putting them to work, much like the Nazi's did in World War Two. Most are returned to the gulag each night, but they have folks with computer skills that we need, and they're to be sent to Jackson next Monday. If we can hack a Russian website and gain access to the classified documents, we can play hell with their plans."

"You'd have to pass up some known items, just to keep them from knowing you have compromised their computer security system."

"What you say is true, but we're putting the cart before the horse. First, we have to attack the gulag and base, rescue some programmers and hackers, and then gain access to a computer with electrical power."

"Then why attack? We don't have electricity and never will." Skeeter asked.

"My civil engineers and others claim we can use batteries, and the computer folks we have assure me a working computer is not only possible, but available. It seems the commander before Willy, I don't remember his name, had computers and electrical power for a period of time."

"The commander was Colonel Parker, sir." John said.

"Yes, that's the man's name."

"What time do we attack?" Skeeter asked.

"Tomorrow night at 0200 hours."

CHAPTER 19

The next evening, at the Russian hospital on Edwards, Major Rusak was arguing with a doctor over his condition. Finally, the angry doctor threw his clipboard on a table and said, "Go on, get the hell out of here, Major, but do not come back crying to us when your pain gets severe."

"I have vodka for pain, doctor, so I will be fine, and what of my flying friend, Paley? He too wishes to return to his unit."

"Captain Paley is to be released back to flying tomorrow and as far as I am concerned, you can take his big mouth with you tonight when you leave."

"Great and thank you, sir."

"Just leave, Major, and let me get back to my work." the doctor replied, picked up his clipboard and left the room.

Gathering what little he had, but making sure he had the quart of vodka, Rusak made his way to Paley's room.

Seeing the newly promoted Captain Paley sitting on the edge of his bed, Rusak said, "Captain, grab your belongings, we are leaving, and now! Both of our charts have been closed by Doctor Pajari and we are free to go, unless you want to stay here."

"Hell no, I will go, but give me a few minutes to gather what little I have. Let us go back to my quarters and have a few drinks."

"Sure, that sounds good to me."

At 2200 hours, they were both in Paley's new quarters and drinking vodka. Paley, loud as usual, asked, "How does it feel to be a Major?"

"I am treated better, but I do not see another promotion in my future. I am too outspoken and I do not play officer politics at all."

"Then I am screwed, because I do not know about the politics and have no urge to play the game. I just want to fly."

Rusak laughed and then said, "You mean fly and steal."

"I am guilty of trading, but I have never stolen anything."

"What about the pallet of plywood that was being lifted into the air when a full Colonel caught you?"

"How was I to know someone owned the wood? It was sitting out in the middle of nowhere and unguarded." the pilot said with a straight face.

"From what I heard, it was inside the supply units fenced in area and you were helping yourself."

"Major, I take care of my troops and I saw plywood sitting there that my people needed. I do not take for personal gain, but to help my men and women. Our unit had wood on order for over nine months and when it came in, a Colonel decided he needed to fix his personal quarters up better. That was our wood I was taking."

"Any legal action taken against you?"

Paley grinned and replied, "No and there will not be. Colonel Dubow told me he wiped my slate clean the day he pinned the rank of Captain on me. The Colonel, a man named Popoff, is dead now anyway and cannot press charges."

"Keep your nose clean, fly like you should, and I see no reason you will not make Major."

Glancing at his watch, Paley said, "I hate to break up the party, but I need to get some rest. I have to report to the unit in the morning and I am sure they will have some busy work for me to do."

As the two shook hands, Rusak said, "Get some rest. I am still confined to my bed, so I can sleep in, but we both know that will not happen." Breaking his grip with the newest officer in the unit, the Major made his way out the door, more than a little drunk. He heard Paley yell a late goodbye.

At ten minutes after 0200 hours, the world around Rusak and Paley turned bright, which awoke the Major, and then came the screams. Climbing from his bed, his vision messed up by the alcohol he'd had, he picked up the vodka bottle and took another big swig to kill his aches. Bottle still in hand, he made his way to his door and opened it.

A small stream of burning fuel ran by the wooden steps leading to his quarters and when he looked uphill, the whole area was in flames. A big siren mounted on a blazing telephone pole, was blaring an attack warning. *That loud sonofabitch is a bit late,* Rusak thought and he turned, tossed the bottle on his bunk and picked up his weapons. He'd just placed his helmet on, when a loud explosion sounded, followed by more screams.

Paley, who was only three buildings down, arrived and yelled, "What in the hell is going on?"

"The siren indicates we are under attack, but I see no one."

"We need to move quickly away from this flowing fuel. It is only a matter of time before it reaches our quarters."

Picking up the vodka and stuffing it inside his shirt, Rusak asked, "Any ideas where to go?"

"Angle off away from the flames and move up hill, maybe. Down this hill is where all the fuel will gather and a good number of aircraft are located there."

There was a huge explosion and a gigantic mushroom cloud of flames and smoke rolled into itself over where the munitions storage area once existed. Looking at the blast, Rusak found it was possible to see individual bodies as they flew through the air.

Paley screamed to be heard over the smaller blasts, sirens and screams of help, "I warned the Operations Officer about outside storage of munitions! Too many bombs stored out in the open."

"Move toward headquarters and let us see what in the hell is going on." Rusak yelled back.

Red and green tracers flew over their heads as they made their way to the base commanders office. Most of the tracers were coming into the base, which indicated they were in fact under attack by a large group of partisans.

At Colonel Dubow's building, runners were moving in and out. Paley and Rusak entered, moved to the Colonel's office, and waited as the man screamed orders over a radio. He then read some papers handed to him by a runner and said, "Impossible, tell him to fight with the men he has."

"Colonel, a guard reports the hospital is in flames, sir." the radio operator said.

"Damn me, can anything else go wrong?"

"The operations officer says he got about fifty percent of the aircraft in the air, but that burning fuel is threatening the remainder."

Paley looked at Rusak and said, "Come, we will take a helicopter ride."

"I do not know how to fly."

"I do, so come with me, and maybe we can save another aircraft."

Out the door they ran and when they were clear of the buildings, a series of loud explosions were heard near the gulag. Tracers were still flying overhead, but now a chopper was in the fight, and sending short bursts of machine-gun fire into the gulag complex.

"There, off our right is a Ka-60, so climb in. You will need to hook yourself into a harness, so if we take a hit you are not thrown from the aircraft."

A maintenance crew was at the start cart and looking nervous as they waited for a crew to arrive. Paley yelled, "I am Captain Paley and a pilot, so I will take this bird into the air."

"I will go with you!" a young Lieutenant said and then continued, "My name is Gura, Lieutenant Gura, and I am a co-pilot."

"Climb aboard, Lieutenant and let us get this thing in the air before the fuel burns us all to death. Major, you will find a headset hanging near the door, so put it on when you board and keep it on so you can hear us speak to you."

"I understand." Rusak said and moved to the opening where the gunner sat.

Ignoring most checklist procedures, Paley began flipping switches and turning knobs as the burning fuel grew near. When it was about ten feet from him the rotors began to turn. Five minutes later, the ground crew gone and fuel within inches of his wheels, he raised the aircraft. Rusak, who'd seen the fire move under the aircraft was in a near panic when he heard the Captain say, "We are clear of the fire and I intend to stay that way. Rusak, I know you outrank me, but on this chopper I am the boss, understood?"

"Sure, what do you need me to do?"

"Fire at any partisans you see and if I point you at a target, take it out."

"Let us do it."

As they flew over the base, Rusak saw the main base, flight line and part of the gulag appeared to be in flames.

"Good God, how many men and women have burned to death in all of this?" Rusak asked, not realizing the two up front heard him speak.

"Most of the barracks for the troops are in flames and they would have been asleep. I am afraid, Major Rusak, heads will roll when Moscow hears of this."

"To hell with Moscow, what of my men and women? How many are dead and who was the bright ass that put the fuel storage tanks on that hill?"

"Some engineer, but it matters little. There, near the fence line by the gulag, do you see the partisans?"

"Got them." Rusak replied and pulled the trigger on his machine-gun. He moved the barrel of the big gun from side-to-side and saw many of the partisans fall.

"Near the hospital, see the group near the front door? Take them out now!" Paley yelled on the radio. One short burst from his machine-gun and the men near the door were down, so he fired into them once again, to make sure they stayed down.

A LAW or RPG flew past the chopper, missing by inches and it brought the Major back to the present. Out of instinct, he started looking for threats. Bullets pinged sharply and made loud thud sounds as they punched holes in the thin skin of the chopper.

Lieutenant Gura suddenly screamed over the radio and when Rusak glanced at the cockpit, the left side of the co-pilots face was in shreds and his eye was laying on a mangled cheek. The windshield in front of the man was shattered and blood was dripping from the armrest to the floor.

"Paley, is Gura dead?"

"No, but he may soon be, because I am staying in the air as long as we have fuel. There, near the town are a bunch of escaping prisoners."

"I will not fire on them, Captain, orders or not. Feel free to report me, if you wish. There, near the motor pool, at your ten o'clock position. I count an even dozen members of the resistance." The Major brought the big gun into play again, knocking all the partisans over, where they lay kicking and jerking. There came a loud bang, followed by cursing by Paley, and the aircraft began to shudder.

"Major Rusak, we are going to have to land, but it will not be a smooth landing. But first, I am going to try and put some distance between us and this base. I cannot tell who is friendly down there and who is not, so I am heading toward Jackson."

Half way to the big city, the aircraft started falling apart and Rusak saw a large sheet of metal fly past the open door near his gun. Over head a few wires suddenly burst into flames, so the Major squirted them with his fire extinguisher and they went out, leaving the smell of burnt rubber in the compartment.

"What was that?" Rusak asked.

"What are you talking about?"

"Wires overhead started burning."

"Uh, I have no idea, but I am going to have to put us down and do the job within the next few minutes. The instrument console is lit up in lights, but mostly with red lights. On the canvas seats you will find a lap-belt, so put it on tightly."

"Is Lieutenant Gura still alive?"

"I have no idea, and I have been too damned busy to check. We will check him out if we walk away from my landing. Brace yourself, we are going down."

Looking out the side-doors, Rusak saw they were lowering straight down to land in a large field or that's what he thought in the darkness. All went well until the last three or four feet when the engine stopped running and they fell hard to the ground. Impact was hard and the aircraft half rolled, then righted itself. Smoke and dust filled the cabin and made seeing difficult.

Paley stuck his head around and asked, "Are you okay?"

"Fine, except my back hurts."

"Mine too. Our friend, Lieutenant Gura, is dead. I think he bled out while we were fighting. Now, we need to egress this thing and make for the woods. Under your seat you will find a survival kit; bring it with you."

Rusak grabbed the kit and made for the trees. His lower back pained him and he had a long cut on his left forearm from wrist to elbow. They'd just entered the trees when there came a swoosh and the chopper burst into flames.

"I turned all the switches to off, but I suspect the engine was too hot and it caused the fire."

A loud explosion was heard and when the Major glanced at the chopper, very few pieces remained on the ground, because the blast had blown most of the aircraft into the air. Pieces began to fall and for a minute, it was raining helicopter, which brought a loud giggle from Paley.

Feeling the vodka in his shirt, Rusak removed it, took a long drink and then handed it to the pilot. Paley took a long snort, passed it back and said, "We need to stay sober out here, so that was for pain. I suggest we move toward the road and wait for a convoy to come by so we can hitch a ride back to what remains of Edwards."

"Well, we helped a little." Rusak said, and he picked up the survival kit and opened it. Inside he found enough gauze pad to wrap his injured arm. Then, turning he asked "Any injuries?"

"My back is really bothering me and my neck. I suspect it was the g-forces from the impact when we landed. But, no, nothing bleeding like you."

"The only weapon I have is my pistol."

"That is all I have for protection, too. I am not real worried about partisans, because I honestly feel most of them are attacking the base right now. I have never seen so many at one time. Here, I brought two sets of NVG's from the helicopter. Put this on." Paley handed him a set of goggles.

"What do you think caused the helicopter to vibrate like it did? That scared the hell out of me at the time." Rusak asked after he donned the goggles as they moved toward the main road.

"I think the main rotor blade took a hit and we were lucky it did not just fly apart on us."

"Not good. I think and hope this was my last battle in the air. Give my old ass the ground any time, because I can dig a hole in the gro—."

"Be quiet." Paley whispered and then pushed Rusak to one knee, "I heard someone."

Rusak turned his head, scanning the countryside cautiously. A few minutes later, he pointed to a group of ragged men and women walking down a well used trail. Due to the NVG's the scene was in pale green and shades of white. Some looked to be injured, while others obviously were, because they were packed on a stretcher. Both Russians remained still and when Rusak glanced back at the chopper, dense black smoke rose to the dark sky and while the Americans might come looking, he didn't think so. The battle had taken the fight out of most of them and they simply looked tired.

They sat unmoving for over thirty minutes, to allow the partisans to leave the area completely. During that time, Rusak wondered if he'd ever return home to his wife Esfir and their small apartment. He'd written her about his promotion and the increase in pay was huge, more than double his old Master Sergeant pay, but already she must have seen his pay in the bank. He could imagine her surprise when she'd seen the deposit amount. Maybe as an officer, he could now start showing her the standard of living she so richly deserved. He knew she'd continue saving the money, so they could add to the small nest egg they'd saved over the years. He could easily live on half his Major pay and save the rest for a bad day.

Paley elbowed him and said, "Let us move closer to the road. Now, when we flag down a ride, do not move too quickly or pull a gun or they will likely shoot our asses. The guards will be nervous and even more so now that Edwards was attacked."

Hours passed and while they kept looking for more partisans, they saw no one. An hour after sunrise a single motorcycle passed and Paley said, "Move to the road and stand at the side. There will be a convoy coming soon now. I suspect the cyclist was pulling point for them."

As the Captain predicted, a convoy soon came into view. The first few trucks passed, but then a staff car pulled to the side and both men ran to the doors. A back door opened and a voice said, "Get in here gentlemen, and we will talk."

Climbing in, it took Rusak a minute or two to realize he was sitting next to a Major General, so he quickly sat at attention. Paley, unsure what was going on, glanced around the Major and then did the same.

"Relax, gentlemen, because I suspect you have had a long night. Was it your helicopter that went down last night near this road?"

"Yes, sir. Edwards was attacked and we fought as long as we could, but I eventually had to leave the area due to battle damage." Captain Paley replied.

"How did it look when you left?"

"Not good, sir. Burning fuel was running down a slight incline and it torched everything I could see. We got airborne just seconds before our aircraft would have been engulfed by flames."

"Then you are a hero, both of you, and today we need heroes. I was on a staff assistance visit to Jackson when I heard of the attack. I wanted to visit and see for myself how a bunch of civilians could do so much damage to our army. Do either of you have any ideas?"

Careful, Rusak thought, *he is trolling for reasons we lost the fight. It very well may be Dubow and his men will be shot for failure.*

Paley said, "Sir, most of Moscow seems to forget these Americans are all, or most anyway, born with a gun in their hands. Many of them are successful hunters and then when you add their veterans, you have the largest unorganized army in the world. Well, they are organized now."

Grinning, the General look at Rusak and asked, "Do you share his opinion?"

"Pretty much, sir, except I think they are still loosely organized. See, they usually run in small squad size groups, which we call a cell. Well, last night I had never seen so many partisans in one spot in my life. There must have been a thousand cells all around Edwards, the gulag and the air base."

"Surely you jest Major; that would be over 10,000 men."

"I know exactly how many men it would be, sir, because I saw them."

"Do you agree with his estimate, Captain?"

"To be honest, sir, I have no idea how many were there, because I was a busy man at the time, but I have never known Major Rusak to exaggerate. If he claims he saw ten thousand men, then I am damned inclined to agree with him."

"Guard, please hand a bottle of vodka back here so these men can have some much deserved refreshment."

A Sergeant extended his arm and in his fist was a bottle of first class Russian vodka. Since both men were yet in pain, Major Rusak took the drink and said, "Thank you, sir. We both injured our backs upon landing and while I have a bottle, we could not drink enough to kill our pain."

"Driver, when we reach Edwards, take both of these men straight to the hospital."

"Uh, sir," Paley said, "that will not work because the last time I saw the hospital, it was in flames."

"Very well, then. Gentlemen, feel free to share the whole bottle if you wish. I will not have fighting men riding with me in pain."

Edwards was a mess, a real goat-roping mess; structures were black from flames and most of the hard buildings were gone and all of the tents. The hospital was a black spot, still smoking, and the only building to avoid the flames was headquarters, where the General's staff car stopped.

Colonel Dubow was standing in front of his building, hands on his hips, yelling at his men to look for survivors. The first person out of the car was Captain Paley, then Major Rusak, and finally the General. Master Sergeant Turchin called the area to attention.

The General walked to Dubow, extended his hand a said, "Well, Boris, it looks like you have had a fight on your hands."

"Very much so, sir. Intelligence suggests well over 10,000 partisans hit us at 0210 last night."

"Really? What did they use to come up with those numbers?"

"Well, we discovered over a 1,000 of their dead, sir. Additionally, we took a few prisoners and a couple are talking."

"I would not suspect that many partisans in the whole country, Colonel."

"You would be surprised, sir. Perhaps you would like to sit in on one of our interrogation sessions, sir?" Colonel Dubow asked and then thought, *You pompous ass, come in here right after an attack and start questioning me. How dare you, you arrogant sonofabitch!*

"I would like that, Colonel, very much. When is your next session?"

"Master Sergeant Turchin, pull the prisoner named Esom. Why... right now, sir."

CHAPTER 20

Esom was in bad shape, with a broken left leg and an arm dislocated from his last questioning. He was hanging tough, but it was taking all he had not to break. The Russians were vicious during interrogations and he'd only been questioned once. He knew if they discovered he was a sniper, he'd be skinned alive. His job had been to hang back and wait for daylight, then try to kill a senior officer. He'd been with the new woman, Amy, and she'd disappeared just before he'd been captured. He prayed she'd escaped. She was a sniper too, so it was possible she was watching his torture sessions, through her rifle scope.

Esom was pulled forward, the broken bone of his left leg seen through his trousers leg. He screamed in pain as he was pulled to Colonel Dubow; Major Taras, one of the few surviving officers that spoke English, stood beside the Colonel. A huge infantry Private stood by with a steel rod in his hand, to break bones, or cause pain.

Dubow would speak, then Taras would ask the question in English.

"How many men are in your cell?"

Esom said, "What is a cell? I live in Edwards and came here to help you following the attack."

Now, Taras spoke to the Colonel, who grinned.

"You are a liar, because you were caught with a gun."

"I found it."

"Private," Colonel Dubow said in Russian, "break his left arm with your metal rod."

The General was watching the whole thing with a smirk on his face. He loved the look of anguish on Esom's black face and he knew the black man would soon experience more pain when his arm was shattered by the rod. As he watched, a black dot appeared in the middle of Esom's face and the back of his head exploded, sending bone, blood, brains and gore into the face of the private. Esom's body fell limp.

The General was still smiling when his back exploded, sending men and women scampering for safety as Rusak yelled, "Sniper!"

The General was down and Dubow made a move for the man, only to receive a bullet in the chest, and as Taras moved for the Colonel, he fell with the top of his head missing, his body jerking and quivering as he died. Paley took a swig from the vodka bottle and remained squatting behind the staff car. Rusak, extended his hand and the bottle changed ownership for a few minutes. *Damn,* Rusak thought as he looked around, *I am the senior man here.*

"Master Sergeant Turchin, take two squads and find that sniper."

"Yes, sir."

"And, Abram?"

"Yes, sir?"

"Watch your ass because this sniper knows the business."

Turchin laughed and took off at a run toward his men.

Paley asked, "Why did the sniper shoot his own man?"

"To keep him from talking, maybe, or the man might have been a friend and the sniper wanted to end the suffering. Who knows?"

"The black man was brave."

"In case you did not notice, the black man is dead. In the end we will all end up in a grave, but some ways are better than others."

"My, you have turned cynical on me since we got here, my friend. And pass me the drink. Better yet, let me open the door and get a fresh bottle. You can keep that one."

The door opened, but the movement brought a shot, and a bullet narrowly missed Paley to hit a stone, and then it zinged off into space.

"Got it!" Paley said with a stupid look on his face.

"No more moving until the sniper is caught." Rusak said, while wearing a drunken grin.

Twenty minutes later, as the two men passed the vodka bottle, a series of shots were heard in the distance, near where the snipers shots were fired.

"They got the sniper, or so I would bet." Rusak said.

"Maybe."

"Master Sergeant Turchin just radioed and the sniper was a woman; she is dead."

Major Rusak took charge, "Someone get a medic for our injured. You, Private, find some blankets to cover the faces of our dead. Lieutenant, I want you to gather some men and let us see about turning this place into a military base again."

A medic looked up and said, "Colonel Dubow and the General are dead, sir."

"Check the Major."

The medic moved to the man, but the top of his head was missing, "Major Taras is dead, too."

Rusak, who a year ago was a Master Sergeant, was the surviving ranking officer. He took charge, cleaned up the base, and released the prisoners from the gulag, except those guilty of serious crimes. Then he waited, knowing new commanders were coming and the situation would change again, maybe for the better, but likely not.

He'd discovered hundreds of deaths, most burned to death in the fire from the leaking fuel. His first task assigned to the civil engineers squadron was to find a safe place for fuel storage. Three days after they started construction, he walked into his office and saw three Colonels and a Lieutenant Colonel waiting to speak with him. All of them were from Russian Headquarters Mississippi and assigned to Jackson.

Standing when Major Rusak entered, a thin Full Colonel said, "Major, I am Colonel Duboff and have been sent to take overall command of Edwards Air Force Base."

The Colonel extended his hand and said, "With me is Colonel Ivanov, the new Gulag Commander, Colonel Eline, the new Anti-terrorist Commander, and Lieutenant Colonel Kot, your new Infantry Commander. You have been promoted to Lieutenant Colonel, for your efforts during the recent attack, and assigned as the Deputy, or Executive Commander, of our infantry. You are second in command of our troops, behind Lieutenant Colonel Kot."

"Welcome, gentlemen, and if you will give me an hour, we will have a staff meeting and I will introduce all of you to your staff. Colonel Kot, we are very short of men right now and I am unsure when Moscow will send replacements."

"Additional men will be here by the end of the day. Right now, they are in Jackson, waiting for transportation to Edwards." Duboff said and then grinned.

"Good, because right now, we have less than a company of men and hardly need two Lieutenant Colonels in charge."

Over the next month, the base was strengthened, more and more men arrived, and the gulag became full again. Colonel Ivanov, improved the diet for all prisoners, allowing about 1200 calories a day. Food was served twice daily; once in the morning and then each evening. Those working in some way, received three meals a day and were getting about 1800 calories.

This morning, Duboff was conducting his morning staff meeting. The partisans had disappeared following the attack and were not to be found. It had intelligence stumped and Duboff mad.

"We must go on the attack once more, but first we have to find the resistance." Duboff said and then asked, "Colonel Eline, do you have any idea what has happened?"

"Well, I am unsure, but have some ideas. Intelligence in both Alabama and Arkansas have reported an increase in terrorist attacks and strength of the partisans. It is my thoughts that our members of the resistance have moved to those states to assist, and they may be planning a major attack. We have concluded that the attack on Edwards, earlier this year, was not done by Mississippi partisans alone."

Duboff thought for a moment and then asked, "What can we do right now?"

"Well, sir, it is unlikely we will have any major battles, but we can look for their supply bases, support groups, or simply deactivate mines and booby-traps. I suggest we look for supply bases and wipe out their support groups."

Colonel Kot said, "They must not figure we are much of the threat to them, if they have left the state to fight with others."

"We are not sure what they think of us, but keep in mind that a major combined operation would take months to organize, so this may have been planned way before Edwards was attacked."

Colonel Duboff said, "I like the idea of looking for their supply bases and those left behind. While it will be hard, tedious work, any army needs supplies, and to wipe them out may help us a great deal in the long run. Gentlemen, as of 0600 tomorrow we will enter the field looking for any signs of the partisans. All supplies found, especially weapons or munitions will be destroyed in place. We will not risk the lives of our men by returning guns or explosives to supply to be reissued. Partisans are known to tamper with gear and leave it to be found."

Colonel Eline said, "Well said, sir, and you are correct. Over the last year alone, we have had over 50 cases where our gear was tampered with and left for us to find. Usually it was a firing pin removed from weapons, C-4 placed in cartridges after the powder was removed, or grenades with the time delay set to zero, which is rough on the user. If we can find their supplies and wipe them out, the resistance will be reduced, but not killed as a fighting unit."

"I do not understand." Colonel Ivanov said.

"If the resistance loses, let us say 60% of their supplies, they will do one of two things. They will either speed up their attacks on our convoys, trains, or supply areas. Or, they will get additional gear from the resistance in other states. As long as there are Americans that hate us being here, they will find a way to fight."

"Enough of this kind of talk. Gentlemen, I want all of you prepared to start this mission at 0600 hours tomorrow, especially my infantry and aircraft commanders. If you have any questions, see me in my office. Dismissed."

"Ten-hut!" Master Sergeant Turchin said, from the very pit of his stomach, and everyone stood as the Colonel left the room.

At 0600, Lieutenant Colonel Rusak stood on the flight-line with his troops. Choppers were to take them deep into the woods and release them as squads. Rusak would go as well, wanting to keep control of his men, and to be on the scene to verify their findings. For many of the men, it was their first combat mission, so they were understandably anxious.

Rusak addressed his men, "Once in the field, listen to your Sergeants and Officers. They know what it takes to survive in a battle. If you are given an order, follow it to the letter and remember, to do less would let your comrades down. Keep in mind, you are all members of the best army in the world, the Russian army."

The choppers had their engines running and the wide rotor blades were turning overhead. A senior member of the aircrews, walked to Lieutenant Colonel Rusak and said, "Bring the men out, sir, squad by squad. You have too many men, so it will take three trips to get all of you in the field."

"Lieutenant Markov, get the men to the helicopters, a squad at a time."

As the men loaded, Rusak looked at them and wondered how many would still be alive when they made the return trip. Out of habit, he then glanced at the sky, saw no clouds, felt a light wind, and was thankful for good weather. Moving to the first aircraft he climbed in and put on a headset. His helmet he positioned between his legs.

Twenty minutes later as they flew over a deep wooded area, the pilot said, "I have smoke from what looks like a cooking fire at my 2 O'clock position. I suspect it is a partisan camp."

"What is the estimated distance from right now?"

"Eight Kilometers or close to that."

"Put us down here but give me a compass heading to the smoke before you leave."

"Copy, sir, and not a problem. I have a wide field off my left, so I will put you down there."

Fifteen minutes later, Rusak was on the ground with his men, and wanting to get away from the landing site, he said, "Sergeant Sliva, take the point and Corporal Belsky, you pull drag. Move us out on a north by east direction, using compass heading of 050." Then looking at his nervous radio man, he said, "And, you, Private Pac, I want you close enough to me to be my shadow."

For a mile all went well, but then Sliva stopped and motioned Rusak forward. Pointing, the Sergeant indicated a thin line of fishing line across the trail, so the Colonel slowly moved forward. The line was tied to a stick pounded into the ground at one end, while the other end of the line was tied to a grenade pushed into a can. The idea was a walking man would catch the line on his boots or shins, which in turn would drag the grenade from the can. Since the pin on the grenade was pulled, the spoon would fly off, and an explosion would be the result.

Rusak marked the line with a stick stuck in the dirt and sent his Sergeant forward.

Near noon he stopped to allow his men to have a meal. Moving had been slow, because many mines and booby-traps were encountered, and each time they were marked. They'd moved off the trail and were eating under a large oak tree. He'd allowed no fires to heat the meals and some of the men were complaining.

Laughing inside, because he knew from his days as a Master Sergeant, his men weren't really mad. It was just harder to eat a meal with a good quarter of an inch of grease on top cold. They had small chemical tabs for burning, but when he said no fires, he meant it. All it would take is for a sniper or other eyes to be drawn to them and they'd have a fight.

I hope we can reach the source of the smoke and take them out quickly, because it'll make the men all more confident, he thought as he ate his simple meal.

About an hour later, very near the source of the smoke, Rusak stopped the men and then made radio contact with base. He discovered some aircraft were in the air and near him, but he wanted to see what the target looked like first. If aircraft support was needed, it was nice to know he had it overhead now.

"Sergeant Sliva, lead us to where we can see the camp and then stop."

The Sergeant gave a nervous look and then moved forward. A little later, from the top of a slight incline, they could see a small camp below. He counted twenty people, but most weren't carrying weapons or looked to be fighters. Near the camp, covered with brush, he spotted ten medium size tents. *This must be a supply point or why so many tents?* Rusak thought as he double checked the camp.

Leaning close to his Sergeant he said, "I want you to toss two grenades and I will do the same. Once they explode, we charge in shooting. Try to get some prisoners for Colonel Eline to interrogate, okay?"

The Sergeant, facing only the second combat situation in his career, nodded and removed two grenades.

"Now, throw them." the Colonel ordered.

Both grenades were tossed well, landing in the middle of the people working near the fire and Rusak threw his to land on the ends of the group. A loud scream was heard, followed by four explosions almost immediately after. After the blasts, more screams were heard from those injured or dying.

The Russians entered camp with guns blazing and the new men were shooting anything that moved. A small naked male child, not much over three, stood crying beside a woman's body until a bullet struck the kid in the chest and down he went. Two resistance men fired at Rusak, just missing him by inches, but before he could return fire, a long line of automatic fire stitched them across the chest and they fell screaming. Private Yudin moved ahead of the group and a bullet caught him in the neck which knocked him to his knees. His injury sent blood streaming through his fingers as he was grasping at it, hoping in some way to stop the flow of blood. The Russians moved past the injured Private and the opposition was quickly silenced.

"Sergeant!" Rusak called out.

"He is dead, Colonel. He was the first man to fall, I think." Private Jur, the medic, said.

"What do you need, sir?" Corporal Belsky asked.

"Open each of these tents and see what is inside." Lieutenant Colonel Rusak ordered as he walked toward the fallen form of Sergeant Sliva. He discovered the man on his back with four bullet holes in his body. Three bullets had struck his chest and one in the head. Rusak knew any one of the shots would have been fatal. He walked back and watched as his men checked the Americans for any signs of life. Jur was seen moving from person to person looking each over closely.

Finally, Private Jur walked to him and said, "We have three captives, but the others are all dead or soon will be. I counted fourteen dead beyond any doubt and two more will join them within minutes."

"What of Yudin?"

Private Jur grinned and said, "It looks much worse than it is. The shot actually missed a major artery and he will live. I have him patched up, shot him full of morphine, and he is fine until we can get him picked up."

"Colonel, you need to see this, sir!" the Corporal yelled from near the tents.

When Rusak neared the man, the Corporal said, "Explosives, ammunition, and a big supply of medical supplies."

The Lieutenant Colonel had Belsky inventory and write it all down. Most of the gear was Russian, but some had Chinese marking, which confused him.

Turning to his radio man, Rusak said, "Contact base and tell them we have hit a huge supply depot and some of the supplies are clearly marked in Chinese. Also let them know we have three captives, all women, an injured Private, and one man killed."

"Will do, sir."

It was while he was speaking to Belsky, the radio man said, "Colonel, they want all the Chinese items sent out by helicopter. Additionally, secure the captives for transportation, as well as our wounded and dead."

Rusak had it all completed by the time the "whop-whop" sound of the Ka-60 approaching was heard. Belsky popped a smoke flare and guided the chopper to a perfect landing. Within five minutes, all was loaded and the chopper moved away.

"Colonel, the helicopter pilot asked for you to remain here until he could deliver you two replacements for the men we lost."

"Let him know we will do that, because we have some supplies to destroy."

CHAPTER 21

*D*amn me, Sandra thought as she looked around the inside of the Russian chopper and made eye contact with Margie. Both were left behind when John and the rest had moved into Alabama to assist in attacks on gulags. She had no idea they'd end up prisoners and now she'd be beaten and raped. Margie, who was near an opening on the side, where the door had been removed, suddenly tilted and fell from the aircraft. She'd screamed, "Victory for America!" before she fell.

The gunner yelled and the aircraft circled once and then assumed a straight course, which Sandra thought was to Edwards.

I can't follow you, Margie, or I would. I'm packed in the center of this chopper, Sandra thought and then shook her head slowly. *John will want to come for me, but will Colonel Tate allow it? I doubt it, because there were just three of us taken captive. John, no matter what happens, baby, I love you.*

The Chopper sat down on the Edwards Air Base flight-line a few minutes later and the captives were taken to the gulag and placed in individual cells. Sandra soon discovered her room was exactly four paces wide by eight paced long and she estimated the ceiling was eight feet high. The walls, ceiling, and floor were all concrete and the bars looked to be steel. The door was of solid oak and heavy, the hinges reinforced with long bolts through the door frame. The lock was simple, a huge padlock on a wide hasp on the outside. At the bottom of the door was a slot, that she knew food was placed in her cell through, and the honey bucket in the corner was passed through for emptying. She knew immediately she'd not get out of her cell.

That day and night, no one bothered her and it frightened her more not be interrogated, because her mind was working double time on what they might do to her. She'd heard horror stories, the most recent from Colonel Tate, about how brutal the Russians were with prisoners. She fully expected to be raped, beaten and maybe executed. While she expected rough treatment, it was how the torture would be done that scared her.

Near dark the slat on the bottom of her door opened and a tin plate was passed inside. It contained about a cup of beans and a few slices of some sort of meat. The meat was sliced paper thin and easily missed in the meal. As she suspected, it was pork. The jailer slid a cup of water into her cell next and then closed the slat.

Standing on her metal bunk, she looked out the only window in her cell, through the bars. It was then she felt a light wind blowing and realized the window had no glass. She saw no source of heat in the room, no overhead vents, or radiators near the floor. Her overhead light was without a shade and had been burning since she arrived. It would never go out the whole time she lived in the cell.

She prepared herself for death, because few ever escaped the Russians, and it was likely she'd be tortured to death during an interrogation. While she knew her mind was strong and her body was pretty damned tough too, she knew all people the Russians questioned broke at some point. The resistance asked all partisans to try not to break for 24 hours, because that would allow them time to move fighters or relocate supplies. Most of the members of the resistance had no idea where they were half the time and it was done that way on purpose. A person couldn't tell what they didn't know and the whole idea was to keep members in the dark.

Her head quickly snapped toward the door as she heard keys rattling and few minutes later, the cell door swung open.

A huge, muscular looking soldier in uniform said in poor English, "Come."

Sandra stood and moved toward the door, praying God would give her strength for what was to come. She knew she'd return to the cell beaten and in sad shape.

The walk to interrogation was short. The room used to question prisoners was in the same building, but the room was dark. As she entered, Sandra noticed one low wattage bulb burning overhead, the walls were padded, and three metal chairs were bolted to the floor. The chairs, all of them, had straps and chains attached to them. The guard pushed her roughly to a chair and said, "Sit."

Sandra sat in the hard chair and immediately the guard buckled straps around her wrists, ankles, waist, and neck. He then left her alone in the room. From her chair, she could vaguely see a table, just out of the dim light, and it had a number of items intended to inflict pain on those who did not answer questions promptly.

Nearly an hour later, Colonel Eline and the big Russian Private entered the room. Not a word was said as the Colonel lighted a cigarette, inhaled deeply and the released the smoke from his nose. Smiling at Sandra he asked, "Well, looks like my first client is a beautiful woman."

Here it comes, and Lord, give me strength, she silently prayed.

Eline walked to Sandra, ran his hand down her face, and continued moving down until he cupped a breast in his hand. He smiled and said, "I have a few questions, before we get to know each other better and you will answer them, my dear, one way or the other. See, I have ways to make you talk. Some of my techniques cause extreme pain and others will maim you for life. It would be a shame for a beautiful woman like yourself to finish life blind, no tongue, or your face severely disfigured."

At the last sentence he'd lowered his face almost to hers, so Sandra spat in the Russian's face. He gave a mad laugh, wiped his face off with a handkerchief pulled from his coat pocket. Then partially turning, he swung his right hand hard and punched her on the side of the head. She saw stars and actually thought she'd pass out, but wasn't that lucky. She felt blood running down her right cheek.

Colonel Eline said in Russian, "Private Artyom, use a metal rod and break her right arm. Then, leave the room and find ten men who want to use an American woman."

Hours later, alone in her cell, Sandra felt dirty, used, and in pain. Her right arm throbbed. She knew it was broken, she'd been raped countless times, and both of her ears were missing. She'd held on for as long as she could, but eventually passed out.

I can't return to John like I am. He'd take me back easily enough, but I feel so filthy and dirty now. The arm and ears I can do nothing about, but endure the pain. Lord, why are you allowing this to happen to me? I ask you to help me, She thought as she looked around her concrete room.

A few minutes later, either from fatigue or pain, she fell asleep.

The day the women from his cell were taken, John and the rest returned from Alabama to find their camp a black spot in the woods. All the supplies were gone, numerous dead were left unburied, and the only survivor, a young man of seventeen said three women were taken away by the Russians. The witness went so far as to name the three women and John almost panicked when he hard Sandra's name spoken.

His head quickly turned to Colonel Tate, who said, "We can't make a rescue attempt, John, the place is too secure since our last attack. Hell, they've even placed tanks in the compound and we'd be torn to bits trying to get to her."

"She's my wife, Colonel, so I have to try!" John said, as his head spun in different directions.

"You will *not* try and that's an order. We can't rescue her, but we might be able to end her suffering and trust me, she is suffering."

"Kill her? Is that what you mean?"

"Exactly, because right now, that's the best we can do for her and the other two, or did you forget about them?"

"I . . . I'm overwhelmed, sir, and not thinking clearly."

"Give it some thought, John, serious thought. However, for each hour you're considering her fate, she's in pain. As a prior guest of the Russians, I can assure you, she'll be raped and then tortured, because I've seen it happen before. If there was a way to get them out, by God I'd do it, but there is absolutely no hope."

With tears in his eyes, John sat on a blood-stained log, pulled Dolly close, and cried. He'd never considered that one of them would die and he'd felt he and Sandra had years left. His body shook and quivered as he realized he would soon be alone in the world, with no one talk with or convey his dreams, fears, and hopes. Then his mind switched to Sandra and he gave thought to her situation. She was a strong woman and she could recover from rapes, but it was unlikely, as a member of the resistance, she'd be allowed to live. Usually partisans were executed on the spot, but their intelligence section must be interrogating them for new information.

It was then a cell entered the camp and the leader, a man named Smith said, "We found the bodies of our dead dumped in a clearing about five miles from Edwards, Colonel. The dead from the attack on Edwards."

"Were you able to identify them?"

"Most, but some were torn to hell and back. Oh, and both snipers you left behind are dead. We found the woman and the black guy among the dead." Smith said and then handed a sheet of paper to Colonel Tate as he added, "Here is a list of those we could identify, the rest will have to be listed as missing in action."

"Thank you, Smith, and have your cell relax for a bit. As soon as we get our thoughts lined up, we're leaving here."

Smith shrugged and sat on the end of the same log John was on.

A light rain blew in and everyone constructed a temporary shelter, except John remained sitting on the log. Even when it turned to a short, but hard, downpour, he didn't move. His mind was on Sandra, his love for her, and the hopelessness of her situation.

Two hours later, the sun broke through the clouds and John said, "Colonel, I request permission, sir, to take what remains of my cell and terminate the prisoners."

"Disapproved, however, you can take what remains of your cell and join Captain Smith as he makes sure the prisoners no longer suffer at the hands of the Russians."

"We'll never get close enough to kill anyone, so how are we to do this, sir?" Smith asked as he crawled out from his poncho shelter. John never noticed the raindrops falling from the trees or the chill in the wind.

"We have some LAW's here and two of your men are carrying Russian 40 mm semi-automatic grenade launchers, and I'm sure between the two weapons, you are capable of ending the suffering of our people. Just with the launchers alone you have twelve shots. Do you know your way around the camp, Captain?"

"I know where they keep prisoners that are newly caught and where they do the interrogations, if that's what you're really asking me, sir."

"It is. Your orders are to completely destroy that facility. Then, do not return to us, until you've entered Alabama. We want this to look like someone else was behind it."

Looking at John, Smith said, "If you move with me, I call the shots, okay?"

John nodded.

Smith looked around camp and met the eyes of his men before he said, "Let's get our shelters down and prepare to move. I want to be in place by dark. We'll launch our attack right at 2200 on the dot, so let's move, people."

The walk to the gulag was uneventful, except John had to fight back tears. In all his years, never had he been forced to accept such deep pain. He loved Sandra with his very soul and now he was going to assist in killing her.

A half a mile from the camp, Smith stopped, looked at his watch and said, "When we're near the target, I want the LAW's and grenade launchers ready for action. I expect the Russians to come after us and they'll be fast, as well as pissed. So, I want three

LAW's fired and both grenade launchers empty before we leave. The building should be completely destroyed or on fire before we leave. Any questions?"

Since there were none, they continued to move. All wore NVG's and a light mist was falling as they neared an electrical fence that surrounded the whole camp. Smith placed his men on a slight incline, hardly a hill, but elevated enough they were slightly higher than other terrain in the area.

John, glad it was dark and raining, with tears in his eyes, extended the first LAW and then placed it by his feet. He then prepared the other two for firing.

He'd just raised the first LAW to his shoulder, when Smith touched his shoulder and pointed at a guard nearing outside the fence and he had a dog. One of Smith's men, a tall thin man called "Slim" removed a crossbow from his back. Loading one arrow, he placed the other on the ground beside him, and took careful aim.

The *twang* of the bowstring was light and hardly heard in the night air. Slim pulled the string back, loaded another arrow and sighted in on the guard, now bent over his dog. Again he fired and his target fell quietly to the mud.

Whispering, Smith said, "Fire the LAW's now and both of you with the launchers, wait for the first explosion, then join the dance. The rest of you, get ready to move and quickly. "

John had been praying, asking for forgiveness for killing his wife, but now turned all professional as he sighted in the center of the concrete structure and fired. The Law struck the building with a loud explosion and almost immediately the sound of a siren was heard. Search lights, mounted on the tall search towers began crossing the darkness outside of the fence. The second LAW struck right at the rear of Sandra's cell and blew a huge hole in the cinder blocks and concrete. The force of the blast blew her up against the door and she heard the guards screaming and yelling. Dust, smoke and debris filled the air.

Moving slowly, Sandra made her way through the hole and outside. The interrogation center was now under heavy fire as the Russian 40 mm semi-automatic, 6-shot grenade launchers did their damage. Seeing the light from the weapons as they fired, Sandra made her way toward the fence. One of the men using a grenade launcher, punched a hole in the fence and then started firing at towers, and other targets of opportunity.

A squad of Russian soldiers rounded the destroyed building, moving right for Sandra. The partisans fired and men began to fall. Sandra was close to the fence and John, not knowing the figure was his wife, moved to the hole in the protective wire.

"This way!" John screamed as he neared. Suddenly there was a huge explosion and something in the building they'd fired on exploded. Sandra was knocked off her feet, but John was quickly at her side. By the green light of the NVG's, he recognized Sandra and yelled to be heard, "Move and do it now. If you don't, this will have been all for nothing."

She stood, took four or five steps and then collapsed. John scooped her up in his arms and moved for the treeline.

As soon as he neared the partisans, Smith yelled, "Move dead east and do it now!"

They broke contact just as a bright search light from one of the towers found them. Guns were fired and the light quickly went out. John, dropped his back pack and with Sandra on his back began to move with the others. They'd covered less than a mile, when the sound of an approaching chopper was heard.

"Under your poncho's now! If this bird is infrared equipped, we're dead meat." Smith yelled as he pulled his poncho from his pack. Then, falling to the ground, the partisan's covered their bodies with the waterproof material.

John, realizing he'd left his pack, with his poncho, threw his body on Sandra's. *Please Lord,* he prayed, *don't let this chopper have sensor gear.*

The chopper flew in lazy circles a few times and then moved back toward camp. As soon as the bird moved away from them, the partisans were up and running east.

After about five miles, Smith said, "Give your wife to another man, John, you're slowing us down."

"I need to look at her injuries."

"Not yet, you won't. I'll not risk the lives of all of us for the sake of one person. Now, hand her to Thomas and let's move. I plan to stop in a couple of hours."

Time crawled by as John moved beside Thomas and when Smith finally called for a short rest, John looked Sandra over. Night was turning to day and the NVG's were removed and placed in packs.

"Oh, baby, what have they done to you?" John asked in tears as he saw her face. She'd been beaten hard, her nose was broken, teeth were chipped, and both ears were missing. Someone had stuck something hot to her beautiful face to the point she was no longer attractive. Shivering at the damage done to her face, John quickly discovered a broken right arm, a bullet hole to her upper right shoulder, and numerous small burns and cuts to her body. Reaching into a small pouch he carried, he pulled out a syringe of morphine and slid the needle into her right thigh. He then patched her bullet wound and smiled when he saw Captain Smith making a stretcher from some tree limbs.

"We're semi out of danger, so we'll let her travel in style now." Smith said, gazing into John's eyes. Then he asked, "You understand I couldn't endanger all of us for her, don't you?"

"Yes. I was pissed at the time, but I would have made the same decision as you, if our roles were reversed."

"Good. My wife was killed right after the fall, so I know what it's like to lose a loved one. It hurts, but the pain grows less over time."

"I lost my first wife and it turned me into a drunk for a few days, but then the booze ran out and I had to sober up." John said.

"Good; now Pete and Jim, I want you two to carry this woman until you get tired. Once you're beat, I'll have you replaced."

All day they moved toward Alabama, but they varied their course so often the Russians couldn't know where they were actually heading. It was late after noon when they heard a chopper and since they were crossing a clearing, the aircraft had them cornered.

"Scatter!" Smith yelled and the men moved off in all headings of a compass. Sandra was dropped and John moved to her side. A loud hammering sound was heard and men began to fall, with one of the first being Smith in an explosion of red mist. When the chopper started turning, after completing a pass, most of the men were in the trees. The bird lined up once more and started an approach.

Smith was screaming from pain and one other man was down, but silent. The chopper fired the mini-gun once more and the Captain's screams grew quiet. The chopper returned a third time hovered in the air near Smith, as it looked for other targets. Five minutes later it gained altitude and the aircraft turned west, likely returning to Edwards with a grossly exaggerated body count.

Finally, after many long minutes, John check Sandra, found her breathing, so he moved toward the two downed men.

Smith was dead, with most of his head missing and his left leg gone at the knee. The second man was hit hard, but he'd live. John discovered the man's right foot gone and a chunk of flesh was missing from his left ass cheek. Standing, John called the other men to him and quickly realized he'd only lost the two men, when it could have been much worst.

"I want a man on point, one on drag, and two others carrying the litter."

"Let's move, because the whole Russian army will know our location now."

"Which direction?" One of the men asked.

"Back toward Edwards. I doubt they'll expect us to head that direction, and move quickly."

They continued to move for three hours after darkness and it was a tired group that stopped for the night in some thick pines. They'd just stretched out when the guard said, "Company coming."

CHAPTER 22

Colonel Duboff was livid as he walked around the completely destroyed cell block, chain smoking cigarettes in the early morning light of a new day. He'd suffered ten dead, all guards, and both Colonel Eline and a big Private named Artyom were dead on top of that. A brand new facility had been blown away, with only a black spot and some bricks to show it ever existed.

"Colonel, dog teams have the partisans moving east, toward Alabama." A radio man yelled from the communications building.

"Send everything that will fly into the air after them."

"Yes, sir."

"Catch the bastards and bring them back to me to question, by God, and I will get some answers."

"Sir?" Colonel Ivanov asked.

"I am talking to myself, Colonel."

"I do that as well at times. My guards estimate, from the prints in the dirt and bent grasses around our camp where they shot at us, an even twelve men, but that figure could go up or down a man. We found three empty LAW launchers and brass from a Russian RG-6, our 40 mm semi-automatic, 6-shot grenade launcher."

"Damn it, Ivanov, I know what a damned RG-6 is, for heavens sake. Did you find anything else?"

"One of the prisoners escaped, but I do not think she was the reason for the attack. And, sir, to answer your next question, we have no idea which of the women got away at this time. I am waiting for laboratory results to give me names. We noticed spots of blood leading from the building so we know she has been injured."

"It matters little if one woman got away and you can be sure if she was a guest of Colonel Eline, she was injured in more ways than one. I want a hundred prisoners shot this morning and within the hour."

Snapping to attention, Ivanov said, "It will be done, Colonel."

John, now leading the group, moved about ten miles into Alabama and took shelter in an old house. He'd decided, at the last minute, to keep moving east and not return west yet. While he'd fixed Sandra's broken arm by setting it, and then securing it in place using two pieces of wood, her face was a real mess. The shoulder injury was healing, but he suspected she'd faint when she saw her face. The tip of her nose was missing, long and deep knife cuts were in both cheeks, and her forehead was a mass of knife marks. He was scared the damage done would kill her will to live. Sandra had once been a stunning woman.

"John, what are you thinking about?" She asked from a blanket beside him. Dolly had her head in Sandra's lap.

"Baby, you've been cut pretty bad on your face."

"I know, because I felt it every time the knife blade struck me, and Colonel Eline promised to make me ugly."

"He could never make you ugly, but you will have some scars." He pulled small mirror he used to shave with at times and handed it to her.

Sandra took and mirror in her hands. After she raised it, she said, "Well, the Russian was a man of his word, because I'm for damned sure ugly. Nonetheless, I'm alive and that sonofabitch isn't."

Silence was heard.

"John, if you don't want me anymore, I'll understand."

"Baby, I fell in love with the you inside, not the packaging. I still want you and love you, so don't worry about that at all. It's your very soul I love, really, and it's still there."

"John, I was raped. I was used so many times I lost count at twelve."

He pulled her close, noticed she was silently crying, and it almost broke his heart. Kissing her chin, he said, "It still changes nothing. You, Sandra, mean more to me today than at any other time in my life. I thought I'd lost you and I feel so blessed that God returned you to me. No, you'll recover and we'll always be together."

He hugged her closely and felt her body shudder as she cried.

After five days, John awoke early and said, "Everyone up. I want to be moving back into Mississippi within an hour."

Sandra still in pain, took a pain pill from John's first aid kit and climbed to her feet. Her shoulder wasn't as painful as before, only it wasn't strong enough to carry a pack yet. As they donned their heavy packs, he said, "Skeeter, I want you on point and Ware, you pull drag. Now don't think the Russians have given up looking for us, because they haven't. I suspect most of the air traffic looking for us is over, because it's too expensive to search for us by air very long. You can be assured, there are ground troops still looking."

When they crossed over into Mississippi no one knew, not really, because there were no signs or markers deep in the woods. They continued to walk until threatened by darkness and then John called it a day. Sitting by the fire, he watched Sandra swallow another pain pill. Dolly, usually with John, spent the day beside Sandra and at times the dog would look up at her to make sure she was okay. He suspected dogs had a way of knowing when the humans they cared about were hurting or worried. Dolly evidently knew something was wrong with Sandra.

"We should be nearing the Pearl River, the day after tomorrow and our meeting place with Colonel Tate."

"Good," Sandra said, "because I need some time to heal."

Squeezing her hand, which he'd been holding, he replied, "Let's hope you get some time to rest. I have no idea if the man is still there, so we may have to keep moving."

"I'll do what it takes."

Two days later, Ware dropped back and said, "I see Colonel Tate and some others I recognize under the overpass."

"Were they armed?" John asked.

"Relax, they looked like they always do, tired, hungry and armed for bear."

"Lead us to the man."

Tate grinned when he saw John and his group returning and the frowned when he realized he lost two men. "So, tell me, John, how did it go?"

"Very well, or at least the attack did. We lost two men later, after a Russian Ka-60 popped up on the horizon and fired a Gatling gun. I was, I'm happy to say, able to rescue my wife."

"What of the Russian facility?" Colonel Tate asked then looking at Sandra he quickly added, "I see, my dear, that you've been a guest of the Russians. Thanks to them my chest and back are deeply scarred and I have one less testicle than I had before I met them. Rough hosts, the Russians are."

"Well, I'm not sure, sir, but I think the no good bastard that removed my ears and cut my face is dead. Then, there was a huge Private named, Artyom. I hope he burns in hell forever. I had the privilege of seeing the Private on fire, so I know he's gone."

"Colonel, the building is gone, but it'll not even slow the Russians down. I'm sure they put up a tent or will start interrogating in the field." John said.

"Again, John, you fail to see the big picture. What matters is the destruction of Russian property and the killing of her men when we can. Now, some Colonel is going to have to explain to Moscow how a bunch of backwoods rednecks killed their men and destroyed their interrogation center. Moscow will be pissed and maybe even mad enough to remove some commanders."

"So," John said, "that has nothing to do with us."

"Son, it has everything to do with us. Eventually, we'll wear the Russians down and they'll grow tired of burying their sons and daughters, rebuilding, and hunting for American phantoms. They'll one day realize what you and I know, that most Americans are dedicated to living in the best damned place in the world."

"It's hard to prove it, by looking at how we live now."

"We'll get up and dust our asses off, become determined, and in a couple of years we'll have our country back. One thing about Americans I don't want you to *ever* forget, we are not a nation of quitters and in the end, well, the Russians will realize that fact as well."

"But, what do we do in the mean time, sir?"

"Why that's easy, John, we keep killing the Russian sonsof-bitches as fast as we can. We blow up their trucks, planes, buildings and we fight their asses tooth and nail. Always keep in mind, we are Americans and we're winners."

The End of Book 3

The Fall of America:
Premonition of Death
Book 1

*Now available as an audiobook at iTunes,
or at Audible.com.*

About the Author

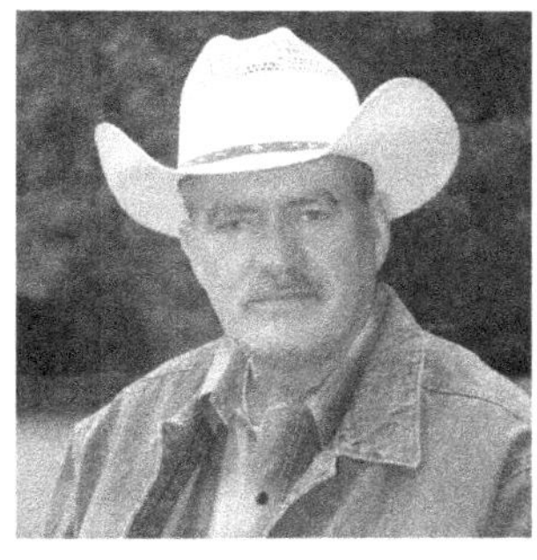 **W.R Benton**, a pen name, is a retired U.S. military senior Non-commissioned Officer with over twenty-six years of active duty service. He grew up in the Missouri Ozark Mtns., where hunting, trapping, camping, and other outdoor activities were the norm. Additionally, he spent more than twelve years teaching survival and parachuting procedures to U.S. Air Force personnel as a Life Support instructor. Mister Benton has an Associate's Degree in Search and Rescue, Survival Operations, a Bachelors Degree in Occupational Safety and Health, and a Masters Degree in Psychology near completion.

Mister Benton is a member of the America Authors Association (AAA). You can visit W.R. Benton online http://www.wrbenton.net or his War Paint Site at http://www.warpaint.info.

Visit him on Facebook at
www.facebook.com/wrbenton01

"**Simple Survival -** A Family Outdoors Guide" is more than a book—it is an outdoor resource bible that every family should have a copy of. This is one of those books that you should have in your camping bag along with the tent and other equipment. However, reading it at home before you go off on some outdoor adventure would be a great help when potential situations happen.

Available at Amazon and other online bookstores

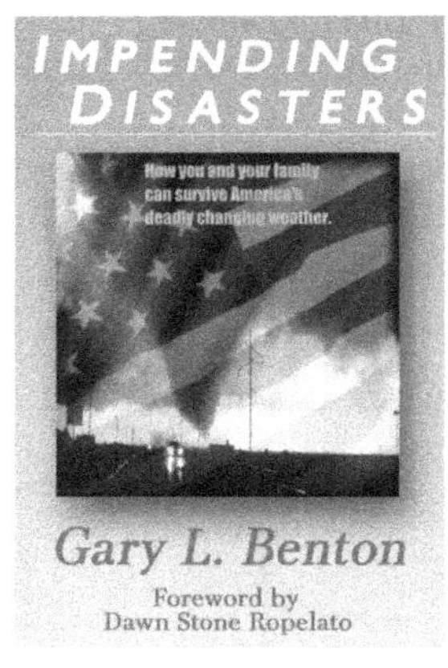

This helpful and comprehensive book covers most major disasters and how to stay safe if you decide to evacuate or stay. It has a section on prolonged survival, which will assist keeping you alive after the natural disaster has done its damage. Many people die following natural disasters, from one mishap or another, but you can learn to survive.

Learn to deal with Tornadoes, ice storms, hurricane, flooding, blackouts, riots, and much more. Contains easy to understand information, and critical gear/equipment lists you will need.

Available at Amazon and other online bookstores

www.ingramcontent.com/pod-product-compliance
Lightning Source LLC
Chambersburg PA
CBHW070924190726
48292CB00004B/1097